P9-BZD-666

❖

"Aaron Elkins is notable among mystery writers in that he can take a heap of nasty old human bones and turn them into suspense and humor."

—*Washington Times*

❖

"He not only makes one think how interesting it would be to be an anthropologist, he almost persuades one that a certain amount of fun could be had out of being a skeleton."

—**Sarah Caudwell,
author of *The Sirens Sang of Murder***

❖

"Ingenious and original."

—*Library Journal*

more . . .

❖

"Aaron Elkins's anthropologist detective, Gideon Oliver, has dug out a niche all his own. A latter-day Dr. Thorndyke, he's a forensic whiz known as 'the skeleton detective.' Show him a few bones and he'll not only describe who died, and from what, but how he or she lived."   —*Detroit News*

♦

"Aaron Elkins is witty and oh so clever."
                              —*New York Daily News*

♦

"Elkins writes with a nice touch of humor . . . Oliver is a likable, down-to-earth, cerebral sleuth."
                              —*Chicago Tribune*

♦

"A solid blend of deduction, adventure, romance."   —*Kirkus Reviews*

♦

RAVES FOR
CURSES!
AND AARON ELKINS'S
GIDEON OLIVER MYSTERY SERIES

❖ ❖ ❖

"*Curses!* is a traditional, entertaining whodunit with quirky characters and clues."
—*Chicago Sun-Times*

❖

"You go digging around in a Mayan tomb, disturbing all those ancient bones and riling all those righteous gods, so what do you expect for your trouble? A curse, is what; or, more precisely, *Curses!* . . . The hero's enthusiastic lectures on human bones make him fascinating company."
—*New York Times Book Review*

❖

"*Curses!* may be the best yet . . . a real detective story, with all the clues placed fairly before the reader, but we'll bet Elkins will keep you guessing."
—*Denver Post*

❖

"A thoroughly entertaining whodunit."
—*Travel & Leisure*

Please turn the page for more praise of the Gideon Oliver Series . . .

"Wheeee! Holmes himself could do no better . . . Elkins conjures up the scene so vividly that it is like a visit to the Yucatán."   —*Houston Post*

❖

"A delightful, semiserious romp through science and an exotic police culture."
                              —*Publishers Weekly*

❖

"This series has great appeal . . . and if you love knowing odd facts, you'll be fascinated with everything that old bones can reveal."
                         —*Atlanta Journal-Constitution*

❖

"Readers who like their humor dark and their gumshoes smart are sure to enjoy the 'bone bash.' "   —*Richmond Times-Dispatch*

❖

"Well-written and fully clued mystery. . . . Aaron Elkins belongs to the old school. His detective, anthropologist Gideon Oliver, will remind mystery experts of R. Austin Freeman's classic turn-of-the-century detective, Dr. Thorndyke." —*Virginian-Pilot*

"A fascinating, cerebral detective. . . . Glistens with the same Sherlockian deductive feats, the powerful sense of atmosphere and character, and the understated wit that brought critical acclaim to his first book."

—*Booklist*

"Aaron Elkins is one of the best in the business and getting better all the time: when his new book arrives I let the cats go hungry and put my own work on hold till I've finished it."

—**Elizabeth Peters, author of**
The Snake, the Crocodile and the Dog

The Professor Gideon Oliver Novels

FELLOWSHIP OF FEAR*
THE DARK PLCE*
MURDER IN THE QUEEN'S ARMES*
OLD BONES*
CURSES*
ICY CLUTCHES*
MAKE NO BONES*
DEAD MEN'S HEARTS*

Also by Aaron Elkins

A WICKED SLICE (with Charlotte Elkins)
A DECEPTIVE CLARITY
A GLANCING LIGHT

*Published by
THE MYSTERIOUS PRESS

ATTENTION: SCHOOLS AND CORPORATIONS

MYSTERIOUS PRESS book, distributed by Warner Books are available at quantity discounts with bulk purchase for educational, business, or sales promotional use. For information, please write to: SPECIAL SALES DEPARTMENT, MYSTERIOUS PRESS, 1271 AVENUE OF THE AMERICAS, NEW YORK, N.Y. 10020

ARE THERE WARNER BOOKS
YOU WANT BUT CANNOT FIND IN YOUR LOCAL STORES?

You can get any MYSTERIOUS PRESS title in print. Simply send title and retail price, plus 95¢ per order and 95¢ per copy to covermailing and handling costs for each book desired. New York State and California residents add applicable sales tax. Enclose check or money order only, no cash please, to: WARNER BOOKS, P.O. BOX 690, NEW YORK, N.Y. 10019

AARON ELKINS

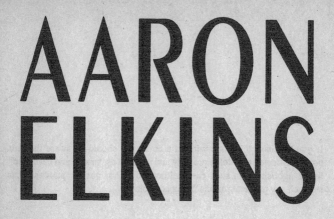

CURSES!

THE MYSTERIOUS PRESS

Published by Warner Books

A Time Warner Company

If you purchase this book without a cover you should be aware that this book may have been stolen property and reported as "unsold and destroyed" to the publisher. In such case neither the author nor the publisher has received any payment for this "stripped book."

MYSTERIOUS PRESS EDITION

Copyright © 1989 by Aaron Elkins
All rights reserved.

Cover design by Krystyna Skalski
Cover illustration by Mary Ann Lasher

The Mysterious Press name and logo are registered trademarks of Warner Books, Inc.

 Mysterious Press books are published by
Warner Books, Inc.
1271 Avenue of the Americas
New York, NY 10020

W A Time Warner Company

Printed in the United States of America

Originally published in hardcover by The Mysterious Press.
First Mysterious Press Paperback Printing: February, 1990
Reissued: August, 1994

10 9 8 7 6

Para Pedro Crespo, gran compañero de viaje

1

I can't understand it," Julie said, lifting a dog-eared pile of term papers and theses from the chair at the side of the desk. "You are basically a neat and orderly man. You don't throw your socks on the floor. You don't leave your underwear hanging on chairs. You clean up your own—"

"Careful," Gideon said. "This is going to my head."

Julie looked unsuccessfully around for someplace to deposit the pile. Gideon pointed to the back left corner of his desk, already three inches deep in paper. "Jam it up against the wall so it doesn't slide off."

She did, began to sit down, and winced. From beneath her she extracted a metal nameplate: "Gideon P. Oliver, Professor of Physical Anthropology," the plastic insert said. She propped it on top of the papers.

"So why," she continued, "do you live in an office that looks like this?" Her gesture took in the entire cluttered space: the desk, the gray metal file cabinet, the two standing bookcases, the wall-mounted shelves over the desk that he had hung himself, defying university policy. All of it was overflowing with paper and books. Many of the books were open, lying helter-skelter with their spines up and bristling with torn-paper markers.

"It's a pedagogical device. Students get uneasy if professors' offices don't look the way they do in the movies."

"No," Julie said, "I think this is the real you. The monster beneath the surface."

"Grr," Gideon said, and leaned over from his chair to pull her face down and kiss her softly on the lips. For a moment he kept his eyes open, looking up at the smooth, lovely face. Then he closed his own eyes and kissed her some more, moving his lips to nuzzle the velvet of her cheeks, and then her jawline, and then her throat.

"Gideon," she said, pulling back a few inches, "the door's open. What if one of your students came by?"

"Are you serious? On a Sunday during winter break? No students for miles. No teachers either. Only me, trying to get this damn monograph in shape." The thought of it effectively broke the spell. He sighed, leaned back in his chair, and slapped the uppermost sheaf of papers on the desk.

"And are you?"

"Getting it in shape? I don't know. I've lost the rhythm or something. It all seems stale. Or I seem stale." He lifted the top sheet. " 'A Reassessment of Middle

Pleistocene Hominids,'" he read aloud. "'Taxonomic Reconsiderations Based on Recent Second Interglacial Evidence from Eastern Europe.'" He grimaced. "What do you think, does it grab you?"

"Uh . . ."

"Me neither, and the title's the best part."

They both laughed and Julie squeezed his hand. "Come on, it's your birthday. I'm taking you out for lunch."

"I thought you had to work."

"Olympic National Park can get by without me for a few hours. Why don't we drive into Seattle? We could be there by one."

"I don't think so, Julie. We wouldn't be back till late. I'd really like to finish up this paper and get it out of my hair. Then I can do something else for the next three weeks."

"Like what?"

"Oh, I don't know. Build some bookcases for the study . . . maybe clean up all those fir cones in back . . . get the garage straightened out . . ."

"Oh, poor baby, you really *are* in the dumps, aren't you? Okay, we'll just go someplace here in Port Angeles. How about a steak at the Bushwacker?"

He shrugged and hauled himself to his feet. "Okay, sure."

"What's wrong, Gideon? Is it just the forty-first birthday blues?"

Yes, he supposed it was. That and the misty gray rain that had been sifting continuously down for nine dismal days and looked as if it wouldn't let up until summer. He was a confirmed lover of rain and fog, but the dreary, dark winters of western Washington were going to take some getting used to.

And then there was the fact that it had been a year and a half since his last dig. A year and a half without the renewing process of hands-on anthropology, a year and a half spent in classroom and office. And no prospect of fieldwork in sight. He felt, he explained to Julie, as if his career were standing still.

"Let me remind you," she said crisply, "that in that year and a half you've started here at a new school, you've gotten your full professorship, you've solidified your formidable reputation as 'the Skeleton Detective of America'—"

"Watch out now, don't push your luck."

"—and you've published three papers."

"Four. I know, Julie, that's all true. I guess I need to do some real work, not just paperwork. And I don't mean identifying dismembered skeletons for the FBI."

"Well, couldn't you get in touch with some of your archaeologist friends? Wouldn't they be glad to have you on a dig?"

"If there were some human bones involved, sure. And if some other physical anthropologist wasn't already part of the team." He shrugged. "I guess that's what I'll do." And then he'd wait months, years maybe, before anything came to pass. Popular accounts notwithstanding, human skeletal remains didn't turn up on digs very often.

"Fine. Good. Anything else bothering you?"

"Julie, do you know how old Rupert Armstrong LeMoyne is?"

"Ah, now we're getting to it. Who's Rupert Armstrong LeMoyne?"

"The dean of faculty. He's thirty-nine years old. Two years younger than I am."

"Gideon, would you *want* to be the dean of faculty?"

"Of course not. That's not the point."

"Would you like to be soft, and white, and self-satisfied like Rupert Armstrong LeMoyne?" She pushed him back into his chair, dropped into his lap, and put her arms around his neck.

Gideon submitted happily. Married two years and still his skin tingled when she touched him. "How do you know he's soft, white, and self-satisfied?"

"Come on, with a name like Rupert Armstrong LeMoyne?" She opened the top two buttons of his shirt and slipped her hand inside. "Does Rupert Armstrong LeMoyne have a furry, warm chest?" She kissed the bridge of his nose, flattened when he'd boxed in college. "Does he have a manly and attractive schnozz? Does he have a square, sexy jaw straight out of *Superman* comics?" That too was kissed, and she looked into his eyes from three inches away, her eyes slightly crossed. "How am I doing? Is this cheering you up?" Her hand was still on his chest, the fingers moving in slow circles.

With his hands on her hips he shifted her, seating her more firmly on his lap, and then stroked her thigh through the twill of her National Park Service trousers. Had he really been sitting there, listless and dispirited, just a few minutes ago? "I don't know if cheering me up is exactly the way to put it," he said, "but it's doing something. Why don't we forget about lunch and drop over to the house for an hour or two?"

"Tell me," she persisted, "is Rupert Armstrong Le-Moyne the author of the best-known book on comparative early hominid phylogeny?"

"The *only* book on comparative early hominid phylogeny."

"Don't quibble. Now," she said, and kissed his nose again, this time on the tip, "did I or did I not just get a pretty good offer on how to pass the next two hours?"

"You bet. And then let's give some thought to going someplace for a few days where it's not raining."

The telephone rang as he began to rise with her still in his arms, and they both sank back into the chair. "This," Gideon said confidently, "will be a very short call. You answer it. Tell them I'm on my way to an extremely important consultation."

"Is this the way your secretary answers the phone? From your lap?"

"It'd be a thought if I had a secretary."

She picked up the receiver. "Dr. Oliver's office . . ." She leaned her head back and laughed. Her hair brushed his temple and he aimed a kiss at it but missed. "Well, hello!" she said. "Yes, he is, right here."

"Thanks a lot," Gideon grumbled.

Julie continued to listen on the telephone. "You're kidding!" she said, turning her head to look at Gideon. "He's not going to believe it."

She handed the telephone to him with a peculiar grin. "You're not going to believe it."

"Hello, Gideon?"

The old man's thin voice promptly brought out a smile. Abraham Irving Goldstein, his onetime professor and continuing mentor. Avram Yitzchak Goldstein of Minsk, who had begun his career in America as a seventeen-year-old peddling ribbons from a pushcart in Brooklyn, and ended it as a distinguished scholar. Abe Goldstein, longtime friend.

"Abe, hello! Where are you calling from?"

"Where should I be calling from? Yucatan. Listen, how would you like to come down here to Tlaloc for a few weeks and give me a hand on the dig? Julie, too, if she can get some time off."

Gideon covered the mouthpiece with his hand and looked at Julie. "I don't believe this."

Abe, as a member of the board of directors of the Horizon Foundation for Anthropological Research, was at a Horizon-sponsored excavation about sixty miles from Merida, near Mexico's Gulf Coast. Tlaloc, a small Mayan ceremonial center, had been discovered only ten years before, and work had begun in 1980. But when a scandal had made the site notorious in 1982, the Mexican government's Instituto Nacional de Antropologia e Historia had shut down the excavation. "For all time," they had declared somewhat histrionically, "to bury the memory of this shameful hour." Gideon had been there at the time, just finishing up work on the collection of human bones that divers had recovered from the cenote—the sacrificial well—a few hundred feet from the buildings, and he had been as shocked and disgusted as anyone else by what had happened.

Afterwards, the site had remained locked for over five

years while Horizon and the Institute engaged in recrim-
inations and negotiations. Eventually, Horizon had made
handsome amends and the threat of a suit had died
quietly away. Then six months ago the government had
relented further, allowing Horizon to begin work again,
"subject to stringent review by the Institute." One of the
express provisions was that Dr. Abraham Goldstein (who
had had no part in the original dig) would personally
direct the start-up, lending his impeccable reputation and
expertise to an operation that had been sadly botched the
first time around.

This, Gideon had no doubt, had been subtly engi-
neered by the "retired" seventy-eight-year-old professor,
who had left Sequim for Yucatan in early December to
begin laying the pre-excavation groundwork. Gideon had
not been asked along; the dredging of the cenote was
finished, and no further burials were expected.

"What's up, Abe?" Gideon asked. "Don't tell me you
turned up some skeletal stuff after all?"

"That's right. You remember the building they called
the Priest's House?"

"Southeast of the temple, all buried in vines? The one
we hadn't worked on yet?"

"That's the one. Only now we got some of the vines
cleaned off and, guess what, there's a body a couple of
feet inside the entry. I made them leave it alone to wait
for you. You can come?"

"What's the weather like?" Not that it made any
difference. He could already feel the excitement of a dig
building in his chest. But he felt that he ought to show at
least a semblance of thinking it over.

"Like it always is here. Hot. Sunny. Humid. Just the way you don't like, but the dig is a pleasure."

Gideon gazed out the window at the rain streaming from the leaves of the soaked rhododendron thicket that backed against the Sciences and Humanities Building. "When did I ever say I didn't like it hot and sunny?" he asked dreamily.

Abe laughed. "Boy, you got a short memory. So, you can come or you can't come?"

"I can come." With bells on, he could come. He squeezed Julie's leg and smiled at her. She had plenty of vacation time saved up. She could come too.

"Ah, wonderful!" Abe said. His pleasure warmed Gideon. "That's fine!"

"What's the crew like?"

"The crew . . . I didn't tell you?"

"Tell me what?" Gideon asked warily.

"Don't be so suspicious. They're all amateurs, that's all. Old friends of yours."

"I thought the government was insisting on professionals this time."

"When we get down to the technical stuff, yes. But for the first couple of weeks it's just clean-up and preliminaries, so we gave the ones who were here in 1982 a chance to come again if they wanted to. On us. From the original nine, five came back, including your old student Harvey Feiffer. We thought we owed it to them, considering the *tsuris* they had before."

Tsuris was trouble, of course. Gideon's knowledge of Yiddish had grown considerably in the last ten years, for Abraham Irving Goldstein had not forsaken the accent, let alone the vocabulary, of his pushcart-peddling days. Sometimes impenetrable, often hardly noticeable, it had never completely disappeared. Whether this was a statement of identity, a whimsical eccentricity (one among many), or a plain, honest-to-goodness accent, no one knew for sure, not even Gideon. Maybe not even Abe. If anyone had the temerity to ask how it was that a world-renowned scholar, a master of seven languages, sometimes spoke with an accent out of *Abie's Irish Rose*, Abe's response was unvarying. His eyes would grow round, his forehead furrow into a million parchmentlike wrinkles. "Accent?" he would echo, astounded. "What kind accent?"

"So?" he said. "When you'll be here? Tomorrow?"

"Tomorrow?" Gideon laughed. "We have to get our things organized, get tourist cards—"

"You can't do that this afternoon?"

"This afternoon is already taken up." Gideon rubbed the small of Julie's back and smiled up at her. The fact that he was desperate to be on a dig hardly meant that he had lost all sense of proportion. "Besides," he added firmly, "there's a monograph I want to finish up. We'll be there at the end of the week. Friday. How's that?"

A fractional hesitation. "Friday? You couldn't make it a little sooner?"

"Like when?"

"Like tomorrow?"

"What's the rush, Abe? The bones will still be there Friday."

"It's not just the bones. Something's bothering me here. I need your opinion."

"Well . . ."

"Also," Abe said with the singsong wheedle that meant the clincher was on its way, "we turned up some new Mayan written material. Garrison from Tulane rushed down here to work on the translation, and she's almost finished. I asked her to hold off on her presentation so you could be here for it, but she has to go back the day after tomorrow. I don't have to tell you it's a historic thing, but, of course, if you can't make it, you can't make it."

Gideon was silent.

"Of course it's only a few leaves, post-Conquest," Abe pressed on, "but still, something like this doesn't happen every day."

Or every year, or every decade. Well, Gideon could always take the monograph along. "Okay," he said, "I'm convinced. We'll be there tomorrow."

"Good. Wonderful. There's funding to pay your fare— Julie's too, if she's willing to do a little work— and we'll put you up at the hotel. Meals too. A salary I can't come up with. I'm not getting paid, why should you?"

"No problem." Gideon was more than satisfied. He'd have paid their own way if he'd had to. "Abe, tell me, what's bothering you there?"

"Listen, Gideon, this call's costing plenty. When you get here I'll explain. Let me know what time you'll be here and someone will pick you up at the airport in Merida."

"Okay, Abe, thanks. See you tomorrow, then. If we can get a plane."

When he hung up, Julie clasped her hands lightly about his neck, her forearms resting on his shoulders. "We're going to Yucatan?"

"Uh-huh. How about that?"

"It's wonderful. I've always wanted to see it. But what are *you* so happy about? I thought you hated the tropics."

"Where do people get these ideas? A dig is a dig. And January won't be that bad down there." He pulled her head down to kiss her. "Anyway, Yucatan is something else. It's unique, you'll see. The jungle, the ruins . . . once you get away from Merida there's a raw, primitive elemental sense of isolation, a—"

"Did you know," she said, never one to be moved by lyric prose, "that you have dried shaving cream behind your ear?"

They were five hours into the flight, high in a clean blue sky above a cloud layer of undulating white.

"It's like looking down on a giant bowl of Cream of Wheat," Julie observed in one of her weaker conversational attempts.

"Mm," Gideon said. He had worked intermittently

and unproductively on "A Reassessment of Middle Pleistocene Hominids" while Julie dawdled with equal lack of result over her quarterly report. Now they both stretched and yawned at the same time.

Julie closed her manila folder and made another stab. "Does Tlaloc mean something, or is it just a name?"

Gideon willingly gave up on the monograph and shoved it into the pocket on the back of the seat in front. "It's the Nahuatl term for the god of rain; the one the Maya called Chac."

"Nahuatl?"

"An Uto-Aztecan language, closely related to Pipil."

"Oh, Pipil," Julie said. "Thanks for clearing that up. Tell me, if it's a Mayan site, why doesn't it have a Mayan name?"

"Because, as anybody who's studied anthropology should know—"

"I was merely an anthro minor. I'm afraid I never got around to Pipil and Nahuatl."

"Well, in the tenth century, the Toltecs, who were Uto-Aztecan, came down to Yucatan from central Mexico and conquered the Maya—or were assimilated by them, depending on whether you take a short or a long view. In any case, most of the famous Mayan ruins in Yucatan are more Toltec than they are Mayan. Chichen Itza, for example."

"Are you saying that Tlaloc isn't really a Mayan site, then?"

"No, it's Mayan all right, but with a Toltec overlay. Oh, the way you might say Strasbourg is really a German city, but with a French overlay."

"I'm not sure how much the French would appreciate that."

"I'm not sure how much the Maya appreciated it."

The lunch cart, which had been making its halting way up the aisle, had finally reached Row 24. Neat little plastic trays with hinged plastic lids were set down before them: a salad of salami, cheese, red peppers, and string beans; a roll; a two-inch cube of chocolate cake; a dozen red grapes in a pleated paper cup.

The thick-bodied man in the aisle seat next to them stared through the transparent lid of his portion with a cold and bitter eye. "Jesus Christ," he muttered at it accusingly, "can you believe this?"

But to Gideon it looked fine; just right for two o'clock in the afternoon, thirty-five thousand feet above the Gulf of Mexico. Julie thought so too, and they polished it off enthusiastically (their seatmate ate the cake and left the rest) and hailed coffee from an attendant.

"Now," Julie said firmly, "how about filling me in on all the sordid details of the famous scandal that closed Tlaloc down in 1982?"

Gideon twisted uncomfortably in the narrow seat. "How much do you know about it?" he asked reluctantly.

"Well, I remember reading about it in *Time*. Somebody stole a Mayan codex, right?"

"That's about it." He tore open the paper seal on a container of half-and-half and poured it into his coffee. "The director, as a matter of fact. Howard Bennett."

After ten seconds of nothing but the drone of the

engines, Julie raised an exasperated eyebrow. "And that's all you're going to tell me?"

"That's all there is."

"But you were *there*. I want the *important* details. What was Howard Bennett like? Was he actually a friend of yours? Was there a woman involved? Did you ever suspect . . ." She stopped and frowned at him. "In fact, why haven't you told me all this long ago?"

He shrugged. "It didn't seem pertinent. It happened before we met."

"You," she said, "are the most closemouthed person I know. You never gossip. It's disgusting. I'm going to be working on this dig now, so it's pertinent." She settled back expectantly, both hands around her cup, and shifted sideways to look at him. "Now tell me all about it. Start from the beginning."

Gideon settled back, too, looking down at the cloud sheet, and let his mind run back. The events at Tlaloc were painful to think about professionally as well as personally. He was, though he would hardly say such a thing aloud, a dedicated anthropologist, devoted to the field and intensely protective of its standards and reputation, both of which were gratifyingly high, generally speaking.

But Howard Bennett had violated those standards in an almost unimaginable way, and since then Gideon had rarely spoken of it. Most people he knew would have been surprised to learn he had been on the scene. Still, Julie had a point. She had a right to know more about it. Anyway, judging from the determined glint in her eyes, he wasn't going to get away with keeping it to himself any longer.

He started from the beginning. "You know what I remember most when I think about it? How hot it was."

3

"Hot" didn't begin to describe that memorable afternoon. It had been like a steam bath, only worse because there was no way to get up and walk out. The temperature had been a hundred degrees, the relative humidity had been a hundred percent, and breathing had been like inhaling through a wad of warm, wet cotton.

The brief rain had ended twenty minutes before, one of those hot slashing torrents that fell on the jungle canopy like a waterfall and then stopped as if someone had turned off a tap. Already the half inch of water that had slicked the ancient Mayan ceremonial plaza of Tlaloc had disappeared, sucked down through the porous soil of Yucatan and into the great natural limestone caverns below. The moment the rain had stopped the sun had reappeared, enveloping the world in vapor. The dense green foliage that pressed in on the plaza from all sides, the thousand-year-old stones of the crumbling temples, the thatch-roofed archeologists' shed—all hissed and steamed in the rain's aftermath.

Gideon was sitting on the veranda of the shed, at the rickety work table nominally under the protection of the eaves, but now mostly in the sun. Like everything else, he was, if not hissing, at least steaming. It poured from his sweaty khaki work clothes, from his curled, stained straw hat, from his very pores. He took another swig from the scarred bottle of warm grapefruit soda, grimaced, wiped his perspiring forehead with an equally wet forearm, and thought wistfully and fleetingly of Yosemite in the snow, and of the cool and windy Mendocino coast. Then he sighed and returned his attention to the brown, roughly globular object, also steaming, on the work table in front of him. It was the latest find brought up by the divers from the cloudy green depths of the sacrificial cenote: a human skull, the fourth so far.

He turned it slowly in his hands. Like most Mayan sacrifices it was young. None of the sutures had even begun to close, which meant it hadn't lived to make it out of its twenties. Nor out of its teens, he thought, running his finger over the chewing surfaces of the teeth. One of the third molars had fallen out after death, but the other one was freshly erupted, as cleanly sculpted as a dentist's model, with no wear on it. That would make eighteen or nineteen a reasonable guess at age. And guess was the right word. Third-molar eruption was wildly variable, but what else was there to go on? After the first twelve or fifteen years, the skull has precious little to reveal about age until the thirties. That left a lot of room for guesses.

"All right, Harvey," he said to the pudgy, balding twenty-five-year-old with the studious manner who sat attentively beside him, "what would you say about age?"

Harvey Feiffer adjusted his posture alertly. "Um, eighteen to twenty?" he ventured. "The left third molar—"

"Good. What about sex?"

"Um, female?"

"Right again. How do you know?"

"Gee, lots of things. There's no supraorbital ridge, and the occipital protuberance is practically nonexistent. And those mastoid processes are just smooth little bumps."

Gideon nodded his approval. In some ways Harvey was one of his better graduate students. He worked hard and he was enthusiastic about anthropology. He had jumped at the chance to accompany Gideon to Yucatan as a research assistant.

"What else do you see when you look at it?" Gideon asked. "*Whom* do you see?"

"Um, whom?" Harvey chewed on the corner of his lip, wiped sweat from under his collar with a handkerchief, and timidly took the skull, being careful to cradle it in his palms in the approved manner. No fingers in the eye sockets. "There are a lot of interesting things, really," he said, buying time. "It's on the small side, and definitely brachycephalic, although not as much as the cranial deformation makes it look." He darted a glance at Gideon to see if he was on the right track and received a noncommital nod. Then he glided his stubby, nail-chewed fingers lightly over the surface as Gideon had taught him to do. "The, uh, superior and inferior nuchal crests are poorly developed, and the temporal lines . . ."

Here in a nutshell was Harvey's problem; an overmeticulous concentration on minutiae, a relentless focus on detail at the expense of pattern and meaning. He had been a late convert to physical anthropology, switching as a junior after hearing Gideon give an all-university lecture on the evolution of the primate hand. Until then he had been a sociology major, and Gideon wondered if both fields hadn't been bad choices, for Harvey Feiffer had the precise and exacting soul of a good accountant.

Once, in an unusually loose moment over a couple of beers, he had said to Gideon, "You know what's so great about physical anthro? There's nothing to argue about; there are right answers. In sociology, if you say, like, familial norms determine infant behavior, the first guy you meet on the street will tell you that's wrong; his kid had a personality all his own from the minute he was born. But if you point at a bump on a bone and announce it's the anterior obturator tubercle, boy, it's great—nobody says *peep*."

". . . and the nasal bones are typically Mayan," Harvey was now rattling on, "and there seems to be a hole drilled in the upper left incisor. Oh, and there are some Wormian bones at the lambdoidal suture, and—"

Gideon repressed a sigh. "Harvey, hold on. Step back from it a minute." Obediently, Harvey leaped up. "No," Gideon said with a smile. "I meant step back mentally. Try to look at the skull as a whole, as part of a person. What can you say about *her?*"

Harvey slid back into his cane chair and frowned terrifically. "Um, about *her*? Well, I'm not sure . . ."

"Do you think she was a pretty girl?"

Harvey wriggled uncomfortably. It wasn't his kind of question. No right answer. "It's hard to say. From the Maya's point of view, I guess she was."

It wasn't a bad answer. By today's standards she would have been far from pretty, but surely the Maya would have thought her beautiful with her delicate, broad skull and those extraordinary, convex nasal bones. To make her prettier still her forehead had been artificially flattened when she was an infant, so that the top of her head was squeezed into the pointy hump they found so attractive. And the hole bored in her tooth had certainly been for a faceted jade pellet that was probably still at the bottom of the cenote. No doubt her ears had been pierced for pendants, her nasal septum for a plug, her left nostril for a gem. Very likely, her eyes had been permanently crossed in childhood by long months of focusing on a little ball of pitch dangling from a string tied to her hair. All to make her desirable.

He let out a long sigh. Amazing, the number of ways you could mutilate and deform human flesh and bone, given a little ingenuity. All that work and pain to make her desirable, and then they had killed her before she was twenty. And all Harvey saw was tubercles and protuberances.

"Okay," Gideon said gently, "let's see if we can't look at her as a human being now, not just a mass of skeletal criteria. For example—"

"Gideon! Dr. Oliver! Hey, where are you?"

He recognized Leo Rose's bellow of a voice and sighed again. Tlaloc was one of those Horizon Foundation excavations that was supervised by professionals but staffed by pay-for-the-privilege amateurs who worked for two weeks or a month and usually turned out to be both the chief pleasure and the chief pain of the dig. Pleasure because of the artless, enthusiastic interest they showed in almost anything at all; pain because this same interest meant the professional staff rarely got ten minutes in a row to work on something without having to answer a well-meant but often inane question.

"Over here, Leo. We're behind the shed."

Bearlike and rumpled, the California real-estate developer lumbered into sight around the corner of the thickly overgrown Priest's House. Or what they called the Priest's House. Anthropologists didn't really know what these buildings had been, any more than they knew what *any* ancient Mayan building had been, or what the Maya had called their great cities and ceremonial centers (if they were actually ceremonial centers), or even what the Maya had called themselves. There was a hell of a lot, when you thought about it, that anthropologists didn't know and probably never would.

Leo was bouncing with excitement. "We found a fake wall, can you believe it? With a kind of little hidden room behind it, and this fantastic stone chest in it. Come on, we figured you'd want to see this. Oh, hiya, Harvey."

Gideon didn't have to be asked twice. He was up at once, carefully placing the girl's skull on the bean-bag ring that served as a cushion. Was there anyone on a dig, amateur or professional, who didn't harbor secret hopes of sealed rooms behind false walls? Not since Howard Carter knocked down that wall in 1922 and walked into the untouched tomb of Tutankhamen, there wasn't.

"Where? In the temple?"

"Underneath. In the stairwell."

Clearing the rubble-filled stairwell was the major ongoing task of the Tlaloc excavation. Since the dig had opened more than two years before, the director, Howard Bennett, had worked steadily at it with changing crews, boring down into the flattopped pyramid on which the little Temple of the Owls sat. Gideon, on leave from his teaching post, had come to Yucatan only two weeks before—when they had begun to bring up bones from the cenote— but he had long since learned that Howard's enthusiasm was centered on the buried passageway. Howard had staked his reputation, such as it was, on the unearthing of some great find when they finally got to the bottom. Why else, he wanted to know, would the Maya go to all the trouble of packing a perfectly good stairwell with tons of debris, if not to hide something of tremendous importance?

Gideon had been doubtful. Sometimes there were treasures at the bottom of such rubble-packed passages; much more often there was nothing. The Maya had made a practice of enlarging their pyramids by using an old one as the core of a new one erected on top of it. The Pyramid of the Magicians at Uxmal had five such masonry "envelopes," one inside the other, like the layers of an onion. And when the Maya built this way, they usually blocked up any hollow spaces in the original pyramid;

for structural soundness, not to hide anything. But a false wall and a sealed room—that was something else again.

"Did you reach the bottom, then?" Harvey asked as they trotted across the grassy plaza toward the pyramid.

No, Leo explained, huffing for breath, they hadn't found the base of the stairwell yet, although they had now dug down twenty-four steps. No, the hollow wall had been discovered on the landing that was just twelve steps down from the temple floor, at a level that had been exposed and unremarked for a year. Someone had noticed that the mortar on one of the walls was different, more crumbly, and when Howard had probed between the blocks of masonry with the point of a trowel, they had come loose.

At the foot of the pyramid Gideon nodded to the two straw-hatted Mayan laborers enjoying their break— cigars and lukewarm tea— on the bottom steps. In return he received two decorous, unsmiling nods. He jogged up the steaming, worn steps, Harvey bumping along beside him and Leo gasping behind, then entered the small building on the pyramid's flat top: the Temple of the Owls, so-called on account of the frieze that ran along its lintel. (They didn't look like owls to Gideon, but no one had much liked his "Temple of the Turkeys" suggestion.)

Inside, the structure was bare, with the look of a burned-out tenement. Ceilings, walls, and floor were coated with a limestone stucco made dismal and blotchy by centuries of intrusive plant growth, since removed, and a millennium of damp heat, still very much present. Only near the roofline were there a few faded streaks of green, blue, and red to suggest what it might have looked like in A.D. 900. The one unusual note was the square opening cut in the floor, and that, of course, led into the stairwell.

On the landing twelve steps below, most of the west wall had already been taken down, with the removed blocks neatly stacked and numbered with felt-tipped markers. The crew and another Mayan laborer were gazing mutely at the opening. Two portable lamps on the landing threw their garish yellow light into the small, astonishing room before them.

It is one of the great thrills of anthropology to look at something that was sealed up a thousand years ago, by the people of a great and vanished culture, and has lain unseen ever since. But this was something more, something out of a fairy tale . . . the Crystal Cave, was it? The room was a jeweled, sparkling white, made all the more dazzling by its contrast with the grimy stairwell—a fiercely glittering ice grotto in the heart of the Yucatan rain forest. But the ice was crystalized calcium carbonate, of course: stalactites on the ceiling, stalagmites on the floor, and a glistening, petrified sheen of it on the walls.

In the center was a waist-high stone chest three feet square, made of four massive slabs standing on their sides, and capped by a great, overhanging stone lid eight inches thick. The lid too was coated with crystal deposits, but through the milky veneer Gideon could see an intricately carved surface of extraordinary beauty. There were Long Count dates around the rim, and in the center a lovingly worked figure of the *halach-uinic*, the True Man, emerging from or disappearing into the jaws of an

Underworld serpent. The red paint had faded to a pale rose. Other than that, the chest might have been finished that morning. The lid was magnificent, in itself a find of the first order. Gideon hardly dared think about what might be under it.

Howard Bennett hadn't seen him come in. Shirtless and built something like a sumo wrestler—sleekly corpulent, with thick, soapy flesh sheathing a heavily muscled frame—he was staring avidly at the lid. On his gleaming neck and shoulders, the skin twitched like a horse's. Gideon heard him laugh deep in his throat, softly and privately. The sound set off an odd shiver of apprehension at the back of Gideon's scalp.

Howard looked up to see the newcomers. "What do you think now?" he said, half exultantly, half challengingly. Gideon had not made a secret of his doubts about there being anything to find.

"It's fantastic," he said sincerely. "I was dead wrong. Congratulations."

Under its sheen of sweat, Howard's beefy, dissipated face was deeply flushed. He wiped perspiration from his upper lip with the tip of an old paisley bandanna tied around his throat and laughed.

Howard Bennett laughed easily and often. His loose, jovial personality was an asset for his one-of-a-kind vocation: directing excavations manned by well-heeled amateurs as keen on vacationing as on digging. After a day at the site he was always game for an evening at the nearby Club Med or even a four-hour round trip to Merida, to the Maya Excelsior Bar, or La Discotheque, or the Boccacio 2000. At the Maya Excelsior, in fact, he was a Saturday-night fixture; he sat in with the small band, playing jazz clarinet, at which he was extraordinarily proficient.

He had had a brief university career; three years at three different institutions. He'd been a lackluster teacher, a less-than-responsible faculty member, and an indifferent researcher. But his formidable field methodology put him in demand as an excavation supervisor, and he was, to Gideon's knowledge, the only person who did this sort of thing for a living. He'd been on Latin American digs for over ten years now, the last two at Tlaloc. In that time he'd been back to the United States only twice, to renew his passport and visas. For more than a decade he had lived a gypsylike existence in Mexico, Guatemala, and Belize.

Gideon had briefly worked with him three years before, at a Mixtec site in Oaxaca, and had been worried about him then. Now it was worse. Howard's centerless, hard-living existence was showing: He was putting on weight, his features were getting blurry, and he was now finishing off a couple of beers at lunch in addition to his evening drinking. And he wasn't very interested in talking about archaeology with Gideon. His conversation ranged from griping about how miserably archaeologists were paid to frank envy of the way some of the rich amateurs could afford to live. For Howard, ten years of rubbing shoulders with high-living stockbrokers and businessmen had not been salutary. He was drinking more, deteriorating mentally and physically, and drifting deeper into professional obscurity.

At least he had been, until this startling find. He

grinned at Gideon, blond eyebrows beetling. "What does it remind you of?"

"Palenque," Gideon said quietly.

"Yeah," Howard breathed. "Palenque!"

It would make anyone think of Palenque, the elegant ruin three hundred miles to the south in the even denser jungles of Chiapas. There, in 1952, in the staircase of a somewhat larger pyramid under a somewhat larger temple, Alberto Ruz Lhuillier had also found a room sealed behind a false wall, also containing a stone chest, much bigger than this one, with a finely carved lid. Inside had been one of the great finds of Meso-American archaeology. It was the skeleton of the ruler known as Pacal, lying regally on his back, swathed in the rich trappings of a Mayan lord: necklace laid upon necklace, enormous earrings, funerary mask, and diadem, all of polished jade; intricately carved rings on all ten fingers; a great pear-shaped pearl; a jade bead delicately placed between his teeth as food for his journey; a jade statue of the sun god at his feet to accompany him.

Howard stared hungrily at the chest. "What do you think is in it?" he asked Gideon and laughed again. His stiff, straw-blond hair was dark with sweat, as furrowed as if he'd been swimming. Gideon didn't like the feverish-looking red patches on his cheeks, or his vaguely reckless manner.

"Not much; the interior dimensions can't be more than two by two," Gideon said reasonably, but Howard's excitement was practically crackling in the dank air, beginning to get to him. He felt the beginning of an ache at his temples and made himself relax his knotted jaw muscles. "If it's another royal burial I'm afraid they've scrunched him up a little to fit him in."

It was meant to ease the atmosphere. Harvey laughed dutifully, and a few of the crew members snickered, but Howard brayed; a nasal yawp that made the others glance uncomfortably at each other.

"You know what I'm going to do?" he said abruptly. "I'm going to get the lid up. Right now." He rubbed his hands together mirthfully while sweat dripped from his chin. He turned to the laborer and spoke tersely in Spanish.

"Avelino, I want a tripod with a hand winch rigged up. And some bracing poles. Go tell the others."

Gideon frowned. This was a tricky operation, better left until the next day when preparations could be more calmly made. He began to say something but changed his mind. No director liked having his authority contested in public, and the leadership of the dig belonged in Howard's hands. Gideon was only there for a few weeks, strictly to analyze the skeletal material. Besides, it was always possible that Howard knew what he was doing.

For the moment it seemed that he did. His directions were concise and accurate, and the tiny Mayan workmen were used to lifting heavy things in cramped spaces. Working efficiently, they spoke quietly to each other in their soft, rustly language. In twenty minutes they had one edge of the lid raised three or four inches, enough to force several wooden rods under it to prop it up.

Howard jumped forward as soon as they were in place, his flashlight already flicked on. He knelt in front of the chest like a man before an altar and shone the light into the narrow opening, leaning forward to get his eyes up against the crevice. For long seconds there was no sound other than the clinking of the metal flashlight barrel against the rim of the chest as he moved it along.

He peered into the chest without saying anything, forearms braced against the rim, forehead leaning on them. The only sound now was an erratic flutter above their heads, like spattering fat: insects igniting against the lights. Nobody in the crew spoke, nobody moved. If they were like Gideon they weren't even breathing. Howard's back was to them, his soft, slabby shoulders buttery with sweat. He looked, thought Gideon, as if he were well on the way to melting into a greasy puddle at the foot of the chest, like something out of H.P. Lovecraft.

"Jesus Christ," he said, tight-voiced and expressionless. "Gideon, look at this."

Swallowing hard, his neck aching with anticipation, Gideon moved forward, not sure whether Howard was looking at the find of the century or the letdown of his life. When he stepped into the recess, stalagmites crunched underneath him, a startlingly crisp sensation in the mucky heat. He dropped to one knee beside Howard while the others watched avidly. Howard shone the light into the chest for him.

Gideon leaned intently forward, profoundly grateful for his life. What other occupation offered moments like this?

Once he got used to the bobbing shadows from Howard's trembling flashlight his reaction was piercing disappointment. There was nothing in the chest but a few dusty, common objects like hundreds of other objects from dozens of other digs: a few jade beads in a heap; a pair of ear ornaments made from scallop shells; two painted plates; and two slim, rectangular, neatly folded bundles of bark lying side by side, also daubed with paint. They all had value from a scholarly point of view, but they were definitely not the find of the century. Why in the world had the Maya gone to such elaborate trouble to hide and preserve this homely junk?

But Gideon was a physical anthropologist; bones were his specialty, not artifacts. Howard was an archaeologist, and he knew better. The flashlight jerked in his hand.

"A *codex*!" he whispered thickly.

Gideon looked again and of course they weren't simple bundles of bark at all. Now he could see the glyphs across the tops of the leaves and the comic-strip–like panels with their gaudy drawings as the beam from Howard's flashlight picked them out. It was a Mayan codex, a pre-Conquest Mayan "book," lying on its spine, opened in the middle so the two halves lay flat.

His lips parted for speech, but he couldn't think of anything to say. Maybe it was the find of the century after all. At least in Mayan archaeology.

4

Literally of the century. There were only three other Mayan codices in existence, and the last one had been found in 1860. All of them were owned by state libraries—in Dresden, Madrid, and Paris—and none were yet completely translated. Assuming that the subject matter of this one was like the others', the fund of knowledge about Mayan ceremony, religion, and language had just been increased by a whopping thirty-three-and-a-third percent.

Howard invited the rest of the crew into the recess to have a look. Whether more than one or two had any idea of the significance of what they saw was doubtful, but they peered through the slit into the stone chest in respectful silence, then backed off a few steps to leave the two anthropologists to their professional talk.

"God, do you know what that must be *worth?*" Howard exclaimed with a rumble of laughter.

A telling comment, but not quite up to professional standards; not in Gideon's view. Its market value was irrelevant; the codex was the property of the Republic of Mexico and properly so. It would never be sold.

"It could be the most significant Mayan find since Palenque," Gideon said stuffily, as much for the crew's benefit as Howard's.

It didn't do much to enlighten Howard. "I could get you two million bucks for that tomorrow," he said. "Easy."

He laughed again and stood up. "Let's get on with it." He turned to give instructions to the foreman on completing the delicate process of levering up the lid and getting it off without damaging the intricate inscriptions.

Gideon retreated to an unoccupied corner of the landing and watched quietly, occasionally wiping the sweat from his eyes. He was no expert in this kind of work, which had more in common with engineering than with anthropology.

Neither was Howard, it turned out. As he and the laborers grunted, pouring sweat, to wedge more poles under the lid, something went wrong. One of the poles was tapped too sharply with a sledgehammer and popped out like a cork to clatter on the floor. The great lid teetered to the right, swayed on its ropes like a colossal pendulum while the workers fought to balance it, and then, with agonizing slowness, tipped and went grinding ponderously over the rim of the chest with a sound like that of the last terrible block sliding into place at the end of *Aida*. It smashed into the wall, one of its richly carved corners crumbling away. That was bad enough, but on its way it also bumped against one of the props that had been erected as shoring while the passageway was dug out.

The prop was knocked off its footing, and for a breathless moment it hung askew, suspended from the crossbeam above it. Then the crossbeam groaned and came down, and it seemed as if half the vaulted ceiling followed with a roar and a billow of sour, choking dust. There were frightened shouts, but when the coughing stopped they found, amazingly enough, that none of the big, wedge-shaped stone blocks had hit anybody, although everyone had been showered with the rubble that the ancient Maya had used to fill their interior walls. Gideon came out of it with another dent in his straw hat and a scrape on the back of his hand. One of the crew had broken his watch; another had chipped a tooth somehow. Almost everyone was coughing and spitting.

While Gideon was still checking to make sure they were all right, Howard hissed sharply; a sigh of relief.

"It's okay," he called shakily, meaning the codex.

It had been shielded by the lid, which still lay across the chest at an angle. Only Gideon seemed to notice that the wonderful bas-reliefs had been chipped by falling rock in four or five places. Add those to the broken corner, and a gloriously preserved find was now just another piece of moldering Mayan art. And it was going to get worse if Howard persisted. But surely he would quit now and sit down to do some planning.

But no. "All right," he said in a way that told Gideon he was just getting started. "All right now."

He spat dirt from his mouth, leaned over the chest, and shoved his sleek arm under the lid as far as he could, grimacing with the effort. But he could only get it in up to his elbow, and with a grunt of frustration he jerked it out. He got to his feet and stared sullenly at the lid, as if it were keeping him from the codex out of stubborn perversity. Two angry-looking welts from the rough stone ran down his forearm, slowly oozing blood. Apparently he hadn't noticed.

"I'm going to need everyone's help," he said. "Preston, Gideon, Leo, you three—"

Gideon decided there had to be a confrontation, like it or not. "Howard—" He had to stop to wipe the dust from his lips with the back of his hand. Perspiration had turned it to a gritty mud. "I think we'd better stop right now and get everyone out of here. This place is going to need more shoring up."

Howard turned on him. "Are you out of your mind? Just leave the codex?"

"It'll wait. Somebody's going to get killed if we stay here."

And that was only part of it. There was the material itself. Howard had already mutilated the magnificent lid, and now he was trying to haul out the codex with all the delicacy of a nineteenth-century grave robber. You didn't simply reach in with sweaty fingers and grab a precious thing like that. Before the contents of the chest were touched they had to be recorded, photographed, drawn *in situ*. And the codex had to be studied to see what its state of preservation was before it was removed and exposed to the outside air. Howard knew all that, damn him. He was letting his excitement get the better of him.

For a moment the director glared at him. Then it was all sweet, slippery reasonableness. "Now, Gideon, don't get melodramatic. Nobody's going to get killed. Don't you think I know what I'm doing?"

Gideon was silent.

"We can have it out in fifteen minutes if everybody cooperates." Howard's voice edged upward. "We can't just leave it here unprotected!"

"We can get guards," Gideon said.

As Howard opened his mouth to answer, a beam let out a sharp, popping crack somewhere above them, and dirt showered from the ceiling onto the top steps. A few pebbles skittered down the stairs toward them.

"Uh, I think Gideon's right," Leo Rose said tentatively. Leo had been a building contractor at one time, and knew about these things. "This whole thing could come down any minute." A few others murmured agreement.

"Guards?" Howard said with a husky chuckle; he was going to try treating it as a joke. "Now just where in the hell are we supposed to get guards we can trust by tonight?"

"Tonight we can guard it ourselves," Gideon said. "We can take turns." He put what he hoped was an implacable expression on his face. The quicker this was over, the better; he just wanted everybody out.

Howard continued to smile at him, but in his cheek a sinew popped. And all at once, he threw in the towel.

"All right, fine," he said genially, as if the whole thing struck him as a silly quibble he could afford to be magnanimous about. "Let's go, everyone."

Once outside, he reestablished his authority. "We'll

take turns standing guard all night; four-hour shifts, two people per team, men only."

"Why only men?" one of the three women demanded.

Howard ignored her. "I'll take the first shift. Worthy, you take it with me."

"Me?" Worthy Partridge was a prunish, middle-aged writer of children's stories. "I'm afraid I know very little about standing guard."

"What is there to know? All right, now—" He stopped, scowling and suspicious. Avelino Canul, the Mayan foreman, was hovering nearby, paying close attention.

"What do you want, Avelino?" Howard asked in brusque Spanish. "You can go home now. You too, Nas. All of you."

Respectfully the foreman explained that they were waiting for their pay. It was Friday.

Muttering and impatient, Howard patted the rear pockets of his tan shorts. "Hell, I forgot all about it," he said, slipping into English. "I left my wallet at the hotel."

"We should wait until Monday?" Avelino asked hopefully. This was not the first time it had happened, and Howard had made a practice of giving them a little something extra for the inconvenience. By Mayan wage standards, it was considerably more than a little something.

Howard nodded curtly and waited for them to go. "Now, the rest of you go on back and get some dinner. Gideon, you and Leo take the next shift. Be back at—what time is it now, anyway?"

"A little after five," Worthy told him.

"Okay, be back at nine. Worthy and Joe, you're on at one to four. Then you and me, Preston, from four to eight." He paused and looked accommodatingly at Gideon. "How's that? Does that meet with your approval?"

Gideon hesitated. He would have been happier taking the first shift himself; Howard could use some time to settle down. And Worthy wouldn't have been his first choice as a partner. But he'd already won the big battle, and he didn't feel like having another argument. Besides, the chances of temple robbers materializing in the next four hours to steal a codex that had been discovered less than two hours ago were remote, to say the least.

"Okay," he said. "We'll see you at nine."

"Something's wrong here," blurted Leo, not normally the most intuitive of men.

It was ten to nine. They had returned to the site under a sultry, darkening sky to find the work shed empty, Howard and Worthy nowhere to be seen. On the work table was the empty, cracked holster of the old .32 caliber revolver that Howard kept at the site as protection against *bandidos*. The lights were on, the generator humming. An opened but untouched bottle of Coca-Cola rested on the floor near a chair.

"They're probably just looking around," Gideon said. "That's all."

"Yeah, sure, that figures."

All the same they glanced uneasily at each other and began walking quickly across the plaza toward the temple. They had reached the foot of the pyramid when they heard scraping noises above them and looked up into the half-darkness to see Worthy floundering sideways down the steps.

"Gideon!" he called. "Leo! My God!"

He came perilously close to slipping on the uneven stones, righted himself after some gawky flapping with his long arms, and continued coming down with more care. "My God," Gideon heard him murmur again. "Oh, dear Lord."

This, Gideon said to himself, is not going to be good news.

When he got to the bottom, Worthy looked apprehensively at both of them. "Where's Howard? Have you seen him?"

No, definitely not good news.

"What do you mean, have *we* seen him?" Leo said. "Where is he?"

Worthy clutched Gideon's arm, an uncharacteristic gesture. "It's terrible up there—it's—it's—"

Gideon was off, taking the steps of the pyramid two at a time. Worthy gave a little whimper and scrambled up behind him, trying to keep up, to catch his breath, and to explain, all at once.

"He said—Howard said—he heard something . . . about an hour ago. He took that wretched gun, and a crowbar too, and went to check . . ."

"You didn't go with him?" Gideon called over his shoulder without slowing down.

"He said not to. He said he'd do a . . . do a patrol himself. You know the way the man is . . ."

Gideon did indeed. He reached the top and ran across the weedy, stonelittered terrace to the temple. In every direction the dense mat of tropical forest stretched to the flat horizon, a bleak irongray in the fading light.

It was black inside the windowless temple. He switched on the flashlight he'd brought with him.

Worthy caught up to him. "He was gone so long . . . I began to wonder. I went to check. And when I got here I found— I found—"

It wasn't necessary for him to tell what he'd found. Gideon stood rock-still, disbelieving, the flashlight beamed directly at the square opening in the stone floor.

There was no landing below. There was no passage. There were no steps, or none after the top two or three. All there was was a square space filled with rubble and jumbled blocks of worked stone.

Behind them Leo clumped bulkily through the entrance. "Oh, shit," he said. "The whole goddamn thing caved in. I knew it."

It was true. The secret passage that the Maya had excavated down into the rubble-packed pyramid—and then filled with more rubble to hide it—had collapsed. The years Horizon had spent digging out the stairway had been undone in seconds. It was all buried again, the way the Maya had wanted it in the first place.

Worthy stared at Gideon. His lips twitched. "Where's Howard?" he said. "Where's the codex?"

5

"And that's the whole story," Gideon said. "Good-bye Howard, good-bye, codex." They were on their third cup of coffee. "Nobody's seen them since. If he's really managed to sell it, he's probably in Rio living like a millionaire. Change that; if he's sold it, he *is* a millionaire."

"But how can you be sure he took it?" Julie asked. "Maybe the stairwell just caved in on it. It was already pretty shaky, right? Maybe the codex is still there, under all the rubble. Maybe *Howard* is still there—"

"No, we dug it out, or rather the police did, all the way back down to the landing. Took them two days," Gideon remembered. "Police dig faster than archaeologists."

"And when they got there they didn't find anything?"

"Well, the chest itself was still there. He'd smashed the lid to pieces to get it off. That was a crime in its own right. It was a hell of a piece of art."

"Maybe the cave-in smashed it."

"No, it was done with the sledgehammer. He left it

upstairs on the temple floor, with some of the other tools. The police matched a couple of the gouges on the lid with the head of the hammer." He shook his head, freshly pained at the memory. "That beautiful, beautiful carving."

Julie commiserated silently, caressing the back of his hand.

"The earrings and plates and things were still inside," he went on, "crushed by the cave-in—or maybe by the sledge for good measure; who knows—but the codex was gone."

"And Howard just disappeared into the jungle?"

"He disappeared into the friendly skies of Aeromexico. While we were all standing around gawking at the cave-in, he must have been doubling back to the hotel. The police found the crowbar near the path. Anyway, he picked up some stuff from his room, ripped off a van from the parking lot, and took off. They found the van at the airport in Merida a few days later."

"What about the gun?"

"Never seen again."

"And now you really think he's living the high life somewhere?"

"That I'm not so sure about. We put together a committee of anthropologists from Latin America and the States—I guess I was the prime mover—to keep him from selling the codex. The Committee for Mayan Scholarship."

Julie giggled. "Sorry, I didn't mean to laugh, but what could a committee do?"

They could do plenty. They had made it their business

to see that every potential buyer of the codex they could think of—every museum, every library, every auction house and gallery, even every private collector—was informed of how it had gotten into Howard's hands. They had contacted over four thousand institutions and individuals, and gotten articles in all the relevant journals and magazines.

"And we did a lot more than that. We made it clear that whoever bought it, or a piece of it, would be prosecuted to the full extent of the law—which was maybe pushing it a little, because there isn't any enforceable international law on buying stolen archaeological material."

"And you were successful? He wasn't able to sell it?"

"Not as far as we know. It wasn't too hard to scare possible buyers, you see, because this would have been the first and only Mayan codex ever available on the open market, or any market. So anyone who bought *any* Mayan codex had to know that he was buying *this* one. No one could claim ignorance."

"I bet Howard was a little annoyed."

"I sure as hell hope so. Look, the clouds have lifted."

The plane was beginning its descent now, sliding down over the huge green bulge of Yucatan. There wasn't much to see. A virtually featureless world, neatly bisected: pure bright-blue sky above, hummocky green jungle below. Not a building in sight; no roads, no electrical towers. No rivers even, for northern Yucatan, lush as it is, has none. All the water is underground, in the enormous caverns yawning beneath the limestone crust. The only variation in the green was an occasional flat, circular gleam of olive brown, like a plastic disk stuck on a relief map to represent a pond. In a sense these *were* the ponds of Yucatan, the famous cenotes; sinkholes where the fragile limestone had collapsed to reveal the water table below.

"I'm still not clear about the cave-in," Julie said. "Was it an accident or what? Why didn't Howard get caught in it himself?"

"He didn't get caught because it wasn't an accident. He purposely knocked down the props to cave it in, hoping we'd think he might be buried down there and waste a day or two digging for him instead of hunting for him. Which we did."

"But how can you possibly know that?"

"He told us."

"He . . .?"

"Told us. He mailed us a letter from Merida before he flew out. Two pages, very cool and offhand. Said he really hated to smash the lid, but what else could he do, and he apologized for taking somebody's van but he couldn't very well call a taxi, could he, and the van would be found unharmed in Slot Number Something at the airport. And of course he'd do everything he could to find someone who'd buy the codex whole so he wouldn't have to cut such a wonderful thing up into little pieces. Itty bitty pieces, I think he said."

"Gideon, he sounds a little crazy."

"I wouldn't be surprised. Not that being crazy lets him off the hook, the bastard."

"The louse," Julie agreed.

The landing patter had begun, muffled by the heavy

thrum of the engines. "The captain has turned on the no-smoking sign. Please fasten your seat belts and return your tray tables . . ."

Obediently Gideon folded the table back into the seat in front of him. "Anything else you want to know?" By now he was glad he'd told her the story. She was right; he should have done it a long time ago.

"Well, I do have one question, but you're going to think it's pretty dumb." She grinned at him. "Something tells me I'm going to have a lot of silly questions over the next couple of weeks."

Gideon smiled back at her. He loved her silly questions. "Your questions are never dumb. Merely ignorant."

"Oh, thanks, that's a relief. All right, then, just what *is* a codex? A manuscript? A book?"

"That's right. From the Latin *caudex*, meaning a split block of wood, kind of like a shingle, which the Romans coated with wax and then inscribed."

She looked at him quizzically. "You know the damnedest things."

"I," he said with dignity, "am a full professor. My mind is replete with scholarly arcana, some of which, I can safely say, are even more useless than that."

"I know. It's ruining our social life. Nobody wants to play Trivial Pursuit with us."

He laughed. "Anyway, the term came into general use to mean anything with pages, as opposed to a continuous scroll. A Mayan codex looks pretty much like a modern book, with covers and pages that turn, except it's made out of one long strip of paper—pounded bark, rather—

that's folded accordian-style. You can pull it all out like a folding screen."

"That's interesting," she said. "And they're really so valuable?"

"They're so valuable that nobody knows what one's worth. There are only three others, and none of them is in private hands. Over a million dollars I'd guess, even on the black market. Maybe four times that if you cut it up and sold the pages separately." He grimaced. "Perish the thought."

Customs at Merida International Airport meant being waved through by a sullen woman in an olive-drab uniform, who was sipping from a can of Dr. Pepper and looking as if she wanted to be someplace else. As they walked through the glass doors into the waiting room and the moist heat of Yucatan, Julie said: "Gideon, there's a man looking at us in a funny way. Is it someone you know?"

Gideon followed her gaze toward a display of giant Kahlua bottles in the window of the duty-free shop. In front of it a bony man with a vaguely vexed expression around the eyes, a severely trimmed but scraggly goatee, and a pinched, prunish mouth was looking at them, one hand raised and motionless, with the index finger primly and economically extended. The sandy goatee was new, but the rest was familiar. Gideon smiled and waved.

"That," he said, "is Worthy Partridge, and he's not looking at us funny. He always looks like that."

"Is that really his name?" she asked, as they made their way toward him.

"I think the whole name is Kenneth Worthy Partridge,

but he just uses the last two. He writes children's books, and he figures it looks good on the covers. You know, Mother Goose, Peter Rabbit, Worthy Partridge."

"A children's writer?" Julie asked disbelievingly. "He doesn't exactly look like a man who loves kids."

He didn't love kids, and he wasn't overly keen on grownups either. Despite Worthy's dazed and ineffectual performance on the night that Howard had disappeared with the codex, Gideon remembered him as a sharply critical man given to faultfinding and sweeping generalizations: "The Mayans were dopes." "All lawyers are crooks." "Children have only two motivations—selfishness and greed."

With allowances made for these sometimes startling pronouncements, Gideon had liked him, or at least enjoyed his presence. He seemed to be one of those people who had decided on a personality role early in life and then found himself typecast, unable to move on to something else. But there were occasional glimmers of a nimble intelligence, and every now and then a wry, dessicated sense of humor would peep unexpectedly out.

He was not feeling humorous this afternoon. When he was introduced to Julie he nodded without smiling, and when Gideon asked him how the dig was going, his reply was dour and terse.

"The dig," he said, "is cursed."

Gideon very nearly laughed, but managed to cough discreetly instead. It was going to take a while to get used to Worthy Partridge again.

6

But this time it wasn't hyperbole. The excavation at Tlaloc had been cursed, literally and emphatically. In the sixteenth century. By the Maya.

And in case there should be any doubt about it they had left a written copy at the site. Worthy gave them the details as he started up the tan Volkswagen van that served as the dig runabout.

"We found it when we started to clear the Priest's House. There was a niche in the entryway, right next to the new skeleton, and in it was this little pamphlet wrapped in bark. A curse," he said with a grimace, as if it had been put there as a personal affront to Worthy Partridge.

"Mm," Gideon said, looking dreamily out the window.

For a while, when he'd been dredging up those rotten memories, he'd wondered if returning had been a mistake. But now, watching the neat, white, all-in-a-row suburbs of Merida give way to brilliant jungle and immense henequen plantations with their colonial haciendas, once grand but now weathering romantically, it didn't seem like a bad idea at all. After the muted greens of the Pacific Northwest, the colors were astonishingly bright and varied under a brassy Mexican sun, and even the warmth—sticky, but nothing like the mind-numbing heat of June—was only a minor annoyance.

"A pamphlet?" Julie said. "Do you mean a codex?"

"I don't believe so," Worthy said uncertainly. "Dr. Goldstein said it was more like the books of Chim Bom Bom or somebody. Sis Boom Bah, Rin Tin Tin, some such absurd name."

"The Books of Chilam Balam," Gideon said. "Post-Conquest books, written by the Maya on Spanish paper. The conquistadores taught the native scribes how to use European script to write down the Mayan language. The idea was to make it easier to teach them Christianity, but of course the Maya jumped at the chance to write all kinds of things."

"Hold on," Julie said. "I feel an ignorant question coming on. Didn't they already know how to write? What about that codex? What about those calendars they carved?"

"Those are hieroglyphs," Gideon explained. "Pictures, basically, or extremely simple symbols—one dot equals *one*, two dots equal *two*. A picture of a house means *house*. They're much more primitive than the spoken language—a kind of shorthand—and there are a lot of things they can't express. They're also harder for us to understand; we still can't read most of them. But these other books are translatable by anyone who understands old Mayan. It's fascinating, really—"

He caught himself and stopped. Unsolicited lectures were one of the professorly hazards to which he was easy prey. "What kind of curse is it?" he asked Worthy. "What does it say?"

"Oh, your basic run-of-the-mill curse," Worthy said with a shrug. "You know, 'He who violates this sacred temple will perish horribly.' This Professor Garrison from Tulane has been down here working on the translation, and that's all she'd tell anybody until she got it completely finished. Scientists," he concluded, "are prima donnas."

As usual, a Worthy Partridge dictum had a way of ending a conversation with a clunk, and Julie and Gideon settled back to watch the scenery go by. They were deep in Mayan country now: thick, scrubby jungle and tiny roadside villages with names like Xlokzodozonot, Xlacab, and Tzukmuk—collections of twenty or thirty primitive thatch-roofed houses with reed or stuccoed walls. No toilets, no running water. Most had no doors, so that the three people in the air-conditioned van could look inside as they went past and see a clay floor, a few sticks of furniture, a hammock, a naked child or two. Pigs, chickens, and skinny dogs wandered aimlessly across the highway, contemptuous of the traffic.

It was Worthy himself who resumed the discussion, but it wasn't much of an improvement. "She's already finished the translation, but we've had to sit around twiddling our thumbs waiting for *you* because Dr. Goldstein wanted you to be there."

Clunk.

Gideon made a try at keeping things going. "How's

the writing, Worthy? Are you still doing that series on the little girl and her fish from Finland?"

"Iceland. No, I'm considering a new adventure series featuring Paco and Pablo—two little boys from ancient Mayan times. What do you think?"

"Uh . . . I hate to split hairs, but I know you like to be accurate, and Paco and Pablo aren't ancient Mayan names. They're Spanish."

Worthy treated him to a brief, mordant glance. "What would you suggest, 'Zactecauh and Yxcal Chac Go to the Fiesta'? 'Ahpop Achih and Gucumatz Find a Friend'?"

Gideon sighed and returned to the scenery.

At a sign that said *"Chichen Itza, Zona Arqueológica,"* Worthy swung around a turkey having a leisurely peck at something in a mud puddle and turned right.

"Chichen Itza?" Julie said. "Are we going to Chichen Itza?"

"No," Gideon explained. "We're going to the Hotel Mayaland, which is just outside the back entrance to Chichen Itza. That's where we all stay. Tlaloc is less than a mile beyond, to the north."

Five minutes later they pulled up in front of the long, yellow main building of the hotel. Gideon remembered it with pleasure; a welcome oasis of cleanliness and civilization in one of Mexico's most undeveloped areas. Through the great entrance arch they could look across the elegant open lobby and down a long veranda paved with gleaming tiles and lined with pillars. Under big lanterns hanging from the veranda roof, groups of people were having cocktails at low glass tables.

"Like it?" he asked as they stepped down from the van.

Julie continued to take in the scene. Small, dark, white-jacketed waiters moved agilely among the tables, threading their way between lush potted plants. At the open-air registration desk a festive party of a dozen or so Germans was being checked in.

"Ah," she said finally, "the jungle; the raw, brooding, primitive sense of isolation . . ."

Waiting for them on the dresser in their room was a wicker basket of yellow dahlias, an ice bucket stuffed with brown bottles of Montejo, the slightly bitter local beer, another ice bucket with glasses in it, and a note from Abe: "Welcome to Yucatan, what took you so long? Relax, wash up, go sit out on the balcony, have a few beers. And save one for me. I'll stop by at 5:00."

They followed his instructions to the letter, and at 4:45 they were in wrought-iron rocking chairs on the ample, deeply shaded balcony outside their room, their second beers at their sides. They had showered and changed to fresh clothes, and now they tipped contentedly back and forth, breathing in the thick, fragrant air and listening to the hollow chuckling of unfamiliar birds in the trees.

Their room was on the second floor, and its balcony overlooked the lush grounds of the grand old hotel—a jungle, but a jungle wrestled into submission, tamed and ordered for the pleasure of discriminating human eyes. Flagstone paths wound from the yellow, vaguely Moorish main building to the outlying bungalows, through thick stands of chicle trees, acacias, and royal palms, some of them a hundred feet high, their fronds and branches matted with trailing vines and flowers. Here and there quiet fountains were tucked away behind massed bougainvillea and frangipani. At the level of the balcony the great arms of a ceiba tree spread out before them, every crotch and hollow overflowing with plant life that had taken hold in the moist bark: spiky, flowering plants, orchids that had trunks of their own, miniature banana palms. Trees growing out of trees.

Drifting appropriately up from the veranda were the soft chords of a guitar serenading the scattered groups of people having drinks. Even the occasional muted snatches of cocktail conversation, mostly in German or English, carried a sense of civilized ease that was more than welcome after a grubby, exhausting journey that had started at 5:00 A.M. The Mayaland, of course, had been built as a hotel for hardy, well-to-do visitors to nearby Chichen Itza in the 1930s. It was mere luck that it was also close enough to the long-hidden Tlaloc to serve as headquarters.

Julie leaned back in her rocker and put her feet up on the low, glass-topped table.

"Ah," she said, "the essential Yucatan. The jungle, the raw, primitive, elemental—"

Gideon laughed. "Don't be tedious. You have to live someplace, you know, even on a dig, and since the Mayaland is so close and there are usually a few spare rooms . . ."

"Yes, but before I met you I was so naive I believed genuine anthropologists slept in tents and lived off the land on snakes and toads. I didn't know they stayed in deluxe international resorts, for God's sake."

"Yes, well, naturally Abe and I, being genuine anthropologists, would prefer bathing in a muddy cenote and eating iguanas, but of course we have to think of our amateurs, who might not be so used to roughing it."

"Sure," Julie said. "Right." She felt on her left for her glass. Gideon picked it up and put it in her hand, and they sat in peaceable silence until Abe knocked on the louvered door to the room at five o'clock.

He was as lean and sprightly as ever. Maybe a little sprightlier, as if two weeks of poking among the tumbled stones of Tlaloc under the Yucatecan sun had done his arthritis good, which it no doubt had. His watery blue eyes sparkled with intelligence and humor above the rectangular glasses he'd recently taken to wearing low on his nose most of the time, and around his neck on a black cord the rest of the time. This after a quarter century of carrying his reading glasses in a pocket and rummaging for them when he needed them. It was one of the very few concessions to age Gideon had known him to make.

"So," he said, after the preliminaries of greeting, when Gideon had poured him a glass of beer and they had resettled on the balcony, "how do you like our curse?" His exuberant sunburst of white hair, backlit by the sun, was like a frizzy halo.

"I can hardly wait for all the lousy jokes," Gideon said. "Every time anybody breaks a pencil or misplaces a trowel it's going to be the Curse of Tlaloc. When does Garrison present her translation?"

"After dinner. Eight o'clock." He leaned forward,

holding the glass in both thin hands. "Listen, guess what. The Institute changed its mind. They're going to let us dig under the temple. I guess I convinced them after all."

"That's great! Congratulations!"

When the Instituto Nacional de Antropologia e Historia had permitted Horizon to reopen Tlaloc, the Temple of the Owls, where the codex had been found (and promptly lost), was expressly excluded. It was to remain locked and off limits, a kind of shrine to iniquity. This, Gideon knew, Abe had been lobbying to have changed, spending several days in Mexico City putting forth a persuasive argument: Somewhere he had gotten hold of an almost unknown volume by the nineteenth-century French artist-explorer Jean Frédéric de Waldeck, in which was sketched a ruined, looted Mayan temple-pyramid he had come upon in the Guatemalan highlands. The structure was virtually identical to the Temple of the Owls—two-level stairwell, concealed room in the landing, and all.

Moreover, de Waldeck had found a *second* concealed chamber at the base of the steps, also regrettably broken into and emptied. Did this mean there might be a second sealed room at Tlaloc, under the first one and now blocked by the debris of the cave-in? If there were, what might it not contain, considering the fantastic find in the one above? No one knew the answers, of course, (and the Count de Waldeck's romantic enthusiasms had been known to get the better of his fidelity to fact), but Gideon was sure that Abe's presentation to the Institute had made their mouths water.

"That's wonderful, Abe," Julie said. "Maybe Horizon can get back in their good graces yet."

With his head tilted to one side, Abe seemed to weigh these innocuous words. "Maybe," he said darkly, "maybe not." He drained his beer. "If you're not too tired from your trip, how about taking a walk to the site? We can be back by dark if we get started now."

"I'd love it!" Julie said.

"Good. And you, Gideon, I want you to have a look at something."

Gideon frowned. "Is something wrong, Abe?"

"That," Abe said, "is what I want you to tell me."

As Yucatecan ruins went, it wasn't much, not in the same league as Coba, or Chichen Itza, or Uxmal; a square ceremonial plaza about three hundred feet down each side, with six more-or-less standing structures. The largest was the one they were on, the Pyramid of the Owls, but by Mayan standards it was hardly imposing: a squat, truncated pyramid only forty-two feet high, with its broad, crumbling stairway of stone steps set at a comfortable forty-degree grade instead of the usual dizzying, near-vertical uplift.

When they had made their way to the top they turned to look back out over the site. Five and a half years hadn't changed it much. Only the eight-foot chain-link fence surrounding it was new. It had been erected by the government a few months after the site had been shut down.

They were facing west into an early-evening sky just shifting from a pale blue to a rich, red-ribbed mauve.

Below them were the rest of the buildings, trailing long shadows and scattered with no apparent design around the edges of the grassy plaza: the thickly overgrown cube of the Priest's House, where the newly discovered skeleton lay; the twin ramps of the modest ball court, where much of the current work centered; the cluster of three small, collapsed buildings, little more than foundations now and unimaginatively dubbed the West Group by Howard Bennett.

The clump of knobby hummocks along the northern border of the plaza just inside the fence had also once been structures of some kind, but the jungle had long ago broken them up and engulfed them. To a casual eye they were no more than irregular humps of dirt and debris covered with soil and sprouting tangles of weeds and bushes. No one would even be able to guess at what they had been until they were cleared and excavated in the years to come.

And that was it, except for the archaeologists' shed of limestone stucco, its thatched roof flaring to salmon as the slanting rays of sunlight struck it. Immediately beyond the square plaza, on all sides, the rain forest pressed in, a lumpy, scrubby mat, endless and impenetrable.

Or so it seemed. Invisible under the green canopy was the trail they had walked to get here. Decrepit now, collapsed and pulled apart by time and roots, it had once been part of the complex system of raised Mayan "highways" that had linked the great centers. This one cut arrow-straight through the jungle for three-quarters of a mile to Chichen Itza, conveniently passing within fifty yards of the Mayaland's grounds on the way.

But from here the Mayaland might have been on another continent. There was nothing to see beyond this silent, thousand-year-old place of ghosts but jungle, nothing to hear but the thickening drone of insects as the evening came on. It was an astonishing thought that they had been drinking iced beers in a posh hotel only twenty minutes before. Even the air was primeval, full of the sharp, burnt-straw smell of Yucatan. Here they still cleared their cornfields for next year's crop by setting them aflame, just as they had done when Tlaloc bustled with life.

"Come," Abe said. "I want you to have a look inside the temple."

The entrances to Mayan temples are generally doorless, but this one had been sealed by the government with a thick plywood barrier, now warped and spongy. A clumsy arrangement of metal bars and a massive padlock held it in place.

Abe grasped the padlock. "Yesterday when they sent me the key, I came up to have a look around. And *this*," he said dramatically, "is what I found." When he lifted the lock it slid apart in his hand.

"It was already open?" Julie said.

Not merely open, but sawn neatly through the hasp.

"Looters?" Gideon wondered.

"Ah, you tell me," Abe said. "Let's go in."

When the wooden barrier was wrenched out of the way, they found a jumble of stones and dirt inside, some of it piled three feet high. The collapsed stairwell in the center, re-excavated down to the landing by the police in 1982, was now crudely dug out a further six or seven steps. A dusty pickax lay at the bottom of the shaft. There was a spade propped in a corner, and a yellow plastic bucket on one of the dirt piles.

Abe turned to Gideon. "So, did it get left like this in 1982?"

"No, of course not. The police cleaned up after themselves, and I was here when the government sealed it. There have been looters here, all right."

"Just what I figured," Abe said with a sigh. Then, mildly, as an afterthought: *"Vay is mir."*

"Woe is me," Gideon abstractedly translated for Julie. He had been through enough crises with Abe to know the expression well. He was kneeling, looking closely at the spade in the beam of his flashlight, using his fingers to break up some clods of earth that had been stuck to it.

"But do you mean the Mexican government hasn't been guarding the site?" Julie asked. "Anyone can see it would be attractive to looters. Where there was one codex they'd think there might be another one."

"Highly unlikely," Gideon said. "Wildly unlikely."

"Sure, you'd know that, but would they?"

"It *was* guarded," Abe said. "One of the guards from Chichen Itza walked over twice a day to have a look around."

"Twice a day? But anybody—"

"Julie, certain things you got to understand. You know how many archaeological sites there are in Yucatan?"

Julie shook her head.

"Well, you're even with everybody else," Abe said.

"Nobody knows. A thousand for sure; probably two thousand. In all of them there's stuff worth stealing, but that's a lot of places to guard twenty-four hours a day."

"But still—"

"They put a fence around it," he said with a smile, "which is more than most of them have. But what kind of robber would it be who lets himself be stopped by a fence?"

"Well, at least they've saved us some work," Gideon said, brushing the dirt from his knees and standing up. "We'd just have had to redig those steps ourselves."

"That's a point," Abe said equably.

"I don't understand you two!" Julie exclaimed. "How can you stand there so calmly? There have been *looters* in here! Who knows what they got away with?"

"They didn't get away with anything," Gideon said. "At least I don't see how they could have. They didn't do any new excavating. All they did was re-dig a few steps that we'd already excavated before the cave-in. We'd gotten down thirteen steps below the landing, if I remember."

"Twelve, according to the site report," Abe said. "Altogether, twenty-four down from here." He looked at Julie. "So all they did was clear away some more of the rubble that fell down when Howard, that bum, caved in the tunnel."

"Oh." Julie subsided, looking unconvinced, and peered down into the dim shaft. "Is that where you found the chest? On that landing?"

Gideon flicked on his flashlight again and the three of them walked down together. "Here it is."

The heavy chest was still in the little chamber, four massive limestone slabs standing on their edges around a fifth slab that served as the base, all of it grit-coated and painfully empty. The mutilated lid, since patched together, was now in the Museum of Anthropology in the capital.

Gideon played the beam of light over the walls of the once-sealed room. No more fairyland down there; no pristine crystal cave. The stalactites and stalagmites were still there, but they had turned a dingy gray, thickly scummed with lichen and pulpy fungus. After a millennium of perfect preservation, five years of exposure to the fecund air of Yucatan had turned what had once seemed like glittering cascades of ice into nasty excrescences. There were even a few pallid, frightened-looking plants in crannies here and there, cowering deep inside a pyramid, ten feet below the surface of a sealed, windowless, lightless building.

"So what were they looking for?" Abe said, as much to himself as to anyone else as they walked back up the stairs. "With a thousand places to hunt for treasure, what's so special about Tlaloc? And why dig under the temple, where it's already been dug once?"

"Could they have heard about the possibility of another sealed room at the bottom?" Gideon asked.

"No, no, this I doubt very much. De Waldeck's book was never translated from the French, and as far as I know there are only two copies, the one I saw at Dumbarton Oaks and one in Paris. No one ever even mentions it in the literature. Only by luck did I stumble on it myself. Besides, another sealed room is a long shot, no more. And even if there is one, who says there's anything in it worth robbing? No, if I was a looter I could spend my time a lot better."

"The two of you keep assuming they knew exactly what they were doing," Julie said, "but they probably just heard some stories about the codex being found here and decided to do a little exploring on their own."

"Maybe so," said Abe. "Anyway, they gave up before they got very far, thank God."

Julie gestured at the tools that had been left behind. "I wonder if you frightened them off when you reopened the dig last week."

"That seems like a reasonable possibility," Abe said agreeably.

It didn't to Gideon. He could think of two reasonable possibilities, and neither of them was the one Julie had suggested. When he had taken a look at the spade he had found that the clumps of dirt sticking to the blade were just that: dirt. No fungi, no webby tufts of mold. So it was highly improbable that it had been lying untouched for very long in this dark, moist dungeon of a room. Even the heaps of dirt and rubble looked fresh, although a few of them were starting to turn a woolly gray here and there.

Assuming that these moldy piles were the earliest, he estimated that the digging had begun—not ended—about a week ago, or even less. And to all intents and purposes it was still going on.

That meant, he told the others, that someone had been burrowing away in here *since* the dig had reopened. So either some very careful looters had been managing to evade Abe, the crew, and the guards, or . . .

Or one of the crew had been jumping the gun and excavating the temple on his own.

"Or her own," Julie corrected.

"Or their own," Abe said, "but let's not jump the gun ourselves. Why the crew? Let's stick with outsiders. Maybe they worked at night when nobody was around. What's so impossible about that?"

"But then where are their lamps?" Julie asked. "If they left their other tools, why not their lights?"

"Because if they came and went at night, they'd need them to get back to wherever they were going." Abe folded his arms and studied the gouged-out stairwell, squeezing his lower lip between his fingers. "If these are all the tools they had, then there's maybe . . . say, ten, twelve hours digging they did here. Eight if they had two people instead of one. Gideon, you would agree?"

Gideon agreed.

"So, that's what, two nights' work at most? Not so hard for some robbers to wait until we locked up and then come in and do their dirty work for a couple nights."

"I agree they probably did it at night," Gideon said, "but I still don't think it was outsiders. Outsiders have had a deserted site to dig in at their leisure since 1982. Why wait till it's crawling with people? No, if this has really been done in the last week, and I'm betting it has, then I'm also betting somebody on the crew's responsible."

"But that just doesn't add up," Julie said. "If anybody

would know that those steps have already been excavated, they would. They were here."

"That's true," Gideon admitted. "It doesn't add up, whatever way you look at it."

Unexpectedly, Abe laughed brightly. "A puzzle," he said. "Come on, it's dinner time, and then we got our curse to hear about." He nudged a pile of rubble with his toe. "This we can talk about later."

7

Bernadette Rose Garrison, Professor of Pre-Columbian Languages at Tulane's Middle-American Research Institute, did not fit the layman's idea of a leading scholar of ancient Mayan. Or Gideon's either. A severe, dowdy black woman in her fifties, with her hair pulled back into a bun, she sported the only set of pince-nez Gideon had ever seen on a live person. She might have made a perfect office manager, diligent and prim, or maybe a supervising social worker, or a sternly uncompromising loan officer. Her manner was unceremonious—"call me Bernie," she had said when they were introduced at dinner—but imposing enough so that only the most self-confident (Abe, for instance) had taken her up on it.

Gideon, easier to intimidate, stuck with "Dr. Garrison," which she seemed to find entirely suitable.

She sat at the head of a huge, grim table of sixteenth-century Spanish design, her neatly typed notes before her. Surrounding the table were ten massive chairs of mahogany and dark, stiffened leather, presumably also meant to evoke the Spanish past, but looking like nothing so much as 1930s-style electric chairs. All were filled, one by Dr. Garrison, eight by the members of the Tlaloc crew, and one by the formidable Dr. Armando Villanueva, deputy director of the Instituto Nacional de Antropologia e Historia, who had arrived unannounced from Mexico City only two hours before for the express purpose of being present at Dr. Garrison's translation. That, and to exercise the Institute's prerogative of stringent review.

This latter function had been made clear at dinner by the portly, outspoken Dr. Villanueva himself. He had stood up at the head of the table and bluntly explained that in his private opinion Horizon had permanently compromised itself in 1982, that he believed it should not have been permitted to reopen the excavation, and that he had articulated these views with great vigor but had been overruled. That being as it was, he bore no grudge but would of course be obliged to see to it that the strictest standards were maintained. To this end, they could expect close scrutiny from him as to signs of irregularity.

After the meal, talking to Gideon and Abe, he had made an attempt at bluff cordiality. "Well," he said, "how do things go at Tlaloc? Is there anything interesting to report?"

Abe and Gideon exchanged a quick, mutually understood glance: This was not the best of all possible times to mention the clandestine digging that had been going on under the Temple of the Owls.

"Don't look at me," Gideon had said. "I just got here."

"Interesting?" Abe had said blandly. "No, no, nothing interesting; all very routine."

Now, with everyone gathered in the Mayaland's reading room over coffee and dessert, Dr. Garrison consumed the last of her banana ice cream and glanced austerely at her buzzing audience, waiting for their undivided attention.

Gideon took the opportunity to look them over too. One of them, he was almost sure, had been up nights digging under the Temple of the Owls, searching for—what? And why?

Sitting directly opposite him was Leo Rose, as rumply and cheerful as ever. A few damp, four-color brochures stuck out of a pocket as usual, ready to be handed out at a moment's notice. Leo ran a land-development firm that seemed to specialize in unlikely endeavors. Currently they were selling lots on the desolate rim of the Salton Sea. ("Desert Shores Flexivillas!" blared the pamphlet he had already pressed genially on Gideon. "Opulent Time-share Haciendas on the California Riviera!") The last time, Gideon remembered, it had been a luxury golf resort on the outskirts of Tijuana.

Leo noticed Gideon looking at him and raised his cup.

"*Bueno-bueno*," he mouthed. It was a joke from the earlier dig. Leo had shown a marvelous ability to get along in Mexico with no communication skills beyond a spirited *bueno-bueno*, a lively arsenal of hand gestures, and a great, honking laugh that first alarmed then delighted the tiny Yucatecans.

Between Leo and Gideon, at the far end of the table from Dr. Garrison, was Harvey Feiffer, Gideon's old student, who had left anthropology for "communication systems technology engineering" a few months after the previous dig. Fearsome and incomprehensible as this field was to Gideon, it had been the right move for Harvey, who had finally found his niche.

So he had explained, bragging understandably to his ex-professor when they had chatted before dinner, and Gideon had seen no reason to think otherwise. Toupeed now, and running to fat, the thirty-one-year-old Harvey had apparently leaped willingly into a precocious middle age. He was married, with one child and another on the way; he had just bought a house in an upper-middle-level-executive suburb; and he was now "in the marketing end of things," soon to be promoted to corporate division head in the Atlanta company he worked for. And that wasn't all, Harvey puffed happily. In fourteen more months he would have worked for CompuServe for five years, at which time his contributions to the retirement plan would be vested, and his stock-option purchases automatically matched, dollar for dollar, which would provide a very tidy nest egg when he retired in 2017.

But his hard-driving new style had taken a toll, he confessed to Gideon. Several months before, he'd gone to his doctor complaining of chronic stomach pains. A pair of incipient ulcers had been diagnosed, and he had been ordered to get away from things, to take a few weeks off from work and family pressures. Luckily, the opportunity to take part in the dig had come along at just the right time.

On Leo's other side were Preston and Emma Byers. Preston was an extraordinarily handsome man, with limpid blue eyes and a profile as chiseled and handsome as Paul Newman's. Naturally, Gideon had taken an immediate dislike to him, but it had been hard to maintain. Preston was the most self-effacing of men, mild, retiring, and sweet-natured, with a perpetual expression of gentle perplexity on his classic features; an unprofound, amiably dull man who seldom spoke unless spoken to.

At fifty, he had changed little. His attractively graying hair had receded a bit in front, but he had made up for this by letting it grow a little longer in back; not in a wild sort of way, of course, but in an unobtrusive little rill that fell neatly over his collar. He was a onetime distributor of commercial kitchen equipment who had answered a start-your-own-business advertisement in a trade magazine many years before and somehow wound up building a modest fortune from a chain of fast-food restaurants in the Midwest. (Burger Bopper? Wiener Beaner? Gideon could never remember.)

Gideon had little doubt that the easygoing Preston owed his business success to the hard-driving woman beside him. Worthy had once referred to them as a Beauty-and-the-Beast marriage in reverse, and with reason; Emma was as homely as Preston was good-looking. Muscular, coarse-haired, red-faced, and plain, she used no make up or jewelry, but made up for her lack of bodily adornment by wearing clothes as up-to-the-minute as a mannequin's. Today she had on a buttery yellow outfit of baggy pants and loose overshirt with buttons in the back, circled at the waist by a wide, drooping belt of red leather.

The effect was surely not what she intended. Emma and her outfits never seemed to go together. They were out of joint, vaguely wrong, even a little unsettling, like a cowboy wearing glasses.

And, finally, sitting on Julie's other side, near Abe, there was Worthy Partridge. Alone among the coffee drinkers, he was having tea, and engaged at the moment in neatly lifting a teabag from the cup, wrapping the string around it to extract the last of the liquid, and placing the bag in a flip-top receptacle he carried with him for the purpose. The saucer of lime wedges that had come with the tea was contemptuously ignored.

Worthy claimed he drank tea because it helped ease the chronic constipation that afflicted him. Worthy was the only American he knew—the only one he had ever heard of—who managed to remain constipated when he came to Mexico.

Leo, Harvey, Preston, Emma, Worthy. Which of them had been up nights excavating the stairwell? He couldn't realistically imagine any of them doing it. What conceivable reason could they have? They had already helped dig it out with their own hands once. Of course they all knew about Abe's idea that there might be another hidden room, but surely they understood that the notion was more sizzle than substance, that the likelihood was slim, and the chance of another treasure even slimmer. Or did they? And even if they did, might they not think that even a slim chance at a million-dollar treasure was worth a few nights' lost sleep?

Either way, it didn't much matter anymore. Abe had engaged guards to watch over the site at night, and the official stairwell excavation was about to reopen. There would be no more secret digging. Still, Gideon would dearly have liked to know what had been going on.

He turned in his chair and gave his attention to Dr. Garrison, who had just cleared her throat meaningfully.

"Copies are now being made for each of you," she said, "but I think we should begin without waiting further. Dr. Villanueva and I must leave for Mexico City in less than an hour. An early-morning press conference has been scheduled."

She straightened her pince-nez and folded her hands before her on the table. "I have rendered this material in as exact and literal a manner as possible, leaving interpretation to others," she explained. "The polysyn-thetic Mayan characteristic of reliance on verbal nouns has necessarily been transformed into our own grammar. Beyond that, I have tried to be consistent with the historical conventions that have applied to previous works. I can assure you," she added unnecessarily, "that I have used no poetic license."

She began to read aloud with a velvety Georgia accent curiously at odds with her precise diction.

" 'The day Katun Thirteen Ahau,' " she intoned.
" 'Itzamná, Itzamtzab is his face during its reign.' "

Julie leaned over to Gideon and whispered: "This is a translation?"

Gideon spread his hands but said nothing. Explaining the Mayan system of dating would be hard enough with a couple of hours at his disposal. There wasn't much sense in trying to do it in an aside.

Dr. Garrison continued. " 'Those who come here to this place Tlaloc to disturb our bones and the dust of our bodies, let them know that many punishments will come to them. These are the punishments that will come to them.

" 'First, the bloodsucking kinkajou will come freely among them.

" 'Second, the darkness will be sundered and turned to light, and the terrible voices of the gods will be heard in the air, and there will be a mighty pummeling of the soul so that the spirit languishes and faints. Their treasures will be lost and their *batabobs* and *ahlelobs* will desert them . . .' "

The pince-nez were plucked off. "I'm afraid I have no wholly unambiguous referents for *batabobs* and *ahlelobs* in this context."

"The *batabob* was the governor of the area, the big chief," Abe said promptly. "The *ahlelob*, I think, was the assistant chief."

She looked at him. So did Gideon, to whom it came as a surprise that Abe knew something about the Mayan language. No, not a surprise; an item of interest, maybe.

Gideon had been astonished too many times by the range of his knowledge to be surprised anymore.

Under Dr. Garrison's uncompromising stare Abe smiled and shrugged modestly. "I guess I read it somewhere?"

"Thank you." With her index finger she found her place again.

"Maybe we can get *him* to play Trivial Pursuit with us," Julie whispered to Gideon.

"Not with me," Gideon muttered back.

" 'Third, the one called Tucumbalam will turn their entrails to fire and bloody flux.' "

This caused Worthy to grimace and push the rest of his ice cream away.

" 'Fourth, the one called Xecotcavach will pierce their skulls so that their brains spill onto the earth.' "

"Yuck, I'm grossing out," Leo announced, shoveling ice cream into his mouth.

Emma leaned stiffly toward him, her face intense. "Sh!" she whispered sharply. "This isn't a joke!"

Gideon frowned. Dim memories stirred. Wasn't it Emma who had belonged to some oddball group dedicated to the otherworldly theories of Von Daniken, or Velikovsky, or someone like that? Yes, it was, he recalled. Once she had cornered him into a long, dippy discussion of how it was that a carved, five-thousand-year-old Japanese Dogu figure wore what could only have been an astronaut's helmet and goggles. ("And, as you must know, Dr. Oliver, goggles hadn't even been invented in the Stone Age!") He had spent much of his subsequent time in Yucatan trying to stay out of her way without offending her.

Leo mimed a good-natured apology and quieted.

Dr. Garrison had paused coolly at the interruption. Now she continued the litany of calamity.

" 'Fifth, the beast that turns men to stone will come among them from the Underword.

" 'And all this will be only the beginning of their vexation by the devil, for the Lords of Xibalba will come and gouge out their eyes, and cut off their heads, and grind and crumble their nerves and their bones, and torment them until they die and are no more.

"Only thus will Vucub-Camé be satisfied, and Holom-Tucur, who has a head but no body, and Balam-Quitzé, and the Lord Hun-Hunahpu, and Gekaquch, and the Lords Zibakihay and Ahquehay, and the Lords . . .' "

"Do you suppose this goes on much longer?" Julie whispered.

"I don't think so," Gideon said. "It's only one page long."

" '. . . Balam-Acab, and Mahucatah, and even Ah Puch, who never tires.' "

"Mayan god of death," Gideon murmured knowledge-ably, impressing Julie with another bit of arcana pulled from who knew where.

" 'And when all this is done and the light turns to darkness for all time, there will be terrible mourning and crying . . .' "

Dr. Garrison paused, letting the somber words hang on the air. By now the lush, rhythmic Georgia accent seemed to suit them. "Mohh-nin' . . . and crahh-in' . . ."

" 'For it will be,' " she concluded mellowly, watching her audience and not the paper, " 'the end of the cigar.' "

"The end of the cigar," she repeated, cutting off any possible incipient ripple of laughter, "is a Mayan metaphor for closure, for the end of life."

She removed her pince-nez and with her thumb and forefinger slowly rubbed the indentations in the bridge of her nose. "For the end," she said, "of everything."

8

Humming to himself, beginning to relax, even enjoying the feel of the sweat pooling at the small of his back, Gideon snipped with the pruning shears here, there, tugged gently at a sturdy brown root, and sat back on his heels to study the situation a little more.

It was good to be working with his hands again, good to have a new skeleton to himself. (He had been guiltily relieved when Harvey somewhat shamefacedly announced his preference for nonskeletal work this time.) He snipped again, tugged again, and with an exclamation of satisfaction freed a gnarled three-inch root segment and tossed it through the doorway behind him. He laid the shears down next to the machete.

Machetes and pruning shears were hardly tools of the trade, but in the scrubby, stubborn jungles of Yucatan you couldn't get very far without them. Vines and roots were everywhere, flourishing and intrusive, and every archaeologist of the Maya had had the frustrating experience of working for days to free something, then becoming preoccupied with something else for a week or two, and returning to the original stela or carving to find it more deeply embedded in vegetation than before. All the major sites employed teams of machete-wielding workmen to chop back the jungle continually. Without them the long-lost cities would be engulfed again in a few seasons—as indeed many of them had been.

The lichen-stained skeleton in the entryway of the Priest's House had been there a lot longer than a season or two; longer than a century or two. The dead gray color of the bone, the dry, crumbly edges, the absence of even a dehydrated shred of tendon or ligament all suggested three to four hundred years. The vegetation was a clue to time too. Intrusive as it was, it couldn't have taken less than three centuries to choke the vestibule the way it had. There were fungous gray plants hanging from the roof— where you could see the roof—pulpy mosses oozing from the mortar of the stone walls, tightly packed trunks and roots and vines everywhere, springing from the inch or two of black soil and rotting vegetable matter that had blown in over the centuries, a grain or two at a time, to cling anywhere it could.

And the skeleton had surely been there longer than the vegetation. That was obvious from the way the roots of some of the oldest plants, gnarled, bulbous, woody monsters with warped and blackened leaves, twined around and through the bones. Sometimes they sprang *from* the bones. Wormlike tendrils crawled from the eye sockets and the nasal cavity, from the shoulder joints and the vertebral foramina; even from the braincase, erupting in a thick, ugly snarl from the foramen magnum, the hole at the base of the skull through which the spine joins the brain. The leisurely violence of their grip had slowly splintered many of the bones and twisted the skeleton into grotesque contortions. The pelvis was cracked and turned backward, the skull almost upside down.

He had used the machete to chop some elbow room for himself, but for the last two and a half hours he'd been working more delicately, with shears, knife, and dental pick. Now, although he still had a long way to go, he'd pruned enough to have his first close look.

The skeleton was on its left side, curled in the fetal position. This was archaeology's most commonly encountered burial position—it required the smallest hole—but this body hadn't been buried. It lay on the stone floor just inside the entryway, squarely blocking it. He could see a few scattered jade beads beneath it, and near one forearm was a thin, crumpled metal bracelet. The clothing had long since rotted away.

It was a male this time; Harvey would certainly have pointed out the overhanging brow ridge, the sturdy mastoid processes, and the rectangular orbits of the skull. And through a net of straw-colored root tendrils, much of the pelvis could be seen. That too was distinctively masculine. Gideon didn't have to apply the anthropologist's literal rule of thumb for the greater sciatic notch—(stick your thumb in it; if there's room to wiggle it, it's female; if not, it's male)—to see that there was hardly room for a pinky, let alone a thumb. Besides, a disc of obsidian gleamed darkly in the dark tangle beneath the skull, and it was the stern Bishop Landa himself who had noted disapprovingly that "the men, and not the women, wear mirrors in their hair."

It seemed to be a man of middle age. Too early yet to come up with anything precise, but the cranial sutures were almost obliterated except for a few spots on the lambdoid, so he had probably been in his forties anyway, an estimate supported by the carious, deeply worn brown teeth. (The Maya had lived on stone-ground corn—which meant that they consumed a lot of corn-ground stone as well—and the result was molars that were often eroded to raw little stumps by the time they were thirty. Anyone who thought that dental cavities had come in with refined sugar had never seen an early American Indian skull.)

He took half-a-dozen flash pictures with the Minolta single-lens reflex and made a quick sketch. Then he turned the skull to see the face better, cringing a little at the sight of the snaky, freshly severed roots bursting from the eye sockets, as in an edifying carving on a medieval coffin. The struggling roots had first pried the bones in and around the sockets apart, then gripped them firmly where they were, so that the face of the skull seemed out of focus, with some parts of it closer than others.

He unscrewed the clamp on the lamp tripod and brought the bulb as far down as it would come, shifting it to throw its light laterally across the skull. All the little bumps and grooves were thrown into sharp, shadowed relief, and he leaned closer to see what there was to see.

He blinked, surprised, then used his sensitive fingertips to explore further, particularly around the eye sockets. Odd, the individual bones of the orbit hadn't been pulled apart over the years at all. They'd been shattered. And most of the cracked shards of bone had been forced *inward*, not outward, which was not at all the way you'd expect roots thrusting out from the braincase to do it.

It was almost as if . . .

Again he sat back on his heels, frowning.

It was almost certainly as if . . .

". . . almost certainly as if the eyes had been gouged out," Gideon said, looking from Abe to the others. "In fact," he added, "there's no 'almost' about it."

The crew was gathered in the lacy shade of a few drowsing acacias, sitting among the masonry blocks of the West Group. It was the only sizeable shaded area in the plaza; the rest was scrubby lawn, open to the sun. As a result it was a favorite place for lunch and early-afternoon snoozing. Most lunches, like today's, were relaxed show-and-tells at which the staff chatted about the morning's progress.

Everyone except Emma and Preston Byers was eating boxed sandwich lunches from the hotel. The Byerses, having forsaken meat some time before, were making an abstemious meal of soy cakes packed in plastic envelopes, mung bean sprouts they claimed to have grown on the windowsill of their room, and bananas.

They had, it seemed, sold their fast-food empire and now ran Wellbeing, a mail-order supplier of New Age essentials for living. Like Leo, they had brought with them an ample supply of brochures, one of which Gideon had been unable to avoid.

"The Midwest's gourmet holistic-macrobiotic supermarket," it said. "Bulk organic grains (whole-milled), rice koji, masa delight, chewable bee-pollen tablets (a proven skin rejuvenator), dandelion thunder, tofu cream cheese, 30 varieties of kelp (unsurpassed for cleansing the colon), nori, fucus tips, 120 varieties of natural nut butter. Books on therapeutic drumming, Tibetan stress reduction, other life-enhancing studies. Wide range of energy-balancing crystals."

At Gideon's words Emma had looked significantly at Preston, who continued to chew, smiling absently at her. Worthy Partridge stopped munching his turkey sandwich and looked up uneasily, as if, whatever this meant, it couldn't be good news. But this was his standard reaction to new things.

Leo Rose also responded in his characteristic way, with his honk of a laugh. "The curse of Tlaloc *lives*," he whispered.

Worthy was unamused. "I don't see anything funny in that. Could it possibly be true, Gideon?"

"Hee-hee-hee-heee," Leo rasped. "Hoo-hoo-h—"

Worthy silenced him with a haughty scowl. "I don't mean, is the *curse* true," he snapped. "I mean, do you think it—he—was left there, you know, as a warning not to disturb the site?"

"That's just what I do think," Gideon said. "I don't remember the words of the curse, exactly, but somewhere in there—"

"I do," Emma Byers said. "Last night I focused my

interpolarity flow on it during my amethyst meditation interval." She flushed and looked defensively at the others, expecting to be challenged. "I have it multidimensionally internalized now," she announced.

"I think that means," grumped Worthy to no one, "that she's learned the curse by heart. God forbid."

Gideon wasn't overjoyed with the idea either. "Well, I don't think it's too important to—"

Emma closed her eyes, ignoring them both. " 'The Lords of Xibalba will come and gouge out their eyes,' " she intoned in a fair imitation of Dr. Garrison, sans accent.

"Right," Gideon said. "Anyway—"

" '. . . and cut off their heads,' " Emma droned on, her eyes still pressed shut, " 'and grind and crumble their nerves and their bones, and torment them until they die and are no more. Only thus—' "

"Thanks, Emma," Gideon cut in. "That's fine. Well, it looks as if somebody did all those things to the poor guy in the doorway."

"Huh?" Harvey said. "How can you tell that his nerves were crumbled? I mean, if all you have to go on are bones—"

Gideon bowed his head to hide a smile. Some things never changed. Trust Harvey to inject some welcome literal-mindedness into things.

"You're absolutely right, Harvey. That was an overstatement. I don't know about the nerves. But everything else holds. The head was cut off—sawed off, rather—with some kind of blade that wasn't very sharp; a flint knife, probably. And a lot of the bones were crushed with something heavy. The hand and foot bones were practically pounded to pulp, as if they laid his hands and feet on a flat stone and—"

"Gideon, enough, you don't have to draw a picture," Abe said, making a face.

"This is sure fun," Julie chipped in. "I'm certainly enjoying my lunch."

Gideon subsided. He didn't much like thinking about it either.

For a few moments the only sounds were the rustling and hiccupping of birds in the shadowed forest a few yards off; people ate their sandwiches or peeled their fruit in thoughtful silence.

"Dr. Oliver," Emma Byers said abruptly, "have you had a chance to read the winter issue of *Holy Anthro* yet?"

"Uh . . . *Holy Anthro*?" What the hell was *Holy Anthro*? Did he really want to know?

She looked at him, surprised. "*The Journal of Holistic Anthropology and Shamanistic Enlightenment*," she explained. "There was an article in it that speaks to us very directly."

"Uh, no, I must have missed it," he said cravenly.

"What about you, Dr. Goldstein? I'm sure *you* saw it."

"No, I'm afraid not," Abe said with a sweet smile. "Unfortunately, I left for Yucatan before my copy came in the mail."

Gideon eyed him doubtfully. With Abe you never knew.

Emma blinked, apparently expressing her own stolid

form of astonishment at the slovenly scholarship of two supposedly professional anthropologists. "There was an article on prophecies by the ancient Maya."

"Oh, my God." Worthy bit gloomily into an orange segment and raised his eyes heavenward.

Emma Byers was an ungainly woman given to spotty blushing and a halting, blurting style of speech. But she was not easily put off. "This was a scientifically controlled study," she maintained, her eyes on the ground, "by the Institute of Transformative Consciousness—"

"Ah," said Abe.

"Sheesh," said Worthy.

"—that proves beyond a doubt that all twelve major changes in the Dow Jones average in the first half of last year were predicted in the *Popol Vuh* to within two points—and the *Popol Vuh* was written by the Quiché Maya in 1550." She flushed and bit tightly into her soy cake.

The only response came from Leo. "Now if it told me about *next* year's Dow Jones, I might be interested."

"Preston," Emma said, "you remember, don't you?"

"What?" Her startled husband almost dropped his banana. He looked about him as if for help. Gideon wondered, not for the first time, just how much say he'd had in the Byers' decision to trade their hamburger empire for the meatless, fatless glories of the New Age.

But of course Preston was infinitely malleable, and unfailingly agreeable. "Why, yes," he said at last. "Yes, I think I do. I believe it pointed out that a thousand dollars invested and reinvested according to the, er, *Popol Vuh* would have brought, er, five thousand dollars in the end." He looked at her hopefully. "Was that the one?"

"*Twenty*-five thousand dollars," Emma said. "Now listen to *this*!" She closed her eyes again, frowning deeply. "This is from the curse. I've been thinking a lot about this. 'Their treasures will be lost, and their *batabobs* and *ahlelobs* will desert them—'"

"Hey, I know that song," Leo said, laughing. "Oh, *batabobs* and *ahlelobs* and little lambs eat ivy–"

"Oh, damn it, Leo!" Emma said with surprising heat. "Doesn't anyone see what it means?" She opened her eyes to gaze intensely at them.

No one did; not even Preston, who was searching hard for its significance, his classic brow furrowed.

Gideon thought he had a glimmer but kept it to himself.

"It predicts exactly what happened here," Emma said. "The curse is being fulfilled. We didn't know it at the time, but it was already coming to pass in 1982."

"The Curse . . . of Tlaloc," Leo intoned metallically into his empty Coca-Cola can, then flinched under Emma's glare. "I think I better shut up."

"Do you really mean you don't see it?" Emma said, addressing them all. Her patchy flush spread and darkened, possibly from the pain of dealing with a crowd of closed-minded dunces. "Howard Bennett was our *batabob*, our leader, and he deserted us. What could be more clear?"

Just what Gideon had been afraid of. This wasn't good. What little he knew about curses on archaeological expeditions he'd learned from the movies, and they usually made the point that it was a mistake to start taking them too seriously.

"This is totally ridiculous," Worthy said bluntly. He dabbed querulously at his small beard with a paper napkin. "I can't believe this. We're in the 1980s. This is a scientific expedition. How can we even be discussing this New Age twaddle?" He pronounced "New Age" as a single word, "newage," rhyming with "sewage."

"Besides," Harvey said reasonably, "you're getting things out of order. *Batabobs* and *ahlelobs*, that was part *two* of the curse, wasn't it? Well, we haven't even had our part *one* yet."

"Absolutely correct," Worthy said scornfully. "Or has anyone seen a bloodsucking kinkajou?"

Leo didn't go along with them. "But you know, it's true, what Emma says," he said, seemingly taken with the idea. Or perhaps he thought it would be more fun to change sides. "Howard did desert us, didn't he? And the codex, that was our treasure, and it's sure lost, right?" He had finished his lunch and was slumped back against the stone platform of one of the ruined buildings, hands clasped contentedly on his ample abdomen. "Maybe the things in the curse don't have to come true in order."

Emma's glance at him was hopeful but guarded. It was hard to tell whether he was serious. If he was ever serious. Leo smiled back at her, Buddha-like. They were dressed almost the same, Gideon noted bemusedly, in trendy, undyed linen shirts and knee-length beige shorts that were fashionably wrinkled and oversized. But Emma managed to look like a Banana Republic advertisement, as long as you didn't get too close; Leo just looked like someone who'd slept in his clothes.

"Leo's right," Emma said. "Who are we to impose our Western construct of time as a linear continuum on other culture planes?"

Worthy made an irritated sound and addressed the sky. "Do you know what this demonstrates? The abysmal failure of our educational system. Anyone who is gullible enough to be duped by the newage claptrap put out—"

"Oh, is that so?" Emma said thickly. Her feelings were hurt. "And you think that *you're* in a position to judge three thousand years of—"

"*Kinder, kinder,*" Abe said. "Children, let's not get carried away. I'm sure nobody really means—"

But Worthy had been stung and overrode him. "This is absurd! If this is all we can find to talk about we'd be better off holding our tongues entirely."

"Well, yes, I agree with that," Preston said, then added amicably: "There are some things we're better off not knowing." He was fortunate to be seated a foot or two in front of Emma; her glower of annoyance spattered harmlessly on the handsome gray wavelet of hair on his collar.

"That," Worthy said icily, "is not at all what I meant."

When Abe had been a professor, Gideon remembered, he had usually stayed out of classroom arguments and let Gideon and his other students fight things out among themselves. Usually. But there was often a point at which the democratic approach was unceremoniously scotched in favor of a firm, fatherly, unqualified opinion from the expert. That point had now been reached.

"I agree with Worthy one hundred percent," he said, looking soberly from one member of the crew to another. "The curse, the skeleton in the doorway, these are very interesting. As archaeological data they're worth talking about." He held up a spidery finger. "But as supernatural occurrences they ain't." He fixed his gaze on Emma, kindly but firmly. "I'll tell you the truth; I'm a little surprised anybody here would take this seriously."

Emma's puffy face tightened. She flushed yet again but said nothing.

"Oh, I don't know," Leo said, not disrespectfully. "You have to admit it's something to think about."

"Look," Julie said gently, "I wasn't here in 1982, so I don't really know what I'm talking about, but it seems to me that we're confusing things. The codex was never our treasure in the first place. And it wasn't *lost*; Dr. Bennett took it. And of course he ran off afterward. You don't need a curse to explain any of that."

"Absolutely right," Abe said warmly. "The law of parsimony in a nutshell. So let's not hear any more about the curse. Case closed. End of cigar. Time to go back to work."

He stood up, a little creaky after sitting on the ground for so long, and brushed dust from his trousers. "On the other hand," he said with his tiniest smile, "if someone runs into any bloodsucking kinkajous hanging around, be sure and let me know."

9

He didn't have long to wait. The next day, on a humid morning under a sullen gray sky, the Curse of Tlaloc struck again. Lurking in the supposedly deserted work shed was a bloodsucking kinkajou.

Or near enough.

Julie, Gideon, and Abe had walked to the site after an early breakfast at the Mayaland, planning to put in an hour of organizing and sorting before the crew arrived. Gideon had unlocked and opened the door, then quickly put out his arm to block the others as the smell of something rank and wild seeped from the stuffy interior.

"What's wrong?" Julie asked. Then she smelled it too, and stood very still and stiff, peering past him into the dim interior.

Something grunted thickly in the darkness, like a pig rooting, and there was a scrabbling sound, as of clawed feet moving over the limestone mortar floor toward them. The hairs rose at the back of Gideon's neck. All three people stepped instinctively back from the threshold.

From the shadows a furry brown animal emerged tentatively, then stopped and backed away again. About the size of a raccoon, with a ring-striped tail balanced daintily above it, it had a face that looked something like a fox and something like an old basketball sneaker. It looked warily up at them.

"Good morning," the neatly lettered placard hanging from its neck said. "I am a bloodsucking kinkajou."

"Good morning to you," said Abe. "I am a broken-down old professor."

Julie laughed. "It's a coati, a coatimundi. And it doesn't suck blood, it eats fruits and berries."

She knelt to coax it near with a fig from her box lunch, and after some indecision the animal approached with rubbery-nosed interest. But as soon as it saw its chance it darted between her and Abe and made for the fence with a rolling, flatfooted gait. In two seconds it was through the opening, and in one more it burst through the jungle's green wall and disappeared.

Opinion as to the perpetrator varied. Julie was sure it was Leo, Gideon thought it just might be a sarcastic comment from Worthy, and Abe wondered wryly if Dr. Gideon Oliver might not be behind it.

Julie stood up for him. "He hasn't been out of my sight since we quit work yesterday," she declared staunchly.

"Oh, yeah, what about when you took a shower?" Abe wanted to know.

"We took it together," Gideon told him. "Abe, on my honor as a serious and responsible scientist, I didn't do it."

"Ha," said Abe, but he switched his vote to Leo.

When the others arrived at eight-thirty and were told about it, Leo was everyone else's favorite suspect too, and was roundly accused, but he swore with his hand on his heart that he'd had nothing to do with it.

"It was the work of the gods," he said darkly. "An omen." He cut his voice to a melodramatic whisper and wiggled his eyebrows at Preston. "There are some things we aren't meant to know."

"Absolutely," said Preston, for whom this seemed to be a guiding philosophy.

"A coatimundi, I love it. Out of sight!" Chuckling heavily, Stan Ard slowly wrote something in a spiral-bound notebook. "Coatimundi, what is that, some kind of lizard?"

Regretting that he had brought it up at all, Gideon told him about the raccoonlike mammal. It was 5:00 P.M. and they were sitting in basket chairs on the shaded, tiled veranda of the hotel, where Gideon had promised Ard an hour-long interview. Earlier, during the lunch break, Abe had told the crew about the free-lance reporter's arrival. He had suggested that they cooperate with him but keep to the facts and try not to say anything sensational; the ever-alert Dr. Villanueva was no doubt on the lookout for lapses of good taste that might appear in print.

Privately, Abe had confided to Gideon that he was worried. A brief talk with Ard had made him wonder about the reporter's judgment, and the man had hedged on what publication would print his article. Abe had considered asking the crew to refuse to talk with him. But he had decided on second thought that Ard was the kind of journalist who wouldn't quit, and might make up his own story if he had to—which was the most worrisome possibility of all.

After five minutes of conversation, Gideon's impression of the reporter was equally unfavorable. Stan Ard was a coarse, blowsy man who gobbled unfiltered cigarettes like someone bent on killing himself as quickly as possible, and who coughed like someone who was succeeding. He had spent the first few minutes of the interview hacking, pounding his chest, and talking about himself, hinting broadly at a shadowy past full of vague and undisclosable associations with the CIA and *Soldier of Fortune*.

He had struck Gideon as not very bright, not very subtle, and not very principled. But he had done his homework. He had a copy of the curse and a binder full of earlier reports about the theft of the codex.

"Look, Stan," Gideon said uneasily as Ard continued to fill up the page with his round, methodical script, "this thing with the coati was just an in-joke, not something that was intended to make the newspapers. If it's all the same to you . . ."

Ard stopped writing and held up a hand in acquiescence. "Hey, no problem. Fine, great, we'll forget all about it." To show his sincerity he ripped out the page, crumpled it, and tossed it into an ashtray. "Okay, Gid, let's get down to brass tacks. Let me tell you what I'm doing here." He leveled two thick fingers and the cigarette between them at Gideon. "I think you're going to like this."

Why was it, Gideon wondered idly, that he had never much cared for anyone who called him "Gid"?

"What I'm doing here is I'm doing a three-part feature for *Flak* on the curse, the dig, the whole schmear. You couldn't ask for better publicity."

"*Flak*?" Gideon said doubtfully, putting aside his questions about the need for better publicity. "Isn't that one of those papers you see at the checkout counters? 'Boy Weds Own Mother to Get Even with Dad over Allowance Dispute'? 'Priest Splits into Four Segments While Addressing Congregation'?"

"You got it."

No wonder Ard had hedged with Abe. "Oh, God," Gideon said, "I can see it now. 'Grisly Curse of Death Stalks Jungle Excavation.' "

Ard blinked thoughtfully. "Hey, not bad." Apparently he meant it, because he wrote it down on a fresh sheet. "Got any other ideas?"

Gideon laughed. "I don't suppose you'd go for 'A Textual Analysis of a Post-Classic Mayan Incunabulum'?"

"You're right, I wouldn't, and neither would the schmucks at the checkout counter." His heavy chuckle turned into a gargly cough and died away. "Okay, look, I was reading the original report you wrote up in '82 and I needed to check some things with you. Make sure I've got it straight." He flipped back a few pages in his notebook.

On the glass table in front of them were a Tecate beer for Gideon—which he didn't really want, but Ard had insisted on ordering him something—and a double scotch on the rocks for the reporter. Nearby, others also chatted and drank, enjoying the relative coolness of the predinner hour. Behind Ard, a few tables away, Emma was hectoring Leo Rose on cosmic consciousness. Leo, in his usual manner, was jollying her along. Or maybe she was converting him. Who could tell with Leo?

"Okay." Ard gulped Scotch. "I want this to be human-interest stuff, not just facts." The face he made showed what he thought of facts. "Let me ask you this." While he chose his words he rooted with a finger in the curly hair at the base of his throat, jiggling the thin gold chains nestling there. "Describe to me how you felt in the . . . in the dark, damp depths of that passageway when your eyes beheld the long-lost Tlaloc codex." He thought a moment, then wrote that down too, visibly impressed.

Gideon decided to have a swallow of beer after all. An hour with Stan Ard was going to be a long time. There were still fifty-one minutes to go. "I don't know, Stan. It's hard to remember. It was a long time ago."

"Yeah, but you must have thought something," Ard said. He decided to clarify the question. "I mean, you must have thought *something*."

"Well, I didn't know it was a codex when I first saw it," Gideon said, aware that he wasn't providing very good copy. "I thought it was just some bundles of cloth."

Ard frowned and shook his head. "Nah, that's no good," he said reprovingly. "What are you, kidding me?" He downed another slug of Scotch, made a pained expression, belched, sucked on his cigarette, and gave himself over to coughing again while he hammered on his chest with the flat of his hand.

"Okay, let's start with basic concrete facts," he said when he could speak again. "The five *W*s: who, why, what . . . uh, which . . . you know. Maybe that'll get us to something we can use. Now, according to what I read, the tunnel started looking like it was going to cave in right after you found the codex, while all you guys were down there, right?"

"Right."

"At 4:12 P.M."

Gideon nodded.

"Great," Ard said without enthusiasm. "How much more concrete can you get than that?" Squinting, he flapped at the cigarette smoke. "So how did you happen to know the exact time?"

Gideon shrugged. "I guess I looked at my watch . . ." He hesitated, seeing a sudden ray of hope. "No, wait, it was *his* watch." He gestured in Leo's direction. "When that post broke and some of the ceiling came down it broke his watch. Stopped it at 4:12. We noticed it later, when we were on our way back to the site."

"Broke his watch? Did he get hurt or anything?" Ard asked hopefully.

Gideon saw his chance. "You know, Stan," he said, "Leo Rose is really the guy you ought to be talking to; you've already got my version in those clippings. But Leo was right there with me, up there on that—that dark, lonely pyramid when it happened. He could give you a fresh perspective."

This wasn't as low a trick as it seemed. By now even the durable, resilient Leo was withering under Emma's remorseless, high-volume barrage (". . . because which reality plane you select doesn't really matter," she was saying. "That's what past-life regression is all about. If you think about it in terms of Jungian synchronicity . . .") For some minutes Leo had been paying more attention to Gideon's and Ard's conversation than his own. His eyes were cast plaintively in their direction for possible escape.

And regardless of what the irrepressible Leo might say, Abe had nothing to worry about. An article in *Flak* was not going to be read by anyone in the academic world; not admittedly, anyway. And even Dr. Villanueva couldn't claim there was any danger that it might be taken seriously.

"Yeah?" Ard said with interest. He reached for the cigarette he'd put down during a coughing spasm, peered interestedly over his shoulder at Leo, and gave him a small, welcoming wave. Leo was quick to take advantage of it. In a flash he was out of his chair, leaving behind a sulking Emma displeased at having Leo's mind expansion interrupted. Four quick strides put him at their table.

"Hi," he said brightly. He blew out his cheeks, rolled his eyes, and grinned at Gideon.

"Leo here was lucky to escape with his life when the ceiling gave way," Gideon said. "It not only stopped his watch at 4:12, it almost took his arm off. There was blood all over the place." It was but a small exaggeration for the greater good. Leo's wrist had, after all, been scratched, if Gideon remembered correctly.

Leo was more than happy to go along. "There sure was," he agreed. "There was blood everywhere."

This obviously appealed to Ard, and Gideon pressed on. "Leo, Stan is doing a story on Tlaloc for *Flak*. He was thinking you'd be a good person to talk to."

"*Flak!*" Leo was clearly impressed. "You work for *Flak*?"

"No, I'm a free-lancer. I work out of L.A."

"L.A.!" Leo was even more impressed. "L.A. is a great place to live. Wonderful. You're only a hundred and fifty miles from the Salton Sea, did you know that?" He slid a chair next to Ard's. "Stan," he said, bulking sincerely at his side, "have you ever thought about the benefits of time-share ownership of a waterfront hacienda in the desert?"

He was reaching for a soggy brochure when Gideon made a discreet exit, and the last he heard from them, as he headed up the stairs, was a brayed "*bueno-bueno*." Leo was calling for another round.

10

Later that evening Julie and Gideon were on their balcony, about as relaxed as people can get without being asleep. After Gideon's abbreviated interview, they had showered and changed, then gone in to dinner by themselves. They'd had sea bass in pesto sauce, with a more-than-decent bottle of Frascati. Later, they'd spent a highly satisfactory interlude in their cool and darkened room, marred only by their working up another sweat. They had showered for the third time that day, and now they were sitting in the wrought-iron rocking chairs, snifters of brandy beside them. Above them the tops of the trees were hidden by the night, but the gardens and pathways were lit with a mellow amber glow from ornate, fern-shrouded lanterns.

"Ah . . ." said Julie.

"I know," Gideon said. "The raw, primitive—"

"No," she said, smiling, "just *ah*. This is lovely."

"Mmm."

"Gideon, I've been doing some more thinking about whoever's been digging in the temple."

They had talked about it several times with Abe and arrived at no useful conclusions. The site was now patroled at night but there had been no sign of the diggers, and Abe had decided to go ahead with the legitimate excavation, or re-excavation, of the stairwell the next day. Four Mayan laborers had been brought on for the heavy work, and Abe had asked Leo, as the only one of the crew who knew something about shoring, to supervise them, at least to begin with. Another crew member, assigned on a daily rotation basis, would be stationed at the foot of the pyramid to sift the fill that would be brought down in buckets on a clothesline arrangement. After that it would be trucked away.

The crew had expressed surprise when they were told about the surreptitious excavating, but little interest. They were more concerned with griping about having to sift the rubble even though the stairwell had already been excavated once before. As always, the screening table was the most unpopular of dig assignments. But Abe was firm, as he should have been. No fill or dirt would leave Tlaloc without sifting.

"What I was wondering," Julie went on, "was whether the codex might not still be down there."

Gideon looked at her, surprised. "That's impossible. Howard's been trying to peddle it for years. That's what the committee was all about."

"Has he? Have you ever actually seen it again? Since that first look you had at it, I mean?"

"No, but there have been reports from all over the world—"

"Reliable reports?"

"Well—"

"That you can vouch for?"

"Well, no, not personally—"

"Has anybody produced any photographs? Or detailed descriptions that you could check for accuracy?"

"Well . . . no, not that I know of, but—"

"Gideon, there are reports from all over the world on flying saucers, and Adolf Hitler, and . . . well, all kinds of things. Even photographs, but that doesn't prove they're really out there."

"No, of course it doesn't, but why would Howard have left it behind? And are you saying he took the codex out of the chest, threw it down the steps to the bottom, collapsed the tunnel on top of it, and then just walked away from it? What would be the point? How could—"

"I don't know, I don't know," she said, laughing and

exasperated both. "I'm trying to be creative. Look, maybe Howard *didn't* cave in the stairwell. That is, not on purpose. Maybe it was an accident. Maybe he—now wait, just hear me out—you said that one of the supports had already been knocked out accidentally, right? Well, maybe they weakened some more when he was smashing the lid to get at the codex, and maybe they just collapsed by themselves. Isn't that possible? Maybe . . . maybe he dropped it and it fell down the stairs, and then the wall caved in on it and he had to leave it because he had no choice."

"Then why not just stick it out and say he had nothing to do with it? Why run off?"

"Well . . . hmm. I'll have to work on that."

"It's creative, all right, I'll say that." Gideon lifted his snifter to his face, inhaled, and thought about it. "If you accept the premises, it even has a certain bizarre logic."

She laughed. "I love it when you get carried away."

"No," he said, smiling back, "I think you have a point. Except—"

"I knew it."

"—why would Howard write a letter to Horizon bragging about stealing the codex, when he didn't?"

"Because . . . " She paused, groping. " . . . because he wanted you all to think it was gone." She brightened, taken with the idea. "He didn't want anyone to look for it and find it before he could come back and dig it up himself. And nobody did," she finished triumphantly. "Did they?"

Gideon lowered his glass to the table and turned to look at her. "No, they didn't, Julie," he said slowly.

"And so you think it's Howard himself who's been digging, trying to get to the codex before we do?"

"Well, he's the only one who'd know it was still there—if it is still there. It makes sense, doesn't it?"

For a moment Gideon almost thought it did. Then he sank back against the chair. "No, I don't think so. Aside from everything else, the timing's all wrong. Why would he wait until now, the very worst possible time, to try to get it? He could have given things a couple of years to blow over, come back to dig it up with no one around, and be long gone by now."

"True," Julie admitted after a few seconds. She leaned back in the chair and began rocking again. "Back to the drawing board. Or, on second thought, I think I'll just let you solve it."

"Ah, come on. Coming up with ideas isn't any fun. I'd rather criticize yours."

On the veranda a fluid tenor had joined the guitarist; a sweet, soft version of "El Venadito" floated up to them. They reached across to clasp hands and slowly rocked, listening to the old folk song.

Soy un pobre venadito que habita en la serrani-i-i-a.
Como no soy tan mansito . . .

Gideon sighed, took a long, sleepy stretch, and stood up. "Ready for bed?"

"Whew, again? The tropics really agree with you, don't they?"

"I was thinking," he said, "of going to sleep." He held out his hand to lift her out of her chair, and pulled her into his arms. She rubbed her forehead against his cheek and slid her hands slowly up and down his back.

"On the other hand," he said, "I suppose I could be coaxed."

Julie smiled at him. "Why don't we finish our brandies and then see how we feel? Or if you're still awake."

"Good thinking."

Inside the room, they pulled the louvered balcony doors shut behind them, and Gideon crossed to the front door to flick on the light and start the slow ceiling fan they liked to have on when they slept. Not for the breeze, which was nil, but the lazy tropical ambience.

"Is that something you dropped?" Julie said, pointing toward his feet.

He looked down to see a white sheet of paper folded into quarters on the red-tiled floor. "No, someone must have slipped it under the door."

The brief message was centered on the page.

Gideon Oliver, leave Yucatan or you will die.
This is not a joke.

—The Gods of Tlaloc

After he had stared at it for a few seconds Julie took it from his hand and read it. "I don't . . . is this supposed to be funny?"

"I don't know. Personally, I thought the bloodsucking coatimundi had more going for it."

"Do you think it's really a threat? A *death* threat?"

Gideon shook his head slowly back and forth. "I

just—Christ, what am I thinking of!" He flung the door open and leaped out into the hallway.

But no one was there, of course. The tiled hallway gleamed emptily at them, peaceful and benign, and the potted plants weren't big enough for anyone to hide behind. When he came back into the room, Julie's face was anxious.

"Hey," he said softly, putting his arms around her again and pulling her close, rocking slowly back and forth with her. "Hey, there isn't anything to worry about, believe me. Really."

She lifted her head from his shoulder to throw him a mute, skeptical look.

"No, honestly," he said. "Threatening letters are just so much bluster. No one takes them seriously. I certainly don't, and with all the forensic work I do, I get a lot of these things."

She looked at him again, this time with surprise. "You do?"

"Sure, all the time."

Well, twice. Once he'd been scheduled to testify that the skeleton of a Mafia figure found in Lake Michigan showed signs of strangulation. The other time had been when he was going to give evidence on the identification of a dope racketeer whose face and fingerprints had been scraped off before he'd been dumped in the desert near Las Vegas. Both times he'd gotten anonymous letters explaining in repellent detail just what would happen to him if he showed up in court.

"And they never amount to anything?" Julie asked, not looking overly convinced.

"Nope, never."

Well, once. The night after his testimony in the Mafia murder someone had fired two shots through the door of his room in the Holiday Inn, but he hadn't been there at the time. It was only Gideon's second case for the FBI, and he had been thrilled.

"What about the time someone mailed you a letter bomb?" Julie said. "What about the time someone set that monstrous dog on you? On us, rather. How about—"

"We're talking about threatening letters," he said sensibly. "People who write threatening letters don't follow through. Never." Or was he laying it on too thick? "Well, almost never."

She gazed at him doubtfully.

"It's an accepted fact," he told her. "No question about it."

It wasn't that he was feeling especially brave, but how could anyone get very excited about this silly note? The two he'd received in the past had been poisonous; explicit enough to bring on a sweat just from the reading. This one was so . . . quaint, so juvenile. *This is not a joke. The Gods of Tlaloc.* Almost certainly a joke was just what it was, probably by the same person who had put the coat in the work shed.

Besides, what he had told Julie was true. People who wanted to kill you, killed you. They didn't write you letters about it.

He grinned at her. "Come on, Julie. Would I lie?"

She was not reassured. "Why," she wondered, addressing a window over his shoulder, "do these things happen to him? They don't happen to other people. They only happen when he's around. Curses, death threats . . ."

"It didn't used to happen to me. I don't do it on purpose."

"I know," she said and managed a wry smile. "It's some kind of gift. My theory is that you give off some kind of electrical field that attracts weirdness. Oh, Gideon! . . ."

She hugged him tightly, then stepped back. "What are you going to do?"

"I don't know. I suppose the police ought to be told. I'll do it tomorrow."

"*Tomorrow?*" She looked at him disbelievingly.

"Julie, we're in the middle of nowhere. The nearest cops who know what they're doing are the state police in Merida. Anyhow, there isn't any hurry. The notes says to leave Yucatan or I'll die, right? Obviously, it can't mean for me to leave right now, this minute. How could I? I'm sure I've got a few days. It's only logical."

"Yes, but I don't think you can assume whoever wrote this is logical."

There he agreed with her. "Tell you what. Let's wait until the morning anyway. We'll talk to Abe about it at breakfast and take it from there."

She started to disagree, then nodded and began to take off her watch. "Okay, you're right. I'm probably making a mountain out of a molehill."

"Note?" Abe said, his eyebrows sliding up.

He reached for it over his breakfast plate of *frutas frescas*—sliced papaya, pineapple, and watermelon, along with an unpeeled little banana; and of course a few lime wedges. He patted first one pocket of his shirt, then the other, then his hip pockets.

"They're hanging around your neck," Gideon offered delicately.

"I know, I know." He propped his reading glasses on the end of his nose. "Of course around my neck. Where else should they be?"

He studied the sheet for a long time. "I don't like it," he said at last.

"I'm not too wild about it myself," Gideon said.

Abe began to unpeel the banana. "I'll tell you what. I have to go into Merida this afternoon anyway, to the university library. I'll stop at the state police and give them this. We'll see what they have to say."

That was fine with Gideon, who began to attend to his scrambled eggs and ham.

Julie, who hadn't gotten used to the muddy brown eggs of Yucatan ("It's because of what they feed the chickens," Worthy had told her darkly), was toying with her toast and coffee. "Abe, it has to be somebody from the crew, doesn't it?"

"I'm sorry to say so, but it looks like it. Who else even knows Gideon is here? Who else knows about the curse?"

"It was in the papers," Gideon pointed out. "Garrison was on her way to a press conference in Mexico City, remember?"

"Yesterday morning. You think somebody read about it in the newspapers and came running to Yucatan the same day to slip a note under your door? No, I'm afraid Julie's right."

Gideon sighed and slid his plate away. "I suppose so." He glanced at a table across the room where a few of the staff sat. Harvey gave him a cheerful wave. Preston smiled and nodded his leonine, empty head. "Which doesn't make me terrifically happy. But I still think it's just another dumb joke. Like the coati."

"And the digging that was going on? That was also a joke, you think?"

Gideon shook his head. He didn't know.

"What do you think, Abe?" Julie asked.

"Mm," Abe said. He was looking carefully at the note again. " 'Gideon Oliver, leave Yucatan or you will die,' " he read aloud slowly. " 'This is not a joke. The Gods of Tlaloc.' " He looked sharply up at them. "Does this seem familiar to anybody else, or just to me?"

"Not to me," Julie said.

But Gideon hesitated. When he'd first read it there had been a momentary glimmer of recognition, a feeling that he'd seen it before. He'd discounted it as a random association; it was not the world's most original death threat.

"I don't think so, Abe," he said.

"Yeah," Abe said after another moment of peering at it. "I'm probably imagining it." He put a hand on Gideon's forearm. "Listen, Gideon, I'm sure you're right, it's just a joke, but all the same you'll be careful, yes? Why take chances?"

"I'll be careful, Abe."

Abe nodded and wiped his mouth with a napkin. "Good." He took a long last look at the letter, holding the glasses to his temples with his hands.

"You're sure it doesn't look familiar?"

11

The Hotel Mayaland is situated near a small secondary entrance to Chichen Itza. It sits on a quarter-mile-long spur of pavement that is little-used except by hotel guests walking to and from the ruins. At a little before eight-thirty on most nights, thirty or forty people from the hotel wander lazily along this pleasant path into Chichen Itza for the English-language sound-and-light show.

Julie and Gideon decided to take in the show. Abe wasn't due back from Merida until ten o'clock, when they were to meet for coffee. The entrance to the grounds was a narrow opening in a chain-link fence erected across the road, guarded by a querulous, one-legged ticket-taker in a wheelchair. The fence itself was draped with tourist merchandise, mostly T-shirts with spurious Mayan motifs. In front of them the genuine Mayan vendors, three dark, round women in nightgownlike *huipiles*, huddled unobtrusively. By the weak light of a few bulbs wound through the fence, some thin children of eight or nine played a scuffling game of soccer with a miniature ball, calling to each other in Mayan and Spanish.

Two slightly older boys with small palm-fiber baskets worked the incoming crowd, displaying a surprising English vocabulary.

"Hello, mister, wanna buy a snake? What kind you want? I catch one special for you. With a stick."

"Who'd want to buy a snake?" a chubby American boy of ten asked the harried-looking woman with him. A reasonable question, Gideon thought.

"They catch them for a snake farm, Jared," the woman told him. "They're not supposed to sell them to tourists, but they do."

"There's no such thing as a snake farm," the boy said with knowledgeable contempt.

"Not that kind of farm. They extract the venom to use for snakebites. Isn't that interesting?"

"You're full of baloney," Jared said.

There were no takers for the snakes, and no one seemed to be buying T-shirts either. The Mayan women slumped passively on low stools, hardly lifting their eyes from the ground.

"Let's buy a couple," Julie said. "T-shirts, I mean."

Gideon nodded. "Let's."

Julie liked one with a reproduction of a mural on it. Gideon pointed out that it was based—loosely—on one from Teotihuacan, not Chichen Itza, but she stuck with it anyway.

"What about you?" she asked. "How about the one of that man all dressed in feathers?"

"Quetzalcoatl? No, thanks, but, you know, I kind of like that one there, with that naked girl spread-eagled on the altar, ready to have her heart cut out. Very artistic."

"You have to be joking. I hope you're joking."

"No, I think it's very colorful. But, okay, I'll settle for the one with the picture of El Castillo."

From the gate it was a leisurely five-minute walk to the site. There was a light bulb strung from a tree every fifty feet or so, enough—barely—to keep them from stumbling off the path and into the scrub but not so bright that they couldn't see the stars.

They had taken the path to the site several days before, but that had been in the afternoon, and the ruins had come gradually into view through the branches. Now, however, at the end of the path the central plaza of Chichen Itza opened before them with throat-catching suddenness, chalky, vast, and silent in the starlight. El Castillo, the great, temple-topped central pyramid, loomed on their right, infinitely more overwhelming than it was in the daytime, a stupendous, bleakly gleaming tower of gray ice. Beyond it, obscured by a wispy night fog, was the blood-soaked Temple of the Warriors and its Thousand Columns. Ahead of them was the immense ball court, and all around, invisible but felt, the jungle, biding its time, waiting to swallow everything up again when the cycle of time decreed.

It was enough to stop Julie in her tracks. "Oh, my," she said quietly. "Will you look at that?"

Gideon squeezed her hand, not above a slow, rolling shiver of emotion himself.

To their left, things were on a friendlier, more human

scale. There was a long double row of battered, folding metal chairs set out on the grass, starkly but ineffectively lit by a single lamp behind. At one end of the rows was a wagon where soft drinks and candy were sold. Most of the chairs were already filled by people bussed in from Merida especially for the show, and the ground was littered with food wrappers and plastic cups, some of them probably left from the Spanish-language performance at seven.

The only seats Gideon and Julie could find together were at the far end of the second row, next to Jared and the harried-looking woman.

"Don't I get any candy or anything? " the boy was complaining as they sat down. "How about a Mars Bar?"

The woman emitted a muttered groan under her breath but got up promptly.

"And a Coke or something!" the boy yelled after her. Then he turned to Gideon and Julie. "That's my mother," he announced. I live in Puerto Vallarta when I'm with her, but I spend the summers with my dad in Connecticut. They're divorced."

"That's too bad," Julie said.

"That's okay, I don't mind," he said tolerantly. "Did you ever see this show before? We saw it last night. It's awesome. It freaked my mother out of her pants."

"That's nice," Julie said after a brief pause.

"Especially the part about the sacrifices. That's really gross. I'll tell you when they're gonna do that part."

"That's all right," Gideon said. "You don't have to bother."

"Oh, that's okay. I'll tell you when to hold your ears too. The music gets pretty loud."

Gideon glanced around, hoping that there might after all be another pair of empty seats they'd missed, but they were all filled now.

"You know what a man in our hotel calls this place?" the boy said, giggling. "Chicken Pizza." He wriggled with amusement.

The woman came back with a bottle of Coca-Cola and a candy bar. The bottle was accepted without comment, but not the bar.

"Snickers?" he said with outraged disbelief. "You brought me a *Snickers*?"

Jared," she said tiredly, "this is Mexico. They don't have all the same candy here. What's wrong with Snickers? Snickers are good. I like Snickers."

"I do too," Gideon said, rooting for the underdog.

The single light behind them went out. From a loudspeaker a horn began to wail a weird, lonely melody. The crowd hushed, except for Jared, who was not finished with his mother.

"You know I hate Snickers."

"This," Gideon muttered to Julie, "is what comes of naming a kid 'Jared.'"

"Jared," his mother said, "it's made by the same company that makes Mars Bars. Look at the wrapper."

Jared did not find this logic persuasive. "I hate them."

"Jared, how can we work this out?"

"We can't," he said,

"Jared—"

Gideon grabbed Julie's hand and together they ran off

through the darkness toward the ball court a hundred feet away. "We can sit on the steps," he whispered. "The view will be better anyway."

The *tlachtli* of Chichen Itza is the most impressive ball court of ancient Mexico, consisting of an enormous open space 545 feet long ("almost the length of two football fields," as American guidebooks endlessly point out) and 225 feet across, enclosed by two thick, high, parallel ramparts, each one with a stone ring set about 25 feet above the ground. Here the Maya had played their ceremonial game of *pok-a-tok*, in which competing teams tried to heave a hard rubber ball through one of the rings. Depending on whom you believed, the successful competitors either got to keep their heads or they cheerfully gave them up and went as heroes to live forever with the gods.

At the south end of one of these walls—the one nearest the folding chairs—is a flight of stone steps to the top. Julie and Gideon made for them and sat down on the lowest one as the plaintive melody died lingeringly away.

"Welcome," boomed an accented, echoing voice, "to the lost and mysterious world of the ancient Maya. Tonight you will learn of the early days of our fathers and forefathers, the days before the foreigners came, the days of the sacred places: of Zubinche and Timozon, of Zizal and Cumcanul, and of the great city known as the Mouth of the Well of the Itzas . . . CHICHEN ITZA!"

The slow, cadenced words slid away into the jungle on the moist breeze, and they were left in black silence.

Then, louder, the voice echoed once more. "*Behold*," it boomed, "*behold the wonders of our ancestors!*"

A crash of drums, and the Castillo leaped abruptly out at them like a colossal faceted crystal, drenched in flaming light, seemingly glowing from within. The grand stone staircase was a deep sapphire blue, the massive bulk of the pyramid a paler, under-the-sea turquoise. The Temple of Kukulcán on top was parrot green, its interior—seen through the rectangular entry-way—a boiling, riveting crimson. The stars, the jungle, the rest of the structures vanished against this brilliance, as if a huge backdrop of black velvet had been rung down.

At the sight there was a distant, collective gasp from the rows of spectators, and Julie impulsively clutched Gideon's hand.

"I'm not sure," she said, "but I think this may be freaking me out of my pants."

Gideon laughed. He himself had felt another slow chill riffle up between his shoulders and stir the hairs at the back of his neck. This was accompanied by a mild sense of guilt. Professional anthropologists were not supposed to get goose bumps from hokey, overloud extravaganzas consisting of bogus music, sham history, and meaning-less colored lights.

"I'm going to watch the rest from the top of the steps," he told Julie. "Want to come?"

She looked behind her at the narrow, rail-less flight of stone steps, steep even by Mayan standards. "Up those? In the dark? Are you kidding?"

"Well, I think I'll go. The view should be terrific."

"Be careful, will you?"

He was, mounting gingerly on all fours and leaning his right side into the wall, as most visitors did even in the daytime. The staircase was at the very edge of the wall; on his left was a murderously sheer drop down to a broad stone platform. The scene from the top was everything he'd hoped, giving him a view of every building in the plaza as the show continued, the lights moving from one ruined structure to another. He settled down on the top step to watch, leaning back on his elbow, only half listening to the windy monologue.

". . . the terrible god Chac Mool, who received the dripping hearts freshly torn from the sacrificial victims . . ."

The sonorous voice vibrated and soared as the lights picked out the expressionless face of the reclining Chac Mool figure atop the Temple of the Warriors and then moved to the grim Platform of the Skulls. ". . . whose heads were then impaled on this, the *tzompantli*, for the glory of the ancient gods."

Gideon himself was sprawled at the side of one of the more famous structures of Chichen Itza: the Temple of the Jaguars, which the conquering Toltecs had superimposed on top of the existing rampart of the old ball court as a shrine to themselves. Inside, wall paintings showed their subjugation of the city. The entrance was a small portico facing into the ball court and away from the other structures, its heavy lintel supported in the dramatic Toltec manner by two snake-columns—thick stone pillars in the form of feathered serpents, with their fanged, three-foot-high heads as the bases and their upraised tails supporting the roof.

At the edge of his sight Gideon could see the reflected lights playing over the fantastic heads of the snakes only a few feet away as the show progressed, so that they seemed to writhe and strain—a further agreeable titillation of his highly unprofessional goose bumps. All in all, he was enjoying the show a great deal.

"And so at last we say farewell to these lost days of grandeur," the voice intoned in its measured singsong. "Farewell to the Toltec and the Maya, to Quetzalcoatl and Kukulcán. Farewell to . . . CHICHEN ITZA!"

The brazen din of horns and drums swelled to an earsplitting finale and the entire western half of the complex jumped into eye-searing relief; blue, green, orange, red, gold, violet. A few feet from Gideon, half-seen, the great feathered serpents surged realistically from the shadows.

He turned his head sharply. Had there been something else? Behind the columns, hadn't there just been some sort of movement, a . . .

The music and floodlights went off abruptly, plunging everything into blackness and silence. He could see nothing. But someone was there, standing in the portico. Gideon tensed, straining to listen.

"Who's there?" he said. "*Quien es?*"

Nothing. Only the pulsating afterimages of the lights, the echoes of the horns. He stood perfectly still, waiting; blind and deaf.

And then a chilling, smooth, chinking sound, metal against metal, soft and sinister. A chain? Someone shifting a heavy chain in his hand? There was a furtive scrape of shoe on pavement.

Gideon had not yet stood up, but now he spun instinctively away from the intruder, rolling onto his right side, toward the edge of the wall. Something rammed heavily into his shoulder, the impact muffled by his own rolling movement. A foot—he thought it was a foot—caught him painfully behind the ear, then kicked again at his head.

He twisted farther away, but he knew he was frighteningly close to the end of the wall. Sightless, he grabbed at the pavement with his left hand to steady himself, but it wasn't there; his arm dropped sickeningly down into nothing. He was at the very edge, sprawled on his belly, hanging over a sheer forty-foot drop to a ledge of stone. His fingers scrabbled down over the vertical surface, managing to find a rough outcropping to brace himself against. His other hand, the right, was jammed under his body. A foot dug into him again, this time over the kidneys, with nauseating force, and then yet again, thumping against his ribs, thrusting him onto his belly, urging him over the edge and onto the rocky terrace below.

Gideon pressed himself into the stone pavement with all his strength, trying to keep from going over. He pushed down against the outcropping, jerked his right arm out from under him, and twisted onto his left side, facing the figure he still couldn't see.

At the same moment he heard the chainlike sound again, and a whirr and then a leaden *chink* as something smashed into the pavement two inches from his eyes, where his head had been an instant before. His forehead was spattered with tiny chips of stone. A hand grabbed roughly at his collar, twisting the cloth. Gideon lashed blindly up and caught his assailant across the hip with his forearm. It was a frantic, backhanded swipe, delivered without much force, but it told him just where the figure was, and his next blow was struck at the middle of the chest, or where he hoped the middle of the chest was. This one had the full power of his bunched shoulder muscles behind it. He felt the semi-rigid sternum under his fist, heard the resonant, solid thump of the impact.

"Ow!" With the shocked gasp there was an outrush of warm, winey breath on Gideon's face. The clutching hand let go of his collar and the figure staggered back—a couple of steps, from the sound of it.

Gideon pushed himself quickly to his feet, crouching, fists still clenched, ready for the next rush. He still couldn't see, and all he could hear was the throbbing of blood in his ears. He was nauseated and unsteady, not sure how far away he was from the edge. He licked his lips. His throat was parched.

"Gideon!" It was Julie's voice, alarmed, from the front of the steps. He realized it was the second time she'd called. "What's going on up there? Are you all right?"

And now he heard his attacker stumbling away from him along the length of the long wall, footsteps quickly receding. Gideon started blindly after him, but with his second step he tripped over one of the serpent heads and had to grab it to keep from tumbling to the stony ledge below. He held on, panting and queasy. But his vision was beginning to return. In the distance, halfway along the wall, he could see someone fleeing over the ancient stones, hunched and apelike under the misty, flat ribbon of the Milky Way. Hunched with pain, he hoped.

"Yes," he called to Julie. "I'm all right. I'll be right down." But she was already on her way up, and by the time he was steady enough to let go of the sculpture and ease away from the edge she was there.

"Gideon—my God, what—"

"It's okay, Julie, I'm all right. The guy just scared the hell out of me, that's all. He's gone now."

She scanned his face anxiously. "You're sure you're all right?"

He nodded. "Other than a sore spot where I got kicked in the head, an ache or two where I got kicked in the ribs, and a few bruises here and there, I'm fine." He grinned, but it didn't feel very convincing. "Aside from feeling generally like hell, that is."

"Sit down," she told him, firmly taking his arm in both hands to guide him to a seat on the temple portico.

"Now," she said, still holding his arm while she sat beside him, "what happened?"

He told her.

"And you're sure you're not hurt?"

"Absolutely. Just a few bruises."

"Thank goodness. Did he get your wallet?"

"No, I don't think that's what he was interested in."

She frowned at him. "What then?"

"I had the impression he was trying to kill me."

She continued to stare at him, then decided not to pursue it. "You couldn't see him at all?"

"No, I couldn't see anything. He jumped me just when the lights went out. It was pitch black." Tentatively, he tried standing up and found that he felt better; the queasiness was receding. "I'm okay now."

She stood too, and for a moment they looked at each other, then embraced without speaking. Beside them the pitted serpent columns gleamed in the starlight.

"I got scared," she murmured into his shoulder.

"Well, no wonder. I was a little on edge myself."

She didn't respond except to burrow a little deeper into his shoulder.

"That was a pun," he pointed out. "On edge?"

"Not funny."

"No, it wasn't," he said softly. "Sorry." He stroked her smooth, fragrant hair and held her a while longer. "Feeling better?"

He felt her head nod against his chest. "Come on," he said, "let's head back."

On Julie's insistence they stopped to report it to the khaki-clad official who seemed to be the Chichen Itza security force and custodial squad in one. At the moment he was busy stacking the chairs and trying to shoo off a knot of people standing around enjoying a smoke after the performance. The brief interview was not highly successful from Gideon's point of view, partly because his rudimentary Spanish was barely up to its demands, and partly because the official's priorities differed from his own; most of the time was taken up with an admonitory lecture about watching the show from unapproved areas. He took their Mayaland address, however, and promised to file a report with the proper authorities. Gideon would no doubt hear from them in due course.

"About trying to kill you," Julie said on the walk back to the hotel, "are you really sure that's what he was trying to do?"

"No," Gideon said truthfully. "But he almost brained me with some kind of heavy chain. And he was trying like hell to kick me over the edge. At least that's the way it felt."

"But why? What possible reason could he have? You don't suppose . . . " She stopped walking. "That threat? The one you said couldn't mean anything, that was just so much bluster?"

He shrugged. "Maybe I was wrong."

"Did you get a look at him at all? Would you recognize him if you saw him again?"

"No, I couldn't see, I couldn't hear. The whole thing caught me by surprise, and it couldn't have lasted more than five seconds. Most of which I spent trying not to roll over the edge."

"But you must have been able to tell something. Was he big? Small? Skinny? Fat?"

"I just don't know; he seemed pretty strong, but there really wasn't any way to tell. I never got my hands on him."

They began to walk again, preferring not to fall too far behind the group of people that had been ousted by the guard. Gideon's ear was beginning to ache, his ribs to pulse with pain. The adrenaline-generated anesthesia of danger was starting to wear off.

"I know what you're thinking," she said. "You're thinking it was somebody from the dig."

That's what he was thinking, all right.

Julie jerked her head. "Gideon, I just can't make myself believe it was any of those people. The threat— all right, maybe. But to actually attack you . . . with a *chain*—anyway, how could they even know we were going to the sound-and-light show? We didn't tell anybody."

"No, but any of them could easily have been following us. They could have trailed us to the show, and then when I went up the stairs they might have sneaked around to the far side of the wall, climbed up, and edged their way along it during the performance. And the whole crew went to the show last week. They'd know just the moment when I'd be blinded—"

He sighed. "Would you say this lacks a certain plausibility?"

"Just a little." She turned her head to look up at him. "Gideon, don't get angry, but isn't this beginning to sound just the tiniest bit paranoid to you? You can't even be sure it was an American. Maybe it was someone who never saw you before. Somebody nutty, or a wino or dope addict who was spending the night up there."

Gideon thought it over. "I suppose it could have been."

"Isn't that a more reasonable explanation?"

Gideon put a hand on either side of her waist. "Yes," he said with a smile, "it is."

"After all, you said you smelled wine, didn't you?"

"Yes, that's true."

"And if it only lasted a few seconds before you scared him off, and it was dark, and you were scuffling, how can you be positive he wasn't just trying to rob you?"

"You're right, I can't."

"And do you really believe all this, or are you just humoring me?"

"I'm just humoring you," Gideon said. "Somebody was trying to kill me."

When Gideon awakened the next morning he stretched before thinking, then followed it with an immediate and heartfelt groan.

"Feeling a little achy?" Julie murmured beside him.

"If you call an inability to move without excruciating pain a little achy, then I suppose you could say I'm a little achy. God, I feel like the Tin Man after a year in the rain."

Julie kissed him sleepily somewhere near the left eyebrow and rolled out of bed, yawning. "I'll get you some aspirin."

"Thanks. About forty should do it."

While she rummaged in the toiletry kit that had been placed on the bathroom windowsill but not yet unpacked,

Gideon lay on his back, careful not to move. Although he rarely fell back asleep once awake, this time he drowsed, slipping into a troubling dream, perhaps the continuation of a dream he'd been having when he woke up.

He was a child again, lying on an operating table, alone in an immense, cold room. He was frightened, his heart in his mouth. Something awful was going to happen to him. There was an ominous grinding noise, and the table, which had wheels, began to slide over the linoleum floor, slowly at first, gradually building up to a blurred speed, then coming to halt in another huge room. There, silent, elongated figures in white surgical gowns and masks glided as if on skates. The smell of ether was strong in Gideon's nostrils.

Terrified, he held himself perfectly still. He stopped breathing. He shut his eyes.

But they saw him all the same. One of the tall, slender figures approached, holding a scalpel in a rubber-gloved hand. The figure mumbled something. As he spoke the mask fell away and Gideon could see that there was no human mouth beneath it; no human flesh at all, but the curved, bony jaws of a fish.

The figure towered over him. The scalpel had changed to a flint knife. He lay the point against Gideon's collarbone and pressed. Screaming, Gideon kicked out at him.

"Ow!" the monster cried.

Ow?

His eyes flipped open. Julie was sitting on the side of the bed, her hand gently touching his shoulder, fingertips on his collarbone. "Are you okay? I think you were dreaming. Here's your aspirin."

He took the two tablets, swallowed some water, and fell back onto the bed, trying to hold onto the dream's fragmenting images.

"Julie," he said slowly, "it was an American."

"You were having a dream, Gideon," she said soothingly.

"No, last night. The guy that jumped me. He was an American."

"Last night? But how could you tell? I thought he didn't say anything."

"He grunted. He said 'ow.' I just remembered. Damn, how could I be so stupid?"

There was a brief pause while she frowned down at him. "And Mexicans don't say 'ow'?"

"No, they don't."

"What do they say?"

"I'm not sure, but even if they said it, it wouldn't come out the same. The initial vowel—the *ah* sound—would be farther back in the palate, and the glide to the second one wouldn't be as marked. It would sound more like two separate vowels, not our kind of diphthong."

"It would?"

"Sure." He demonstrated.

"Come again? They wouldn't say 'ow,' they'd say 'ow'?" She was far from convinced.

"They'd say 'ah-oo,'" he repeated patiently, "if they said it at all. But they don't."

"I don't know about this, Gideon," she said doubtfully. "It sounds pretty subtle to me. He was grunting from a punch in the stomach, after all, not reciting a speech, and I doubt if you were listening too carefully to his diphthongs at the time. Besides, are you sure your Spanish is that good?"

"My Spanish is pitiful, but that doesn't have anything to do with it. I'm talking about the general tendency of Romance-language speakers to—" He laughed. "The hell with it. Just trust me."

Tentatively, he rotated his upper arms. "I think the aspirin's beginning to work. How about some breakfast?"

Gideon had continued to improve through a breakfast of *huevos rancheros* with Abe and Julie, but he knew it would be a mistake to try to work on the skeleton just yet; not in the cramped, kneeling position that was required. Instead, he sent a reluctant Julie off to the site with a concerned Abe and decided to spend the day working on his monograph. But it was hard getting his mind off that "ow" and what it meant. Because if it had been an American who had attacked him, it was just about settled: It had to be one of the crew. There just wasn't anybody else. Well, there was Stan Ard, but that was it.

Or was he imagining that "ow," inventing it after the fact as a result of a garbled, childish nightmare? The episode on the wall seemed as if it had been a long time ago. He sighed, forcing himself back to work. The much-amended monograph was on the writing table in front of him, a nearly depleted pot of coffee at his elbow, and a welter of notes and references scattered over the table, the bed, and the carved bureau. And a few piles of

paper were on the floor in a semicircle around his feet.
Just like home. It was as good as being in his office.

But things were not going well. He stared dejectedly at
the depressing sentence in front of him:

> Albeit the precocious sapience of *H. sapiens
> swanscombensis* is now considered discredited
> by most scholars as a result of recent distance
> function analysis, the question of this interest-
> ing population's origin is yet to be resolved, as
> is its taxonomic niche, particularly vis-à-vis
> the Quinzano and Ehringsdorf populations,
> which are, of course, generally classified as
> proto–Western-Neanderthal.

He drained his cup, shook his head, and sighed. Why
did his academic papers always come out like this?
Christ, "albeit"! And "vis-à-vis" in the same sentence.
And three passive constructions—no, four. Was that a
single-sentence record? Was this what fifteen years of
immersion in the professional journals had brought him
to? If he didn't watch out he would start talking this way.

He substituted an "although" for the "albeit" and an
"as compared to" for the "vis-à-vis," but it didn't help
much. He poured himself the last of the coffee and
mused. Now, how would Stan Ard write this up for
Flak? "From what misty, savage dawn of antiquity did
these robust, heavy-browed humans, the first of their
kind, come stumbling . . ." He smiled. If you asked
him, it had something going for it, but he'd never get it
by the editorial board of *Pleistocene Anthropology*.

He stretched gingerly and pushed his tepid coffee away. The weather had turned sultry as the morning wore on, with the threat of rain now hanging heavily in the air, and the humidity had pasted his shirt to his back. No matter how often he washed his hands his palms stayed gummy. Even the sheets of paper he was working with were limp with moisture. He had turned off the languorous ceiling fan. Looking at it had made him feel hotter, not cooler. For the first time since he'd come, he was starting to think with longing of the cool, gray, cleansing rains of Washington.

At eleven-thirty someone knocked at his door. Grateful for the interruption, he shoved the paper aside and went to answer it.

"Emma," he said, surprised. "I thought you were at the site."

"I was. I took my lunch hour early. There's something I have to share with you. It explains everything."

She was already flushing, which in Emma was usually a sign of dogged resolution. That did not bode well. Gideon steeled himself.

"I know you're just going to laugh, Dr. Oliver, but I felt I had an obligation to tell you. I understand the significance of what happened to you last night."

"How do you know what happened to me last night?"

"Everybody knows," she said carelessly. "The whole hotel's talking about it. But I understand *why* it happened. I centered on it during my amethyst meditation." She hesitated and stuck out her broad chin. "I've established a first-level interface with a personage who calls himself Huluc-Canab."

There was no escape. She was standing in the doorway, blocking the only route to freedom unless he wanted to jump from the balcony. He managed a smile. "Would you like to come in?"

She shook her head brusquely. Social amenities were not Emma's forte. "Huluc-Canab explained it to me. Do you remember what the curse said? 'Second, the darkness will be sundered and the terrible voices of the gods will be heard in the air, and there will be a mighty pounding of the soul so that the—' "

"Pummeling," said Gideon.

" '—a mighty pummeling of the soul,' " Emma continued, unfazed, " 'so that the spirit languishes and faints.' " She looked meaningfully at him.

"Ah," he said.

"You don't see what it means?"

"No." He knew that he was eroding her already slipping estimation of him.

"Darkness turning to light? Voices of the gods? It means the sound-and-light show! and the 'pummeling'— it's talking about what happened to *you*. How could it be any more specific than that?"

Many years before, when he had nervously turned in the first draft of his dissertation to his doctoral committee members, Abe had penciled in some comments across the title page: "Very inventive. Considering the lack of data, the inconclusive results, and the ambiguous statistical analysis, you did a wonderful job. Not everyone can make two hundred pages from nothing. I predict you'll go far."

Emma, Gideon was ready to admit, did not lack for

inventiveness either. "Well, I don't know," he said, choosing, as Abe had, to try humor. "If that was my soul they meant to pummel, they sure left some bruises on the surface."

"Oh, come on, Dr. Oliver," she said sharply, "you know I'm right. 'Darkness turning to—'"

"Emma, there's a sound-and-light show every night of the year."

"Yes, but this was the first one *you* were at."

"Look, Emma," he said reasonably, "why should it matter that it was my first light show? Why should the gods have it in for me in particular? Why put out my cigar and no one else's?"

"Because," she said, and gestured at him, almost jabbing him in the chest, "you're the one who's disturbing their privacy."

"Me? Emma, what do you think we're all doing? What do you think archaeology is about? How can we learn anything about the Maya if we don't disturb their privacy?"

"Yes, yes, but *you're* the only one who's disturbing their bones and the dust of their bodies, and the curse specifically mentions—"

"I remember the curse," Gideon said with a sigh. The conversation was showing no signs of improving. "But whoever jumped me last night was a human being with a snootful of wine. And he grunted like anyone else when he got hit, and then scuttled off in a highly corporeal way."

Her splotchy face had set while he spoke. She was, he

saw, giving up on him. And not a moment too soon, as far as he was concerned.

She nodded sadly at him before turning away. "All right, Dr. Oliver, but don't say I didn't try to tell you. The second phase of the curse has come to pass. You know what's in store next. The—"

"Wait," he said, holding up his hand like a traffic policeman. "I don't think I want to know."

When she left he found that his headache was back. He swallowed a second dose of aspirin and walked out on the balcony to take advantage of the nonexistent breeze. He stood quietly at the railing, looking absently down at the foliage. Surely there couldn't be anything in what Emma had said? Not in the way she meant, of course—but was it conceivable that there was a connection between the attack and the curse? That someone might actually be trying to make it look as if—

Behind him he heard the front door of the room open.

"Hello?" Julie's voice. He perked up at once. "Is my husband in there somewhere under all that paper?"

He smiled and went back in. "Hi, coming to check up on me?"

"Yes, are you glad to see me?"

He kissed her lightly on the mouth. "Mm, you bet I am."

"Besides," she said, "I couldn't face another turkey sandwich for lunch. I thought maybe you'd buy me a square meal in the dining room."

"You're on. How'd the dig go this morning?"

She had gone into the bathroom to wash her hands. "Fine," she called over the running water. "Oh, your friend Stan Ard came prowling around looking for you, slavering to get a scoop on what happened last night. I told him I had no idea where you were." She came out toweling her hands. "And the state police are already on the scene, you'll be happy to know."

"You mean they're here about last night?"

"Yes, and that note under the door. I spent half an hour—" There was a crisp doubletap at the door. "That must be the inspector, right on cue."

"The inspector?"

"Inspector Marmolejo. He said you know him."

"I do," Gideon said, heading for the door. He was surprised; he hadn't expected the Chichen Itza guard to forward a report so promptly. Or a full-fledged inspector to hustle right out.

"Why don't we ask him to join us for lunch?" Julie said. "He seems like an interesting man."

"Oh, he is," Gideon said. "He is."

13

When Gideon had last seen Inspector Javier Alfonso Marmolejo of the Yucatecan State Judicial Police, he had been Subteniente Marmolejo, a puckish, elfin subordinate officer involved in the investigation into the stolen codex. He had been used by his pompous superior for little besides translation; his English was excellent. ("It's because so many of our crimes involve Americans," he had explained to Gideon with sly ambiguity.)

In those days, pseudo-military dress and titles had still been in vogue for Mexican police officials, but Marmolejo, alone among his bemedaled, mirror-booted colleagues, had dressed as neatly and inconspicuously as a salesclerk. Now, having risen in the world, he had not changed his style; he wore the openthroated, outside-the-belt white shirt called the *guayabera*, neatly pressed pale-blue trousers, and well-cared-for oxfords on small feet that barely reached the floor when he was seated.

Although he was not yet fifty, the passage of almost six years had wizened the mahogany-skinned Marmolejo, leaving him with a radiating network of foxy wrinkles around his eyes, so that he was looking a little less like an elf these days and a lot more like a wise old monkey. He had changed in his manner too; increased rank had brought with it a mantle of assured, easygoing authority.

Not that he had lacked an aura of authority in 1982, despite his junior level. There had been times when the police operation had teetered on the edge of burlesque under the fat and incompetent colonel who was in charge; but always, one way or another, the level-headed Marmolejo had been able to bring things back from the brink before they collapsed into *opéra bouffe*.

"A very nice dining room," he said as they sat down at their table. "I always like to come here."

The Mayaland's restaurant was the coolest place in the

hotel, an airy, tiled room a full two stories high, with thick white walls and great, dark, burnished ceiling beams of ceiba wood. Outside the screened windows was a long gallery with a vine-covered trellis that threw leafy, green-tinted shadows onto the walls. Beyond that was the bright blue swimming pool, hugged by a mounded, lavish landscape of tropical plants.

The only thing wrong with the room, from Gideon's point of view, was the enormous mural that covered one end wall; a vivid rendition of the Mayan corn-god legend, painted in garish purples and bloody reds, and full of naked, huge-breasted women, along with human heads hanging from trees by their hair and other unpleasantnesses that were part of the Mayan creation myth. Accurate enough, but hardly a stimulant to the appetite. Gideon and Julie always made sure to face away from it, as they had today, but Marmolejo had seated himself so that he was looking directly at it, and he gazed upon it now with contentment and affection. But of course Marmolejo himself was half Mayan, which no doubt made a difference.

"Well, Inspector," Gideon said as the waitress set down a platter of lobster pâté and crackers, "I'm glad to see you again, even if I had to take a few lumps to do it."

Marmolejo murmured his agreement and nodded affably, removing the unlit, half-smoked cigar from his mouth and laying it carefully in an ashtray. Gideon smiled to himself. Marmolejo's ever-present cigar was rarely alight, and then only briefly. There had been a running joke in the old days as to whether he owned more than one of them, or simply struck the same one in his mouth every morning and put it on the bedside table when he went to sleep at night.

"You're feeling all right now?" the inspector said.

"Fine. A few bruises."

"Good." He spread a cracker with pâté, then bit into it with relish. "I understand you couldn't see your attacker. You couldn't identify him if you were to meet him again?"

"No, I couldn't see anything at all."

"You can give us no clues? You noticed nothing?"

Gideon hesitated. "Well—"

"Why don't you ask the inspector whether Mexicans say 'ow'?" Julie asked brightly.

Marmolejo had shrewd, narrow eyes set so far apart above his flat nose they seemed to look around you on both sides. He raised his eyebrows, drooped his eyelids and looked around either side of Gideon. "That sounds interesting," he said pleasantly.

"Julie," Gideon said, suddenly unsure of himself—he hadn't, after all, had a chance to check this diphthong business in any of his reference sources—"I don't know that this is the time—"

"Come on, prof, put your theories to the test. Put your money where your mouth is."

Thus challenged, Gideon did. What, he asked, would Marmolejo be likely to say if somebody hit him in the stomach?

The surprised policeman paused while a Mayan waitress in a *huipil* took their orders. They all asked for the *comida corrida*, the blue-plate special: soup, red snapper with fried banana and saffron rice, dessert. And bottles of Leon Negra, a dark, musky local beer.

Marmolejo continued to wait until the waitress was well away. Then he asked Julie: "Do you happen to speak Spanish, Mrs. Oliver?"

"No, I'm sorry."

Marmolejo nodded and turned to Gideon. "What would I say if someone hit me in the stomach?" His long, narrow teeth gleamed in a sudden smile. "I would say '*Chinga tu madre*!' He made an emphatic gesture. '*Pinche madre*!'"

Julie looked at him inquiringly. "Do I want to know what that means?"

"They are old Mexican sayings," Marmolejo said blandly. "Very difficult to translate."

Gideon laughed and explained that he didn't mean, what would he *say*; he meant, what kind of *sound* would he make.

"Ah," Marmolejo said, "in that case I think I would say *ay*!'" He considered a little more. "Or perhaps '*ay-ay-ay!*' It would depend."

"Nothing else?" Gideon asked.

"Well, with strong enough motivation, maybe '*hijole!*' I feel certain that some time soon you will permit me to know where this is leading."

"You wouldn't say 'ow'?" Gideon persisted.

Marmolejo's eyebrows inched up a little further. "'Ow'? No, never 'ow,'" he said, pronouncing it as a very satisfactory "ah-oo" to Gideon's ears if not to Julie's.

"Ha," Gideon said.

When the *sopa de lima* came—a tangy chicken broth tongue-curlingly flavored with lime—they ate hungrily while Gideon explained.

"So," Marmolejo said, "what you are saying is that this person who attacked you with a chain—"

"I *think* it was a chain. It sounded like a chain."

"—with what you think was a chain, was not a *latino* but a *norteamericano*."

Gideon nodded.

"But are those the only two possibilities? Could he not have been, oh, a German, an Englishman, a Dane? People from all over the world come here."

"I don't think so. I think he was an American."

"Because he said . . ." The inspector arranged his mouth delicately. ". . . 'ow'?" It wasn't quite the American version, but it was close.

"That's right," Gideon said, rising to the faintly teasing tone, and if you're in the mood for a lecture on comparative linguistics, I am prepared to explain fully."

"Say no," Julie said from the side of her mouth.

"No," said Marmolejo. "I will gladly take your word. But I have another question. You were unable to see your attacker, correct? Then how was it he could see you? Or does this require a lecture on the principles of light refraction, in which case I am again prepared to take your word."

Gideon laughed. In 1982 Worthy had summed up the striking incongruity between Marmolejo's dark Indian looks and his frequently elegant English. "You look at the man and you expect 'I don' got to show you no steenkin' bedge,'" he had said. "Instead you get Ricardo Montalban."

"He was standing in the portico of the Temple of the Jaguars," Gideon said, "blocked from the lights and facing the other way. He jumped me the moment the lights went out. His eyes wouldn't have had to adapt."

"Ah, yes, of course." The inspector poured himself a second glass of beer and rubbed a lime wedge around the rim. The limes had been delivered with the beers. In Yucatan, there was very little that did not come with limes. "Other than the members of your expedition, have you seen anyone you know—any *norteamericanos*—in the vicinity?"

"No."

"Which would seem to lead to the unhappy conclusion that it is one of your colleagues who attacked you. No?"

"Yes, I guess so."

"Did you see any of them there yesterday evening?"

Gideon shook his head.

"Would any of them wish to do you harm?"

Gideon smiled. "No, some of them are a little strange, but I haven't been here long enough to get anyone mad at me yet. Not that mad, anyway."

"Merely enough to tell you to leave Yucatan or die," Marmolejo observed mildly. "I wonder if a little police protection, quite discreet, of course, might not be called for."

"No, thanks," Gideon said with feeling. "If you mean having one of your men following us around and sitting on our balcony while we're sleeping, forget it." He'd had police protection before; all in all he preferred being stalked by a would-be killer, particularly one who was as ineffectual as this one seemed to be.

"Gideon," Julie said, "are you sure it might not be a good idea?"

"I'm sure we can be less intrusive than that," Marmolejo said.

"I know, but—"

"You have your wife to think about too, Dr. Oliver. If there is danger to *you*, then also . . ." He raised his hand, fingers spread, and looked in Julie's direction.

He was right, of course, and it was more than enough reason to take precautions. Besides, Marmolejo would do what he wanted; he was merely being polite. Gideon gave in. "Okay, thanks, Inspector. I appreciate it."

"Good, but I would like your cooperation too. No more wandering off alone; no more climbing mysterious ruins by yourself in the dark. When you go to or from the hotel, it must be with others. All right?"

"Look, Inspector, I don't need—"

"He promises," Julie said quickly.

"Fine," said Marmolejo. "And I promise in return to have no men sitting on your balcony during the night."

While they made their way through the fish course Gideon told them about his talk with Emma.

"Emma Byers?" Marmolejo interrupted. "The woman with the red face? The large, powerful woman?"

Gideon understood what he was driving at. He had been thinking about it himself, particularly since his talk with Emma.

It was Julie who asked the question. "Gideon, is it possible that it was a woman who attacked you?"

"I don't know," he said honestly. "I couldn't swear it was a man. It could have been a woman—a large, powerful woman."

"What about the voice?" Marmolejo said. "You heard him speak."

"I heard him—or her—grunt. It was voiceless, a whisper. It could have been either a man or a woman."

"But you said you smelled wine," Julie said. "Doesn't that rule out Emma? Preston, too, for that matter? All they eat is seaweed and tofu."

"That doesn't mean they have anything against booze. I've seen them drink." He shook his head abruptly. "No, sorry, Emma's peculiar, but I can't see her trying to bash my head in with a chain."

"That," Julie said, "is because you hate to think you might have been beaten up by a woman."

This veiled slur obliged him to explain in some detail how he hadn't been beaten up at all but had actually come off pretty well, considering.

Marmolejo seemed to be thinking about something else while this was going on. "Tell me more about the curse," he said. He listened carefully to Gideon's explanation, asking several questions and growing more grave with the answers. He asked for a copy, which Gideon promised to get for him.

At last the inspector pushed aside his empty plate and picked up his unlit cigar, tapping it absently on the rim of the ashtray. "*Qué cosa*," he said softly, looking at the corn-god mural from under lowered lids that made slits of his eyes.

"Do you know what the local name is for Tlaloc?" he

asked. "I don't mean the *meridanos*, I mean the country people, the *yucatecos*. They call it *la ciudad de maldiciónes*, the cursed city. That is what they called it before any outsiders knew of it. That is what their fathers and grandfathers called it." Solemnly, he stuck the cigar in his mouth. "*La ciudad de maldiciónes*."

Gideon eyed him uneasily. Now what the hell was all this about? Marmolejo was an intelligent, practical man. Surely he wouldn't give any credence to a four-hundred-year-old curse.

Or maybe not so surely. Once, over brandies, he'd told Gideon about his extraordinary past. He'd been born in his Mayan mother's village of Tzakol, which Gideon had seen—a derelict little collection of shacks near the Quintana Roo border, where curses were no doubt as common and unremarkable as the pigs that sunned themselves in the middle of the muddy streets. When he was seven, his father had taken the family to Merida. By eleven, he was one of the army of kids selling walkaway snacks of coconut slices and peeled oranges near the *mercado*.

Against enormous odds he had gone through school and eventually saved enough to buy his way into Yucatan's then graft-ridden police department. Now, after the cleanup, his integrity and abilities had made him a high-ranking civil servant. He had attended the University of Yucatan as an adult. He was one of the few provincial officials to have graduated from the new national police academy. He was an educated man.

But who knew how much of Tzakol he still carried with him beneath that rational, sensible surface?

He saw the way Gideon was looking at him and laughed. "Don't worry, my friend. I doubt very much if it was the gods who attacked you with a chain. If it was a chain."

"I'm glad to hear it," Gideon said.

There was a booming splash from outside. The rain had come at last, crashing onto the surface of the swimming pool like a performing whale falling back into a tank, then setting up a tremendous thrumming on the water, the broad-leafed foliage, and the roof of the restaurant. Julie, who took pride in having grown up in the wettest micro-climate in the United States, had never seen anything like it, and watched with her mouth open.

"On the other hand," Marmolejo said easily, reaching for his cigar, "I wouldn't go out of my way to annoy them."

With the downpour, the viscous humidity went out of the air, as if the rain had pounded it into the earth, and a luscious, blossom-scented breeze flowed into the dining room like balm onto a wound. They shifted in their chairs, bathing in it appreciatively. At Marmolejo's suggestion, they ordered coffee with their caramel custard. A few moments before, hot coffee would have been unthinkable.

"I want to show you both something," he said. He set down his cup, and from the unoccupied seat at his right he took a paper bag and laid it on the table. Reaching inside with care he slid out an old Stanley pipe wrench, much used, its coating of red paint almost worn away.

"Do you recognize this?"

"I think so," Julie said. "Isn't it one of the dig tools?"

Gideon agreed that it was.

Marmolejo looked at Gideon. "It doesn't seem otherwise familiar?"

"Well, I think it's the same one we had in '82, if that's what you mean."

Marmolejo shook his head. That wasn't what he meant. He took hold of the heavy wrench carefully, not on the handle but near the loose jaws, and lifted it. He gave it a single firm shake.

Chink.

It was familiar, all right. Gideon sat up with a jerk. "That's what he tried to brain me with! Not a chain, a wrench!"

With a satisfied smile, Marmolejo carefully laid it on the table again and pointed at the head with his ballpoint pen, to a barely noticeable smear of white powder. "You can see where it hit the limestone when it missed your head."

"Where did you find it?" Julie asked a little shakily.

"Below the rampart of the ball court, at the far end, toward the Temple of the Bearded Man."

Gideon nodded. "That's the direction he ran, all right. He must have tossed it off the wall. Have you gotten any fingerprints from it?"

"Not yet, and I am not hopeful of finding any. Even if we did, what then? Many people must have handled it during the excavation."

Julie stared at the big wrench, fascinated and pale. "It's *heavy,*" she said. "My God, if that had hit you in the head, it would have—it would have . . ."

"Like an eggshell," Gideon said. "Well, that just

about makes it a fact; it has to be one of the crew. The tools are all kept in the work shed."

"So it would seem," Marmolejo said. "Ah, here comes our dessert. How I love *flan*."

For the next few days the dig continued almost as if nothing unusual had happened. Despite Gideon's and Julie's heightened perception, the crew seemed no more menacing than ever. They saw no secretive glances, no suspicious behavior. Nobody was slinking guiltily around. Worthy was Worthy, Leo was Leo, Emma was Emma. A little odd, some of them, maybe a little more than odd, but not a discernible would-be murderer among them.

Marmolejo's protection turned out to be a soft-spoken, uniformed officer who accompanied the crew to and from Tlaloc and hung inconspicuously about the site during the workday. Others, in civilian clothes, were at the hotel in the evening. They were not only assigned to guard Gideon, but also to keep an eye on things in general, which they did quite unobtrusively. Abe had tried to put the uniformed one to work— "as long as you're standing around with nothing to do"—but was politely turned down.

As quietly efficient as they seemed to be, they failed to prevent the next phase of the Curse of Tlaloc from coming to pass. This time Gideon did not bear the brunt of it alone.

At any time from 10:00 P.M. the following Monday night to 4:00 A.M. in the morning, according to their stories on Tuesday, every member of the staff was seized with acute attacks of diarrhea, some of which continued well into the morning. Several, including Julie and Abe, suffered intermittent cramps, and all were weakened and made uncomfortable, so much so that Abe called off the day's work.

It was noon before the crew began to straggle out to join their pale and weakened fellows in sipping tentatively at cups of soup or tea on the veranda, and in talking about this latest evidence of the gods' displeasure.

For, of course, that was what Emma claimed it was, and if she didn't have her audience convinced, at least she had them passive and very nearly inert. Gideon, whose sturdy constitution had kept him from suffering too much, had gone downstairs to get a pot of manzanilla tea to bring up to Julie, who hadn't been so lucky, and while he was waiting at the bar for it he was able to overhear Emma holding forth.

They were seated at the large table the group had more or less permanently appropriated as their own, and Emma seemed to be at the summing-up of her discourse. Nearby a jowly Mexican whom Gideon knew for one of Marmolejo's men sleepily cleaned his teeth with a toothpick and stared placidly at nothing.

"Obviously," Emma was telling the crew earnestly, "the curse is unfolding phase by phase, exactly as predicted."

It was a measure of their suffering that no one took issue with her. Even Worthy, who would surely have risen to the challenge a day earlier, sat in opaque silence, looking as if he'd been pickled in brine for a week.

Harvey, as wan and lusterless as a ghost, stared distrustfully into his soup. And Leo, with all the muscle tonus of a banana slug, slumped in his chair, focusing all his concentration on getting his cup to his lips. Preston, who would hardly have taken issue in any case, sprawled with his eyes pressed closed and misery grooved on his handsome, pallid forehead.

Emma, who didn't look any better than the rest of them, continued: "First, the bloodsucking kinkajou was going to come, and it did. Second—"

But, ill as he was, this was too much for Worthy after all. "Oh, for God's sake," he said sourly, "everybody knows that was nothing but a joke. Are you suggesting the gods hung that placard around the poor creature's neck?"

Harvey took heart from him. "And anyway," he croaked, to set things straight, "it wasn't a kinkajou, it was a coatimundi. Julie said so."

"That's right," said Worthy. "Or don't your all-knowing gods know the difference?"

"What matters is the projection of idea-constructions into our collective consciousness," Emma replied with calm inscrutability. "The fabric of the physical reality is nothing. You have to take it as it comes, Harvey." Apparently she had decided that Worthy was beyond help. "If you analyze everything, you just run into the Heisenberg principle."

Naturally enough, this silenced her critics, and she was allowed to go on. "Second—well, you all know what happened to Dr. Oliver. Third, Tucumbalam was going to turn our entrails to fire—"

"Urk," Harvey said softly, and lay his forehead on the table.

"—turn our entrails to fire and bloody flux—"

At this Worthy shuddered, grew even grayer, and stood up. "Excuse me," he said, and turned to leave, his arms clamped to his sides. Sweat glistened on his scant beard.

Leo pushed open his eyes and tried to grin. "Hey, Worthy, how's it feel to have *turista* like everyone else for a change?"

Worthy stopped to turn and stare at Leo. "All things considered," he said soberly, "constipation is much to be preferred." He broke into a constrained little jog toward his cottage.

Emma went resolutely on. "And now we're up to the fourth phase. " 'Fourth, the one called Xecotcavach—' "

Leo interrupted, shoving himself almost upright in his chair and looking thoroughly out of humor for once. "Emma, what is all this bullshit? Why don't you just burn some tofu or something to satisfy the gods, if you know so much about it? What do you want us to do, get out of here and go home, or what?"

Emma glowered at him. "No, I don't think we have to do that yet. They don't really want to harm us, they want to teach us." Her tongue darted over her lips. A dull flush stained her face, spreading upward from her throat into her cheeks. "You'll be interested to know that I think I've established a high-level flow of bio-psychic energy with a personage who calls himself Huluc-Canab. But," she added modestly, "I can't be sure yet. Maybe it's only a past-life regression."

"Hey, Emma, what are you, you a channeler or something?"

The speaker was Stan Ard, who had been sitting unnoticed by Gideon at an adjoining table, a beer at his elbow and his notebook balanced on a heavy thigh.

"I don't care for the word *channeling*," Emma said, preening at the sight of Ard's slowly moving ballpoint pen, "but, yes, I admit I've had some success at receiving mind-construct energy from personality entities on the other side of the physical-reality void."

"Whoa," said Ard, laughing and looking up from the notebook. "Personality which?"

"Personality entities that don't meet our definition of material actuality," Emma explained helpfully. "I visualize them as—"

"*Su té, señor*," said the female bartender to Gideon.

"*Gracias*," he said and signed the chit.

She smiled. "Manzanilla tea is very good for what ails you," she said in English.

"Let's hope so," Gideon said. "Would you happen to know if there's been a general outbreak of *turista* among the guests?"

"No, *señor*, I don't think so. Only your party."

"No problems with the hotel water supply?"

"*Señor*," she said reproachfully, "this is the Mayaland. No doubt you ate somewhere else."

14

"No," Abe said slowly with a shake of his head, "everything I ate all week came from the hotel. You too, right? And Julie?"

"That's right," Gideon said. "So if it was something in the food, it had to come out of the hotel kitchen."

Abe nodded. He was propped up in bed, fragile and sallow-cheeked, and looking disreputable, as old men in pajamas do when they haven't shaved. But he was hopping with restlessness, crossing and recrossing his thin legs, and poking irritably at the pillows stacked behind him.

When Gideon had brought the tea to Julie, she had taken three swallows, sighed, given him a sweet smile, and slipped into a peaceful doze with her hand on his. Gideon had sat without moving until she had fallen into a deeper sleep, then carefully extricated his hand and gone to see how Abe was doing, stopping first at the bar to pick up a bowl of soup and some bread for him. When he'd seen him at about 10:00 A.M., Abe had been in no condition for food.

"So what kind of soup?" Abe said with a listless gesture at the covered bowl.

"So what kind should it be?"

But Abe wasn't in the mood for this. "From an anthropologist I don't expect ethnic humor," he snapped.

"All right, it's chicken soup."

Abe made a growling noise. "Also I don't expect rote adherence to outmoded stereotypes."

"Wow, you're sure in a good mood. I'm really glad I came and cheered you up. Look, let's call it *caldo de pollo*, if that makes you feel better. And it's damn good therapy. It's bland, nutritious, easy to swallow; it can be tolerated even with digestive problems; it replaces fluids lost through dehydration; it—"

Abe covered his ears and made a face. "All right, I'll eat the damn soup, all right?"

Gideon took the cover off the bowl and set the tray on Abe's lap. "You're very welcome," he said. "No need to thank me."

Abe finally smiled tiredly and relaxed against the pillows. "Thank you very much, Gideon. I appreciate it. It was nice of you to think of it." He brought a spoonful to his mouth and swallowed. "It's good," he said, "I didn't realize I was hungry." For a few seconds he ate in silence, visibly reviving.

"You're right," he said, "I'm not in my usual good-natured frame of mind this morning."

"Really? I haven't noticed anything unusual."

Abe smiled again. "No, I've been *kvetching*, all right, and it's not just because I'm sick." He moved the spoon back and forth in the bowl, scowling down at it. "It's because we're *all* sick. Gideon, someone is trying to make it look as if the curse is real." He waved a listless arm. "Sit down, will you?"

Gideon brought one of the dark wooden chairs from the desk to the side of the bed, swung it around backward, and sat down, his forearms resting on the back. "Yes, Emma's just been explaining that to anyone who couldn't figure it out."

"Unless, of course, the whole hotel got sick, which would throw a different light on things."

"I already checked."

"And it's just us?"

"Just us."

"That's what I figured." He tore a tiny piece from a soft slice of white bread and chewed it, slowly and thoroughly. "You got any ideas how it was done?"

"Well, it's obviously something we ate and nobody else did."

"I agree. Isn't it wonderful to be scientists and come up with such terrific deductions?"

"But I don't think it was *Escherichia coli*, or salmonella, or any of the other *turista* bugs. We're not sick enough."

"Speak for yourself."

"You know what I mean. Everybody seems to be on the mend already—including you—and as far as I know there hasn't been any vomiting or fever. Just some acute diarrhea and a little weakness and cramping; nothing serious."

"Easy for you to say," Abe grumbled. "But you're right; I'll live. So what do you think, somebody just slipped a laxative in our food?"

"Looks like it."

"To me too." He handed Gideon the tray to place on a bureau. He had eaten most of the soup and half a slice of bread, and his cheeks had taken on some color. "So the question is, what did we eat yesterday that no one else in the hotel ate? Not breakfast, because we order that individually from the regular menu, and dinner is the same. So that leaves—"

"Lunch, which is prepared at the hotel, boxed, and left in the bar—unattended—for us all to pick up in the morning. Anybody could easily have doctored it."

Abe was shaking his head. "No, Preston and Emma make their own lunches from bee pollen or sunflower sprouts or whatever, and they were sick too." He glanced sharply up. "So they said."

"If they weren't, they were putting on a pretty good show, right down to the green complexions."

They both did some more thinking, their chins on their chests. They looked up at the same time. "The juice!"

Each morning at nine-thirty a busboy from the Mayaland bicycled to the site with an insulated three-gallon container of cold fruit juice, which was heavily used by the crew and remained all day on a table in the work shed. Unattended.

"So how hard would it have been to slip a few spoons of cathartic into it?" Abe asked rhetorically. "Cascara sagrada, say. You could get it in an over-the-counter laxative and break up the tablets into powder."

"We had unfiltered apple juice yesterday, didn't we?" Gideon asked. "Who'd notice if the cascara made it a little darker?"

Abe blew out his cheeks in a sigh. "Somebody around here certainly has a wonderful sense of humor."

"I can't help wondering if Emma's behind this," Gideon said. "She's sure getting a lot of mileage out of it. Maybe she's giving her friend Huluc-Canab a little help from the other side of the physical-reality void."

"But you don't think she was the one that attacked you."

"No." He paused, then added: "Not that I'd swear to it."

"What about the coatimundi?"

"No, that wasn't Emma. That was something different, a joke."

"Maybe it was different, maybe it wasn't. When a lot of funny things are going on together, they got a way of turning out to be related. Goldstein's Theorum of Interconnected Monkey Business."

Gideon smiled. "Could be."

"Of course. Anyway, you're right about one thing." For the first time a tiny sparkle glimmered in Abe's eyes. "It wasn't Emma who provided the coati. It was someone else."

Gideon leaned over the back of the chair, his chin on his crossed forearms. "Okay, Abe, you know something I don't. Let's hear it."

"Well . . ." Abe leaned comfortably back against the pillows, his hands behind his neck. "Since I had some time on my hands this morning I did some thinking, and I got to wondering about this coatimundi. What I wondered was, where do you find such a thing?"

"They're native to this area. Julie says they're probably all over the jungle."

"Sure, but how often do you see one? Ever? You think you could walk out in the jungle and catch one if you decided to play a little joke on the rest of us?"

"Well, no. They're wild animals; they—okay, where do you get a coatimundi when you need one?"

"Me, I'd call a pet shop," Abe said, "which is what I did. It turns out there are two pet stores in Merida, and the first one I called, on Avenida Colón, said it was very funny but he had one for almost two months and nobody wanted it, and now I was the second *norteamericano* this week who wanted one."

Gideon straightened up. "And you found out who the other one was?"

But Abe liked to take his time coming to the punch line. The coati, he told Gideon, was ordered by telephone and delivered to Piste, which as it happened was the nearest village to the Mayaland, about a mile and a half away; a humble, somewhat tacky little crossroads that had become a center for tourists who couldn't afford or didn't want the Mayaland's luxury. The buyer had taken possession of the boxed animal at the bus stop, in front of the Mayan Cave Bar Disco ("English Spooken Here"), from which he left by taxi in the direction of the

Mayaland. This was, Gideon should take note, late Tuesday afternoon, the day before the coati was discovered in the work shed.

"And the name," Gideon murmured, "of this mysterious gringo was . . ."

"No, Señor Merino didn't get his name, but he could describe him: '*Un hombre con una barba de chivo*.'"

Gideon wasn't up to the Spanish. "A man with a what?"

Abe's fingers tapped his chin. "A billy goat's beard."

"Worthy?"

Abe nodded. "You were right in the first place."

The narration had wearied him. He lowered his frail arms and slid down on the pillows, closing his eyes for a few seconds. "Right now I'm a little tired, but in an hour I'll feel better. I'll get dressed and go and have a talk with him and see what's what. And tell him what's what," he added.

"Like hell you will," Gideon said firmly. "You're staying in bed today. I'll talk to Worthy."

"No," Abe said, shaking his head, "I'll take care of it. It's my responsibility, not yours."

"Then how about delegating it? I'll go see him right now. I want you to take it easy and get your strength back. Come on, Abe, be sensible."

"Maybe you're right," Abe said meekly, and Gideon looked at him with a stab of concern. Docility wasn't exactly his style.

"Abe, I don't think it would be a bad idea to have the hotel doctor take a look at you."

Abe dismissed this with a flap of his hand. "No, no. I'll drink liquids; I'll rest." He closed his eyes again and settled himself down to sleep. "You'll see. I'll be fine."

"All right," Gideon said uneasily and stood up. "I'll drop by later and tell you how it goes with Worthy."

"Check up on me, you mean," Abe said wearily. "All right, thank you."

Gideon had reached the door when Abe called. "Gideon?"

"Yes?"

Abe's hands were clasped tranquilly on his chest. His eyes were still closed. "If you brought another bowl of chicken soup I wouldn't say no."

"Oh, all right," Worthy said peevishly, "I'm the criminal; I admit it. I put the miserable beast in the work shed. It was just a *joke*."

He dabbed his gleaming forehead with a handkerchief. "Couldn't we continue this later? I'm really not feeling my usual self."

"None of us are, Worthy. That's why I'm talking to you."

Worthy eyed him mutely across the table in his room.

"How much does a coati cost?" Gideon asked.

Worthy shrugged. "It was fifty-five dollars American."

"That's a lot of money to spend on a joke." He smiled in spite of himself. "Not that it wasn't funny."

Worthy seemed gratified by this, and even smiled faintly himself. "Well, I *was* trying to make a point, you know, although it may have been a little too subtle for

Emma. Gideon, is there some point to this? You have my confession. What more is there to discuss?"

Gideon sat back and studied him. There was quite a bit more to discuss: Had Worthy been making any other subtle points? Like putting something nasty in the apple juice? (Who, after all, would know more about laxatives?) Digging in the temple when he wasn't supposed to? Slipping death threats under doors? Skulking around Chichen Itza with a pipe wrench?

He decided to lay at least part of it on the line. "I was wondering if you had anything to do with this problem we're all having today."

"If I . . . why would . . ." He stared at Gideon. "You're saying someone did this to us on purpose? Poisoned our food?"

"Well, 'poison' is a little strong, but I think so, yes. I wondered if it was another little joke."

"But that's . . . that's monstrous!" Worthy cried sincerely. The sweat had sprung out on his pale forehead again. Fooling around with the digestive system was no joke to Worthy Partridge. "And you think that *I* . . . that I would . . ."

Gideon didn't know whether to believe him or not. Worthy was an intelligent, subtle man; Gideon didn't doubt his ability to dissemble. He had denied the coati incident convincingly enough on the morning it had happened. Still, his outrage seemed like the real thing.

"Gideon, how can you say this?" he cried. "Do you really think I'd do such a thing? I'm as sick as anyone else. My God, sicker, sicker!"

"Everybody's sick, Worthy. Whoever did it is smart

enough to realize he'd stick out like a sore thumb if he was the only healthy one."

Worthy twisted his gangling, sandy-haired legs around each other, left knee behind the right, right ankle behind the left; an arrangement most men's pelvic anatomy made impossible.

"No," he said after a moment, "I wouldn't say that."

"Wouldn't say what?"

"Wouldn't say we're all sick."

They had looked sick enough to Gideon. "What do you mean? Who isn't sick?"

"Stanley Ard," Worthy said evenly.

"Stanley Ard?"

"The reporter."

"Yes, I know, but why would—" But of course he knew very well why. It just hadn't occurred to him before. As Abe had implied, Ard wasn't the kind of reporter who would have scruples about manufacturing events when it came to improving a story. And if it meant bellyaches for a few others, well, that was a price that just might have to be paid.

"Worthy," he said, "that's an interesting thought."

"Yes," Worthy said, and wiped his forehead again. "And now I really think I should lie down."

When Julie awakened at five-thirty she was hungry and cheerful. They ate omelets for dinner (Julie having overcome her reservations about the brown-yolked eggs) and then brought some more soup to a shaven and largely restored Abe. They had talked about Stan Ard, whom Gideon offered to confront, but this time Abe had been

adamant. It was his job, and he would talk with Ard the
next day about the tainted juice and see where it led. As
to the attack on Gideon, it was agreed that Marmolejo
was the one to follow up on that.

15

It was the end of the next workday before Julie, Abe, and
Gideon got a chance to talk again at length.

They were on their way back to the hotel along the
path. The crew was eighty or ninety feet ahead of them,
out of sight and hearing. Behind, the policeman maintained a discreet twenty-foot distance, ambling as casually as a man strolling through a zoo.

Indeed, they might have been in some wildly extrav-
agant walk-through aviary. They moved along a moist
green corridor impossibly crowded with gorgeous little
birds of blue, red, and orange, which darted by their
heads as nimbly as swallows or watched gravely and
openly from the branches. Motmots, jacamars, cotingas,
manakins, according to Julie. And some she swore were
not in her *Birds of Mexico*.

"How did it go with Ard?" Gideon asked. "I noticed
him around today."

"We had a nice talk. He fervently denied putting anything in the apple juice. He was thoroughly shocked at the idea."

"That's not too surprising," Julie said.

"You want a surprise?" asked Abe. "How's this: the mysterious digger was at it again. Two more steps excavated."

Julie looked at him open-mouthed. "What happened to the guards you hired?"

"I hired them for night duty. But the site was deserted during the *day* yesterday, and someone took advantage." He shrugged. "I didn't think of it. I had other things on my mind yesterday." He retreated gloomily into his own thoughts, walking along, head down, hands clasped behind him.

Gideon shook his head. "What in the hell are they looking for?"

"Well, I hate to repeat myself," Julie said, "but I keep thinking that no one's actually seen that codex since the cave-in . . ."

"Impossible. If that codex was down there and anyone knew it—or even thought it—that stairwell would have been dug long ago. Besides—"

"I know," Julie said, sighing. "I know."

Gideon paused to let a beaded, spiny-backed iguana scuttle across his path and into the foliage. "Julie, you don't suppose that was the point of getting us all sick—so that someone could have the site all to himself?"

She glanced at him. "That just might be. And Stan would have been the only one who was healthy enough to go out there and dig while the rest of us just flopped around at the hotel."

"Oh, I wouldn't say that. I could have done some digging yesterday if I'd had a good enough reason. I wouldn't have wanted to, but I could have. So could most of the others, I imagine."

"Maybe, but Stan makes such a satisfying villain."

Gideon smiled. "I can't argue with you there."

Abe returned from wherever he'd been. "Did you hear Ard's leaving tomorrow night? He says he's got all he needs for his first installment."

"He is?" Julie said. "Shouldn't Marmolejo talk to him first?"

"Don't worry, I'm calling the inspector as soon as we get back." He laughed suddenly. "I almost forgot. I have some good news for you. Emma buttonholed me this afternoon to tell me now she's established a second-level pretersensory interface with Huluc-Canab."

"Terrific," Gideon said. "Maybe he'll tell her what we have to do to propitiate the gods."

"He did. He says we have to be more respectful of personality entities from other culturotemporal horizons."

Julie cocked her head. "Meaning?"

"Sorry, that's as specific as he got."

"Emma," Julie mused. "Emma always gets in her two cents' worth, doesn't she?"

Gideon knew what she was thinking. Just after lunch Abe had passed on some information: Preston had proudly told him that Emma was writing a book on the events of Tlaloc, to be told from the perspective of Huluc-Canab, who had revealed himself to be a tenth-century *ahlelob* from nearby Xlapak. (The fact that the loquacious Huluc-Canab predated the curse by five hundred years did not seem to affect his intimate knowledge of it.) According to Preston, Emma had already spoken on the telephone to a New Age publisher in Los Angeles and gotten a tentative six-figure offer for *Beyond Dreaming: The Tlaloc Dialogues of Huluc-Canab*.

Thus, as Julie now pointed out, Emma would seem to have a considerable stake in the fulfillment of the curse; even more than Ard did.

"I don't know, Julie," Gideon said. "I don't have any trouble imagining her slipping something into our water, but I still can't see her as the one who jumped me at Chichen. I just can't."

"I can," Julie said. "The woman is wacko, if you haven't noticed. But let's be fair. As long as we're talking about eccentric characters, what about Worthy?"

"What about him?" Gideon asked.

"Well, what's he doing here anyway? Does he strike you as the type who thinks sweating over a spade in the jungle is fun?"

"He's working on that adventure series about Mayan kids, remember?"

"Oh, that's right."

"Not to mention," said Abe, "that this dig is all-expenses-paid. Everything's on Horizon. People will go to the most miserable places in the world if it's free. Not that this is so miserable."

"That's certainly true," Julie said with a smile. "All right, what about Harvey, then? Aside from its being free, what draws him here? He's some kind of computer specialist now, isn't he?"

"He has ulcers," Gideon said. "A nice, stress-free vacation in the jungle was supposed to be good for them."

"Not only that," Abe said, "but once anthropology gets into your blood it stays there. And don't forget," he added with a nod in Gideon's direction, "Harvey learned his anthropology from a wonderful teacher. So who does that leave, as long as we're being fair and casting aspersions equally?"

"It leaves Preston," Gideon said, "but Preston's presence doesn't need a lot of explanation."

Abe nodded. "Withersoever Emma goes, Preston goes too."

"It also leaves Leo," Julie said slowly. "Now just what is a guy like Leo doing here? What was he doing here last time?"

"Leo," said Gideon. "Hm."

"Hm," Abe said. "Leo."

They walked on silently for a minute or two, while inquisitive birds zipped and swooped around them. From a pendulum-tailed, cinnamon-colored bird in a branch above them came a shy, liquid *ch-ch-chwipp*. At their feet another iguana shuffled resignedly out of their way, muttering.

Abe was muttering too. "Whoever did it, I can't make it add up. All right, Emma, or Ard, or someone, wants it to look like the curse is coming true. Fine. But where does the threatening note come into it? Tell me what the point of that's supposed to be."

"What's the point of the whole thing supposed to be?" Gideon asked. "Why try to kill me if it was only my soul that was supposed to get pounded?"

"Pummeled," Julie said. "And why use something like a pipe wrench if you're trying to make it look like a Mayan curse? It's so, so . . ."

"Anachronistic," Abe supplied. "And what about the digging? What's that all about?"

There were plenty of questions. There weren't many answers. They were already on the hotel grounds when Julie thought of one more. "What's next?"

"Next?" Abe echoed, deep in his own reflections again.

"In the curse. Setting our entrails on fire was *third*. What's *fourth*."

"Something about Xecotcavach," Gideon said grimly. "I don't think it was very pleasant."

It wasn't. "Fourth," said the copy they examined in Abe's bungalow, "the one called Xecotcavach will pierce their skulls so that their brains spill onto the earth."

They stood looking at it for a long time. Julie moved closer to Gideon, her shoulder warm against his chest.

"I think," Abe said, "I'll give Marmolejo that call right now."

Just before dinner Gideon went down to the hotel gift shop to buy some stamps. Leo was there, browsing among the postcards.

"Leo," Gideon said forthrightly, "let me ask you something. What are you doing here?"

The question seemed to startle him. He straightened up from the revolving postcard rack. "Doing here?"

"At the dig. Why do you come to these things? To tell the truth, I can't say you really strike me as someone who's that interested in Mayan archaeology."

"Mayan archaeology?" Leo's happy honk of a laugh bounced off the walls of the little shop. "Who gives a shit about Mayan archaeology? I come to these things because it's a great way to meet buyers, people who can afford to buy what I sell. What else?"

Gideon blinked. "And do they?"

"You better believe it. Harvey's gonna fly down to the Salton Sea with me next month to have a look-see. Hell, I've been on cruises down the Amazon, I've been turtle-watching in the Galapagos, I've been on a dig in Turkey, and I've never yet failed to make a sale. And it's all tax-deductible. You can't beat it. *That's* why I come."

"Oh," Gideon said. "Well, I just wondered."

He lay on his back watching the ceiling fan revolve slowly in the moonglow. Julie was on her side, facing away from him, her warm, naked bottom against his hip. She was breathing steadily and quietly, but he knew she wasn't sleeping.

"Julie?"

"Hm?"

"I've been thinking."

She turned onto her other side to face him, making rustly, comfortable nighttime sounds. Her fingers found his arm and slid down it to gently encircle his wrist. She waited for him to speak.

"Well, I was just thinking that if you want us to pack up and get out of here, we can. If someone's got it in for us—for me in particular—maybe it doesn't make sense to stay. There's no reason why another physical anthropologist can't take over. Marmolejo's going to increase security tomorrow, so I don't think there's any real danger, but who knows? I was the one who said that threat wouldn't amount to anything."

Her head came up, silhouetted against the louvered windows. "Get out of here?" she repeated, obviously surprised. "Because some miserable rodent is going around slipping vile notes under doors and sneaking around with a pipe wrench? To quote one of the eminent G. P. Oliver's more penetrating statements, " 'You have to live your own life. You can't let the creeps and cruds of the world run it for you.' "

He laughed and stroked the soft, moist line of her jaw, first with his fingertips and then with the back of his hand. Her black, ringleted hair gleamed in the dim light, stirring in the faint breeze from the fan.

"Besides," she said, "I've been married to you for over two years now, and I've gotten used to a certain amount of, uh, adventure in my life."

"Good," he said. He'd known what her answer would be, but she deserved a say. His hand drifted to her throat, to the silky, tender side of her breast, beneath her arm. "Are you having trouble sleeping too?" he said.

"A little." She snuggled down again and draped a leg over his. "Got any suggestions?"

"I don't suppose you packed any Ovaltine?"

"Uh-uh." Her leg slid slowly up and down his thighs.

"Well, then," he said, and pulled her all the way onto him, "I suggest we discuss the matter."

16

Marmolejo's increased security came too late. And it wasn't Gideon who needed it.

He and Julie were almost out the door, on their way to breakfast, when the telephone rang. Gideon picked it up.

"Dr. Oliver?" The voice was tentative, urgent. "Er, this is Dr. Plumm speaking. Perhaps you remember me?"

"Of course. Is something wrong?"

Plumm was the house physician, a gentle, unpresuming Englishman of sixty-five with baby-smooth skin and an immaculately groomed little white mustache. He had retired from practice in Portsmouth, lost his wife to cancer less than a year later, and come to Mexico hoping that a change of locale might help him cope with his grief. He had never gone back. Now he lived an expatriate's lonely life at the Mayaland, providing his services in exchange for a room—a superannuated old Brit, as he called himself.

He was something of a crime buff in his ample spare time. He subscribed to the *Journal of Forensic Sciences* and was familiar with a series of papers that Gideon had written on cause-of-death determination from skeletal remains. He had looked Gideon over the night of the attack and had been transparently delighted to find out the name of his patient. He had been eager to discuss some of the points in Gideon's articles, and they had spent a pleasant hour over coffee the next evening.

"Yes," he said, "I'm afraid something is very much wrong, and your help would be invaluable. Would it inconvenience you to come downstairs? It's in your line of work, and I'm sure you'll find of interest."

What was wrong was Stan Ard. He lay sprawled on one of the more distant and isolated jungly paths that wound through the hotel grounds, some hundred yards from the main building, near the chain-link fence that separated the Mayaland property from Chichen Itza. He was half-in, half-out of one of the white plastic lawn chairs that were placed along the paths. The chair had been tipped over onto its right side, apparently with Ard in it. His body had twisted sideways, so that he'd landed on his back, his bare, fat, hairy legs akimbo. His left knee had wound up hooked awkwardly on the armrest. He was wearing a blue *guayabera*, tan Bermuda shorts, and tennis sneakers without socks. The left sneaker had come loose and hung from his big toe.

His head was a bloody mess.

"A jogger found him half an hour ago," Plumm said. "It's the reporter, isn't it?"

"Yes. Stan Ard."

Not that it was easy to tell. Tight-lipped, Gideon forced himself to look down at the shattered head. There was nothing enigmatic about this, no veiled meanings, no obscure nuances. This was the end of the cigar, brutal and unequivocal.

Fourth, the one called Xecotcavach will pierce their skulls so that their brains spill onto the earth.

Standing guard was a jumpy young policeman in a tan uniform and a brown baseball-style cap. He was resolutely looking anywhere but at the body.

"*No toque,*" he said curtly when Gideon approached it.

He needn't have worried. Gideon wasn't about to touch it, for Dr. Plumm was very wrong—this was definitely not in his line of work, and he didn't find it of interest at all; not in the way the physician had meant. Yes, Gideon did forensic consulting and, yes, he frequently enjoyed his work for the FBI. But he was an anthropologist, a bone man, and the older and the browner the bones were, the better. Body fluids, brain tissue, and torn flesh were things he was constitutionally averse to, and the farther he could stay away from them the better.

"If it's still wet," he'd once told the FBI's John Lau, "call somebody else, will you?" Not that the FBI always obliged.

Stan Ard's head was still wet, and while Gideon didn't react the way he had the first time he'd been called in to look at a corpse with a massive cranial wound (he'd thrown up into a strainless-steel sink in San Francisco's

Hall of Justice, scandalizing the medical examiner's staff), his stomach did turn queasily over.

"Well, I'm not a pathologist or a medical doctor, you know, Dr. Plumm. I'm an anthropologist. I don't really—"

"But you're the Skeleton Detective," Plumm replied, as if that said it all. "I've never been called upon to do this before, you see—to be the physician on the scene of a murder—and of course it's terrifically exciting, but I—well, there are more police on their way from Merida, and they've asked for my report, but I'm afraid I may have missed something that would be terribly obvious to someone with experience. I was hoping you might point out any oversights."

He looked hopefully at Gideon with his mild, friendly eyes. His mustache was so meticulously trimmed it might have been two strips of white felt, neatly pasted on. "I should hate to look like a fool before the police."

Gideon relented. "I'd be glad to help if I can, Doctor."

Plumm relaxed visibly. "Well. I've made an examination, of course, although I thought I shouldn't touch anything before the police arrive. That's the proper drill, isn't it?"

"Right."

"Right, then. Of course, with a wound like that there was no question of resuscitation. The man's dead as mutton." He winced. "Oh, I am sorry. He was a friend of yours, wasn't he?"

"An acquaintance. I barely knew him."

Gideon made himself look at Ard again. Nowadays it wasn't so much the gore, the simple physical nastiness, that made his insides twist. Despite himself, he'd seen enough to get past that. But not enough to do what a seasoned homicide investigator could do: look at murder victims and see nothing but clues, diagnostic indicators, evidential data. For bones, yes; for bodies, no. To Gideon, the overwhelming fact, the only fact for the first few moments, was always that of *murder* itself; of willful, blood-soaked violence; of one person's actually *doing* this to another; of the terrible penetrability of skin, the brittleness of bone. It was always pathetic, always sordid, always horrible.

But Plumm had more experience of human penetrability, if not of murder. For him Ard was just another case, but of more than usual interest. "Well," he said, and rubbed his dry, clean hands together, "let me tell you what I've come up with, and you tell me where I've gone wrong, how's that?"

"That's fine," Gideon said, "but I'm sure you haven't gone wrong."

Overhead a helicopter was clattering its way toward the Chichen Itza landing pad. Plumm peered up at it. "The police."

Together they knelt at the side of the body.

"*No toque*," growled the guard.

"*Gracias, señor. Comprendemos*," Plumm replied politely. "Now," he said, all business, "he must have been killed very shortly before he was found." He pointed to Ard's poor, beefy, flaccid fingers. "There's no sign of rigor yet. There's no lividity yet, either, and the blood is still quite liquid. Of course, Lord knows evaporation takes forever in this climate, but I feel reasonably safe in saying he hasn't been dead more than two hours. More likely only one."

He looked at Gideon. "Er, what do you think?"

"You're the expert, but it sounds right to me."

Plumm permitted himself a little gratified quirk of the lips. "Well, then, let's get on to the cause of death. Not much doubt as to that, is there, even if no one seems to have heard the report. A gunshot wound to the head."

No, there wasn't much doubt as to that. Ard's forehead had literally exploded. Just below the hairline there was a dreadful, ragged wound nearly in the shape of a star, with curling petals of flesh peeling outward from its red center.

Gideon turned his eyes away with a shudder. Maybe he'd never get used to this.

"Now," Plumm said with a mixture of reticence and enthusiasm, "what we seem to have here is an exit wound. Classic stellate pattern. The entrance must be in the back of the head, probably near the occiput, where we can't see it. But you can see that quite a bit of blood has soaked into the ground under his neck."

He peeked at Gideon from under a neat white eyebrow. "How am I doing, Professor?"

"Makes sense to me."

Plumm's pink cheeks shone with pleasure. "May I give you my, er, reconstruction of events?"

Gideon nodded. "I'd like to hear it."

"Well, at first I was misled by the subcutaneous hemorrhaging in the orbits." He pointed to Ard's eyes. The upper lids were blue, swollen sacks, as dark and shiny as little plastic trash bags. "I assumed he'd been confronted here on the path and there'd been a terrific fight; hence the black eyes. But"—he waved at the surrounding ground—"there's no sign at all of a struggle, at least none that I can see. And no other facial damage of the sort you'd expect, although it's impossible to say for sure until he's been cleaned up. So I had to conclude there was no fight, and the orbital hemorrhaging happened when his head hit the ground. He must have struck it quite hard. Does that sound plausible?"

"I guess so," Gideon said slowly, but something was bothering him now. He made himself look at the bullet wound again, at the curving, yellow plate of frontal bone that was visible through the thickening blood. There was something odd . . .

"Now, as to what did happen," Plumm was saying. "I think it's fairly clear. From those marks on the ground you can see where the chair had been standing, and that its back was only a few feet from the fence. He was obviously sitting there and—Do you mind if we stand up? My joints aren't what they were."

Neither were Gideon's. They both rose, snapping and creaking. Plumm rubbed the small of his back. Gideon massaged his ribs.

"At any rate," Plumm went on, "inasmuch as he was shot in the back of the head, his killer had to have been on the other side of the fence. That would seem to suggest—although hardly prove—that it was an outsider; that is, not a fellow-guest at the hotel, but someone who wished to conceal his presence here.

"I understand," Gideon said.

After a moment, Plumm continued. "But you know,

this raises several intriguing questions: The murderer must have been lying in wait, probably in those bushes. How could he know that Ard would accommodate him by coming this way, sitting down right here? How——"

Hurrying footsteps scraped on the flagstone walk behind them. The young police officer stiffened, and Gideon and Plumm turned. Marmolejo, accompanied by two men in civilian clothes lugging a two-handled metal trunk between them, was rounding a curve in the path.

The homicide scene-of-the-crime crew of the Yucatecan State Judicial Police had arrived.

One of the civilians immediately began taking pictures with an old-fashioned press camera. The other snapped open the metal case and began selecting his tweezers, brushes, and powders. Marmolejo stood looking impassively at the body for a long time, rolling his dead cigar from one side of his mouth to the other with his tongue. He looked sidewise at Gideon. "And what might you be doing here, may I ask? Not that I'm anything but delighted to see you."

Plumm replied, "I specifically asked him to assist me. I thought—he's a world-famous homicide authority, you see. Er, Dr. Oliver here is"—Gideon cringed; he knew what was coming.—"the Skeleton Detective."

"Mm," replied Marmolejo. He held out his hand to Plumm. "I'm Inspector Marmolejo, Doctor. What can you tell us?"

With a nervous look at Gideon, the physician began a hesitant, near-verbatim repetition of his analysis, gaining confidence as Marmolejo listened intently, head down, staring hard at the body.

"Thank you," Marmolejo said at the conclusion. "That's very helpful."

"Would you like me to put my, er, findings in a written report? I'd be delighted, if it would be of service."

"Very good. The sooner the better. Could you write it now? Officer Hernandez will give you a form."

When the excited Plumm had gone off, Marmolejo remained where he was, studying Ard. One of the two men in civilian clothes was now sketching in a pad; the other was on his knees, burrowing beetlelike under the fallen leaves, and now and again putting invisible things in plastic envelopes or paper sacks that he handed to the uniformed officer.

Gideon waited until he was sure that Plumm was out of earshot. "Uh, Inspector, this really isn't my field—"

"Very true, very true."

He was decidedly less warm than usual, and Gideon couldn't blame him. World-famous experts were well and good in their place, but who really liked them horning in uninvited? Or even invited?

"Still," Gideon said carefully, "there are some things I'd like to point out."

"Dr. Oliver, I'm going to be very busy here for a while, so perhaps you would be good enough to put your conclusions in a report too? I'll look forward to reading it." His expression didn't suggest much enthusiasm over the prospect. He was looking at Gideon with his eyebrows lifted and his eyelids lowered, almost closed. His long mouth was turned down, with the cigar deep in one corner. "Will that be satisfactory?"

Gideon was being dismissed, and none too subtly.

"Look, Inspector," he snapped, "you don't have to worry about satisfying me. You want to do it all by yourself, do it all by yourself. The hell with it."

Before Marmolejo could respond he had turned and walked—strode, he hoped—away down the path.

He was thoroughly embarrassed before he'd gone ten steps. Was this the way world-famous authorities acted? Since when did the Skeleton Detective resort to childish snits when his vanity was pricked?

No, he would repent and humbly—well, dispassionately—submit the report that Marmolejo had asked for. The fact that the inspector happened to be irritable this morning was no reason for Gideon to shirk what was, in a sense, a duty.

Because, except for the time of death, Dr. Plumm had gotten it all wrong. Every bit of it.

17

It wasn't that Javier Marmolejo didn't like Gideon Oliver. Far from it. Oliver was a very likeable man. In 1982, when the naive, semihysterical *norteamericanos* had threatened to turn the Tlaloc investigation into a farce, it had been his good-humored common sense that had saved the day. More than once, too, but of course he hadn't been *el detective de esqueletos* then, and that was the difference.

He was, as Dr. Plumm had pointed out, a famous forensic expert now, not just another harmless anthropologist fooling around in the old cities, and Marmolejo had little patience with famous forensic experts. Oh, he'd learned at the academy about all the wonderful assistance they could provide, these pathologists and toxicologists, anthropologists and odontologists, and he had even seen them prove useful once or twice. All right, more than once or twice. But more often than not, things were more confusing when they got through than when they'd started. Especially with homicides. If someone gave him the choice, he'd throw them all out and make them earn an honest living in the universities.

For Marmolejo, like most policemen, knew that murders didn't get solved in laboratories or under microscopes. When they got solved at all, they solved themselves. The killer confessed or inadvertently pointed the finger at himself, or else one of his friends crawled out from under a rock and did it for him.

It wasn't "clues" that solved murders, it was informants. And the way to flush the bastards out was with old-fashioned police work—methodical, repetitive, and hard on the seat of the pants.

He leaned forward in the thronelike old swivel chair he'd inherited from Colonel Ornelas in 1984, when the crooked old voluptuary had taken the money and run, only days before the well-deserved purge would have caught up with him. With his small brown hands clasped on his lap, Marmolejo looked down at the gleaming wooden desk in front of him.

Inspector Marmolejo was an extremely tidy man. He took pride in the appearance of his desk. There were no notes, or reminders, or lists of telephone numbers slipped under the desk's thick glass top. And on the glass itself, no stacks of files, no manuals, no piles of unread reports. Nothing but whatever he was thinking about at the moment. And at this moment there were two hand-written sheets of business-size Hotel Mayaland statio-nery perfectly aligned with the front edge of the desk.

He sighed, worked the unlit cigar a little deeper into the corner of his mouth, and slid the sheets closer to him. Gideon Oliver again. A memorandum. He read it for the second time.

To: Inspector Marmolejo
From: Gideon Oliver
Subject: Stanley Ard—Circumstances of Death

I'm afraid Dr. Plumm made a few under-standable errors in his analysis of the shooting. This by no means reflects on his general competence, but only on his unfamiliarity with homicides.

Here are my own conclusions:

1. The wound in Ard's forehead is not an exit wound but an entrance wound. Although a gaping hole like this is usually caused by a slug's wobble on the way out, it can also happen once in a while in the case of a contact

entrance wound—that is, when the gun is held against the skin as it's fired. What happens is that the muzzle gases have no chance to dissipate in the air, and instead expand immediately under the skin. And when there is bone directly under the skin—the skull, for instance—the gases are forced back against the underside of the skin with great force, often bursting through it and producing a jagged, stellate wound easily confused with an exit wound. (However, laboratory examination of the surrounding skin will usually show some powder residue and burning.)

Sometimes some of the gases make it through the bone to the inside of the skull and expand there, blowing out the weakest parts of the cranium, which are the supraorbital plates, and filling the upper eyelids with blood. Almost certainly, this is what caused Ard's black eyes.

As you know, this is not a typical situation. I misinterpreted it myself until I caught a glimpse of the bone beneath, and saw that the hole in the skull itself was an unmistakable entrance wound—small, round, and neat, with the outer table of the bone quite intact around the rim.

2. If what I'm saying is correct, the interpretation of what happened has to be modified:
   a) Ard was shot from in front, not from behind.

b) The killer was not lying in wait outside
the fence, but on the hotel grounds with
Ard. There's no reason to think he'd been
trying to keep his presence here a secret
from Ard or anyone else.

c) Because the wound is a contact wound,
requiring the killer to have been within
arm's length, the killer may well have
been someone Ard knew; very possibly
someone he was friendly with.

I'm sure you and your staff have reached these
conclusions on your own by now, but I thought it
would be best to submit something for the record.
As to what it all adds up to, that's your job. If I can
be of any help, I'd be glad to.

If not, that's fine too.

Marmolejo smiled thinly. Prickly, this Oliver. Well, at
least you could understand what he wrote; not like some
of them.

He slid the sheets away with a grunt of annoyance.
Whoever heard of this expansion-of-gas thing? This was
Marmolejo's eighteenth homicide, and he'd never run
into it before. And they'd certainly never mentioned it at
the academy. As a result he'd initially accepted Plumm's
findings. So had Dr. López, the police pathologist, when
he'd finally arrived. But that afternoon, after the au-
topsy, López changed his tune.

That's what made the whole thing so irritating. Oliver
was right every step of the way.

He stood and walked to the big window. Immediately

below was Merida's colonial Plaza Mayor, a manicured island of greenery lapped on all four sides by the sluggish downtown traffic, most of which seemed to consist of extremely noisy, extremely smelly old trucks and buses.

After the police department clean-up, there had been a scramble for the best of the newly available offices in the Palacio de Gobierno, and to Marmolejo's surprise the heaviest fighting had been for the inside rooms, the ones overlooking the quiet courtyard with its modernistic murals chronicling the rise of the Mexican spirit. No one battled him for the colonel's roomy, old-fashioned office on the outside of the building; too much traffic noise, too much traffic stink. But Marmolejo liked the traffic. It stimulated his mind, made him alert and receptive. He'd had enough rustic peace and quiet back in Tzakol to last him for the rest of his life. He even liked the stink from the trucks, as long as it didn't get too bad.

And he could happily get along without the modernistic murals chronicling the rise of the Mexican spirit.

He walked back to the desk, put the memorandum in the to-be-filed box, pulled a fuzzily photocopied sheet out of a drawer, and stared impassively at it. The Curse of Tlaloc. He laid his finger alongside a now-familiar sentence in the middle of the page.

Fourth, the one called Xecotcavach will pierce their skulls so that their brains spill onto the earth.

Marmolejo didn't believe in curses. Not exactly. He didn't believe that Xecotcavach had come up from the Underworld and pierced Ard's skull. No, that had been a twentieth-century human being with a twentieth-century gun. Nor did he think that it had been Tucumbalam who had personally slipped a little something into the crew's food, or some other Mayan god who'd said "ow" (with a *gringo* accent) when Oliver hit him in the stomach.

Perhaps Emma Byers, who was writing a book on the curse, and with whom he'd spent thirty bizarre minutes the day before, really believed all these things, but not Marmolejo. Not precisely. What Marmolejo did believe—and what he had learned to keep to himself— was that there were a lot of things in this world that nobody could explain. Not the professors, not the doctors, not the priests. And definitely not Javier Marmolejo.

He couldn't explain the Evil Eye, but he had seen it work. Oh, he had seen it work. And he couldn't explain how it was that his uncle Fano, who had been given up on by the doctors and carried home to die in Tzakol, had not died after all. The family had brought in a curer who had propitiated the winds, given Fano an amulet of wood from the *tancazche* tree, and called upon Ix Chel, the goddess of health, to help him. And he had recovered. That very night he had stood up on his feet for the first time in weeks, and he had lived. All right, for six or seven months only, but still . . .

Marmolejo had been just a child, but he had learned something valuable from it. A health official, Dr. Zuniga, had visited the family earlier, when Fano had returned home. With the best of intentions he had explained that rituals were fine in their place, but there was no hope at all for the dying man. What could ceremonies do against bacteria and viruses? The best thing the family could do was to resign themselves and make Fano's last hours comfortable. He would be dead within a very few days.

But when Fano didn't die, Dr. Zuniga's philosophy was undisturbed. Yes, the ritual had been effective, he explained patiently, but not really; not the way they supposed. It had no power of its own. It was all in the mind. Fano had *thought* it would work, and so it had. That was all. Where, Dr. Zuniga had asked with a smile, was the mystery in that?

Marmolejo had been much impressed. First the doctor had told the relatives that the ceremony couldn't work and why. Then afterward, without blinking an eye, he had told them exactly why it *had* worked. This he managed to do in a way that showed he had been right both before and after, and the family had been wrong all along. The fact that Fano had recovered, if only for a while, didn't seem to have much to do with it.

It was the young Marmolejo's introduction to the mind of the scientist, and these many years later it was still his key to how their thinking worked: Even when they were wrong they weren't wrong.

Well, Oliver was a lot better than most. And, happily, what he needed from him now was not more of his forensic expertise, but some plain old-fashioned information.

He picked up the telephone on his desk and dialed the Hotel Mayaland.

"*Hola*," he said to the clerk who answered. "*Puedo hablar con Señor Oliver*?"

18

In five-and-a-half years Merida had changed very little. Animated, noisy, cheerful, the city was teeming with round little people not much over five feet tall, among whom outlanders loomed here and there like isolated peaks sticking up above the clouds.

At five feet, six inches, Julie didn't often get the chance to loom, and she was obviously enjoying it. "I feel like Dorothy in Munchkinland," she said happily to Gideon over the heads of the chattering shoppers who had bustled their way between them.

They were fighting their way out of Merida's great public market, heading for an eleven o'clock meeting with Marmolejo. The inspector's request that Gideon—and Julie, if she liked—pay a visit to his office had come at a good time; they were ready for a change of scene. Ard's death had naturally cast a pall over things, but besides that, they had been in Yucatan eleven days and had yet to get more than a mile from the Mayaland. They had caught the morning bus originating from Cancun at its Chichen Itza stop (one of Marmolejo's men had seen them off), and a two-hour ride had put them at the main Merida bus station on Calle 69 an hour before their appointment, giving them time to walk through the famous *mercado*.

They hadn't intended to buy anything, but had succumbed at a stall selling the celebrated local string hammocks. Yucatecan hammocks were delicate, threadlike affairs and Julie had made Gideon ask the vendor if the large size—the *matrimonial especial*—could really hold the weight of two people.

The vendor had drawn himself up. "I myself have no beds in my house, *señor*," he had told Gideon. "Only hammocks. And I have eight children."

Twice on their walk to Marmolejo's office in the center of town, Gideon had been sidled up to by teenaged boys who recognized him as an American (he loomed more than most) and slipped business cards into his hand. Almost anywhere else they would have been invitations to the Pussy Cat Club or the Eros Massage Studio, but there wasn't much big-city nightlife in Merida, and little in the way of earnest vice. "Welcome, gentlemens and ladies," said one card. "We have finally made handcraf scultures for your examination." The other said, "Restaraunt T'ho inwites you to a happy dining on Typical Yucatan Cookings."

Other young men—boys, really, some no more than nine or ten—hawked walkaway snacks from handpushed or bicycle-powered carts at the curbside: spiralpeeled oranges; mangoes on sticks; sliced papayas and pineapples; brown-kerneled corn doused with chili sauce and eaten out of the husk.

"That's what Marmolejo did when he first came to the big city," Gideon said.

Julie watched a sweating, skinny kid of twelve in a ragged gray T-shirt deftly pare a coconut, then whack it into a dozen wedges, all with a few quick strokes of a *coa*, a miniature machete with a wicked hook on the end of it.

"Then he sure has come a long way," she said.

He sure had.

His office was like something out of *Viva Zapata*, an airy, dusty, once-grand space with tiled floors, high windows, cracked walls, and not enough furniture to keep it from looking like a railroad-station waiting room. What furniture there was was eighty or ninety years old, massively made of dark, heavy wood; a sort of *latino-*Victorian. It was far from crude, but somehow one wouldn't have been surprised to see a couple of crossed cartridge belts hooked over a chair back, or a stained sombrero tossed on the corner of the enormous desk.

Marmolejo himself sat, erect and compact, in a richly carved chair that could have held two of him side by side. He apologized handsomely for his sharpness the day before and accepted Gideon's equally sincere apology. Amends made, they relaxed. Marmolejo asked an assistant to bring in soft drinks, then slid four photocopied typewritten pages across the desk.

"This is from Mr. Ard's room; a copy of the article he submitted to his newspaper several days ago."

Gideon looked at it and winced.

Marmolejo's eyebrows rose. "Is something the matter?"

"No, nothing."

Just that the title was "Grisly Curse of Death Stalks Jungle Excavation."

"Perhaps you would look the article over," Marmolejo said. "I thought that as the only member of both the 1982 excavation and the current one"—he inclined his head courteously—"the only one above suspicion—you might be in a position to see if there is something in it that would throw some light on things."

Gideon had wondered where Marmolejo's cigar was, but now the inspector opened the upper right-hand drawer of the desk, revealing a white onyx ashtray. He took a two-inch stub from it, stuck it in the corner of his mouth, and settled down to wait for Gideon to read the article. The drawer was closed with the ashtray still inside.

Gideon quickly read the article. There were no secrets in it, no clues as to why Ard might have been killed. It was a predictably lurid account of the curse and its "terrifying realization." It mentioned the mysterious appearance of a "strange, unidentified jungle animal that whispering native laborers secretly swore was a kinkajou." (There was no mention of the placard around its neck.) It described the "night of fiery agony, when Tucumbalam's revenge was extracted . . . and which even the scientists have yet to satisfactorily explain." And it gave three overwrought paragraphs to a segment that began:

On the night of January 5, Professor Oliver, who had more to fear than most (for who else was so intent on disturbing their sleeping bones?) was driven by an unnameable compulsion to climb the stony, deserted steps of Chichen Itza's ancient ceremonial ball court under a moonlit sky. It was a brave but foolhardy thing to do, for, as this is written, Dr. Oliver is still recovering from the effects of an attack by an unseen, unheard presence . . .

Gideon sighed and moved quickly on. The article's ending, given what had now happened, had a poignance it didn't have when Ard had written it.

And now what? Will the fourth covenant really come to pass, as the first three have? Will skulls be crushed and brains be spilt? Or will Huluc-Canab intervene with the mighty Xecotcavach, as Emma Byers says he promised?

Deep in the jungles of Yucatan, the diggers of Tlaloc eye each other nervously and wait. And wonder.

The previous dig was mentioned only in passing, and there was no reference to the codex. That, apparently, was what had been planned for the second installment, for a postscript promised, "Next: The Strange, Tangled Story of Howard Bennett and The Tlaloc Codex."

Julie had been reading the article too. She tapped the postscript with her finger. "Could it be that someone killed him to keep him from writing the next part?"

"I don't know," Marmolejo said. "Could it?"

"I doubt it," said Gideon. "The story's been printed a hundred times. There's nothing new to tell."

"What about the rest of the article?" Marmolejo asked. "Is there anything at all that might provide a clue? Perhaps someone meant to keep him from revealing something, not knowing it had already been submitted."

Gideon shook his head and passed the article back to him. "Sorry, Inspector, I don't think so. I can't see anyone committing murder to keep something out of *Flak*. It's not the kind of newspaper anybody rational pays attention to. And even if someone did pay attention, what is there to get Ard killed? There's nothing here that half the people in the hotel don't already know, thanks to Emma."

The drinks were brought in. Julie and Gideon had the locally bottled Cristal grapefruit soda; Marmolejo had Coca-Cola. The cigar went back in the drawer, none the worse for use. Not only did he fail to smoke the things, he somehow managed to keep the tips dry.

"I have something else to show you," he said. "Do you recognize this?" He took a small yellow Pen-Tab notebook from a brown paper envelope and held it up.

Julie shook her head.

"It's Ard's," Gideon said. "He was taking notes in it when he interviewed me."

"Ah, good," Marmolejo said with satisfaction. "I thought as much, but I'm glad to have you confirm it; it was found under his body." The notebook too was slid across the desk. Marmolejo was so small and the desk so broad he had to get halfway out of his chair to do it.

There were only about a dozen pages left in the spiral-bound pad, and just one entry, at the top of the first page; "Return to the scene of the crime," it said, written in ballpoint in Ard's round, uncomplicated hand. The final *e* disintegrated into a distorted hook that the point of the pen had jabbed through the paper, then became a scrawl that ran crookedly off the page. At the top right-hand corner of the page there was a smear of what appeared to be dried blood.

"I don't suppose you have any idea what it means?" Marmolejo said. " 'Return to the scene of the crime?' "

"No," said Gideon. "A note to himself? Something about the next installment?"

"This—this scrawl," Julie said, frowning uneasily down at it. "This stain. He must have been—was he writing it when he was killed?" Her hands were in her lap. She wasn't about to have them anywhere near the notebook.

"Yes, it appears so," Marmolejo said. "The notebook was open to this page, and his pen was under him, with the point in the unretracted position."

"Well . . . is it possible it was meant as some sort of clue to his killer? You know—I know this sounds silly—a way of telling us who the murderer was?"

"I don't think so, Julie," Gideon said. "The writing is slow and careful, just the way he usually wrote. No haste, no sign of agitation. That has to mean he didn't know he was about to be killed. It also means there's not much doubt about his killer being somebody he knew, somebody he wasn't afraid of."

The inspector nodded his agreement.

"Whoops," Julie said. "What did I miss? How does that follow?"

"The wound was a contact wound, as you know," Marmolejo began.

"No, I didn't know."

Marmolejo looked surprised. "Forgive me. I assumed that Dr. Oliver confided in you—"

"I do confide in her," Gideon said. "I just spare her some of the messier details."

"Which I appreciate, believe me," Julie said. "But now I'm interested."

"A contact wound indicates the gun was held against his head," Gideon said. "So obviously his killer was standing next to him, right in his space. But Ard wasn't bothered enough to stop writing. And he couldn't have had any idea he was about to be shot or he wouldn't have been making those nice, round letters. At least *I* wouldn't have."

"I see," Julie said. "But that's a little strange, isn't it? Even if you know somebody, how do you press a gun to his forehead and kill him without his being aware of it until you pull the trigger?"

"Oh, not so difficult, I think," Marmolejo said. "Here is our Mr. Ard. He is sitting in the chair at the side of the path, writing. He hears someone coming down the path. He looks up, recognizes the person, nods, perhaps says good morning, and returns to his writing. The person casually draws level with the chair, his hand already on the gun in his pocket. At the very moment he comes abreast he quickly pulls it out, presses it to his head, and—well, as you know."

"But why assume it couldn't have been a stranger?" Julie asked. "Why does it have to be someone he knew?"

It was Gideon who replied. "Because he was still writing when he was shot, Julie. Surely if someone he didn't know was getting that close to him—a foot, foot-and-a-half away—it would have made him uneasy; he would have looked up, stopped writing. But an acquaintance strolling by? Nothing to worry about there."

"Yes," Marmolejo said approvingly. "Exactly as I see it."

"I don't know," Julie said doubtfully. "Maybe he did look up. Maybe he stopped writing. That doesn't mean he had to lift the pen."

"You're suggesting he was killed by a stranger?" Marmolejo asked.

Julie backed off. "Well, no, not *suggesting*. Just—" She grinned. "I'm not sure what I'm suggesting. I think I better leave it to the experts."

Marmolejo nodded briskly. That was fine with him. "The bullet's path," he told them, "is consistent with our little scenario. It passed through his head in a downward direction, entering just below the hairline and emerging from the base of the skull—"

"Which fits in with his sitting in a chair, head tipped forward, while the killer stood," Gideon agreed. "Did you ever find the slug?"

"Yes, and the cartridge as well; a .32–caliber rimfire. Probably from a Smith & Wesson revolver, an old model, although I don't have a final report yet" He sipped from his glass of Coke. "You wouldn't know if any of the crew members possess such a weapon?"

"No idea," Gideon said.

"Couldn't you search their rooms?" asked Julie.

"Not without warrants," Marmolejo said, and smiled. "Requisite as it was, police reform has had its cumbersome aspects." He set down his glass and looked at his watch. "One-ten. Perhaps you'll join me for lunch, and then I'll be happy to drive you back to the Mayaland."

"Lunch sounds good," Gideon said, "but we don't mind taking the bus back."

"But I'm going there anyway. There are several people I want to talk to."

He stood up. The cigar was retrieved from the drawer and reinserted in his mouth. "If you like, there'll be time for you to buy a hammock before we leave."

Gideon's hand went to the plastic bag beside his chair. "Now what makes you think we'd want to buy a hammock?"

"Don't all Americans buy hammocks when they come to Merida? I thought it was a folkway of some kind."

"We've already bought ours," Julie said, laughing.

"Not in the *mercado*, I hope?"

"Well, yes, in the *mercado*," Gideon said defensively. "Why not?"

"What did you pay?"

"Thirty thousand pesos." Gideon darted a glance at Julie. There was no point in telling Marmolejo they had paid twice that. "But it's a good one; well-woven."

"Too bad," Marmolejo said. "I could have gotten you a fine one for half that. Come on, we'll have lunch at the Café Exprés; I think you'll like it."

* * *

Their meal and the ensuing drive consisted of three frustrating hours of trying to comprehend the events of the last eleven days. How were they to apply Abe's Theorem of Interconnected Monkey Business, to which they all subscribed? How to make sense of Ard's murder, of the attack on Gideon, of the threat, the secret digging, and the rest of it—let alone relate them? Halfhearted, half-baked ideas were discarded as quickly as they were produced.

The only thread holding them together seemed to be the serial fulfillment of the curse, and when that subject was raised, Emma came naturally to mind. She had the most at stake, personally and financially, in the curse's sensational fulfillment, and a gory murder was certainly not going to hurt the eventual sales of *Beyond Dreaming*. But would she really take the terrible step—and the terrible risk—of killing Ard, all for the sake of marketing strategy? Was she that cold-blooded?

In the end, even Julie drew back from the notion. It was simply too fanciful, too preposterous.

Marmolejo approached it from another angle. "What if she's doing it not to sell her book but because Huluc-Canab is instructing her to do it?"

The three of them looked at each other. "That," Gideon said, "is a horse of another color."

They had gotten back to the hotel after four, too late to do any useful work at the site. While Marmolejo left to talk to some of the hotel staff, Julie and Gideon stayed in their room, Gideon working listlessly away at his monograph, Julie at her quarterly report. The ringing of the telephone at five-twenty was a welcome interruption.

"That'd be Abe," Julie predicted, "just back from the site, wanting to know how things went with Marmolejo."

It was. The talk had gone fine, Gideon told him, but not much new had come out of it.

"Well, I got something new for you," Abe said when Gideon had finished. "Let me wash up, then meet me in the bar in fifteen minutes. You'll order me a Montejo?"

"What have you got, Abe?"

"Ha, wait and see."

Gideon could practically see the sparkle in his eye.

The Lol-Ha Bar, like most of the Mayaland's public rooms, had open-grillwork gates and shutters instead of doors and glassed-in windows, so the occasional whispers of early evening breeze carried in sounds and fragrances from outside. Julie and Gideon sipped their beers and listened to the guitarist on the veranda warm up for his evening's work with a cool, simple version of "Sheep May Safely Graze" that was unexpectedly compatible with the lush tropical plants and purling fountains.

As the last strains of Bach faded away, Abe came striding purposefully out of the foliage along one of the paths. His slender, upright head was well in advance of the rest of him, with his feet churning to catch up. He was clamping a heavy loose-leaf binder to his chest with both arms.

"Something tells me," Gideon said to Julie, "that we're on the verge of a major breakthrough here."

Abe sat down, slid the beer to the side to make room, and put the binder on the table, turned so that Gideon and Julie could read the page it was opened to. Next to it he laid a photocopy of the threat that had been slipped under their door the previous week.

"So what do you think? Is there any doubt about it?" He leaned back in his armchair looking keenly satisfied.

The binder contained the daily field catalogue from the first dig. It was open to a page dated June 18, 1982, and signed by Howard.

Julie looked blankly from the page to the brief note. Gideon did the same, wondering what there wasn't supposed to be any doubt about.

Gideon Oliver, leave Yucatan or you will die. This is no joke. The Gods of Tlaloc.

Again, the faint tug of familiarity, the sense of having seen this before, but nothing more. He shook his head. "I don't think . . ."

"The *a*s," Abe prompted, and swigged impatiently at his beer.

"The *a*s . . ." Gideon's head swung from the catalogue entry to the threat and back again. And it finally hit him. "The tilted *a*! These two were done on the same typewriter!" He leaned excitedly forward. "The missing arm on that *w*, the nick in the *e*s, they're the same on both sheets!" A glance at a few other pages in the catalogue showed that the same machine had typed them all. "Abe, this is fantastic!"

Abe laughed. "It kept bothering me why it was familiar, and then finally it dawned on me what it was."

"I'm sure this is all very wonderful," Julie said, "but I wish somebody would take the trouble to let me know just why we're all congratulating ourselves."

"Because," Abe said, "we just figured out—you notice I use the self-deprecating 'we'—that this friendly little letter to your husband was written by none other than Howard Bennett." He paused dramatically. "Howard Bennett is here in Yucatan."

"Wait," Julie said, "could we just hold on a minute? I'm all for having Howard the bad guy in the piece too, but how does the fact that these were typed on the same typewriter prove Howard typed them both?"

"It's his typewriter," Abe explained. "A Brother EP–20, a little portable; the kind you can fit in an attaché case. Believe me, I know the police report by heart. When he ran off, the typewriter went with him, isn't that right, Gideon?"

"That's right. He doubled back to his room and got it, along with a few other things."

"But how can you be sure *he* took it?" Julie persisted. "For all you know somebody else—"

"No," Gideon said. "That letter he sent us—you know, regretting the unfortunate little affair of stealing the codex—was typed on it. The police established it at the time." He tapped the note on the table. "And now here are those crooked *a*s again. He's here all right."

Julie took this in, chewing on the inside of her cheek. She turned slowly to Gideon, one eyebrow raised dangerously. "Am I imagining it, or haven't I been saying since last week that he was here? And didn't you give me a hundred reasons why he *wasn't* here, why he *couldn't* be here, why—"

"A good scientist," Gideon explained, "modifies his operational hypotheses to accord with fresh data. When additional—"

"Why don't you just say you were wrong?" Abe said.

"I," Gideon said humbly, "was dead wrong. All wet. In the right church but the wrong pew."

"Yes, you were," Julie said, "and pretty snide about it, too, as I recall."

"Well, I apologize. Sincerely. We should have listened to you."

"*We?*" Abe said. "When did I get involved in this?" He laughed brightly, then wondered aloud: "But what's he doing here? What does he want?"

"The codex," Julie said.

Abe stared at her. "What?"

"That's another one of Julie's hypotheses," Gideon said. "She thinks the codex might still be down there under the rubble, and now Howard's come back for it."

"But that's impossible. We *know* he took it— he *said* so. And we heard reports from all over. And—"

"That's just what Gideon said," Julie replied smugly.

"Anyway, even if it was there, why would he come back for it now, of all times? Why wouldn't—"

"Gideon said that too. It was part of the same lecture in which he patiently explained to me how there couldn't be the slightest possibility that Howard was within a thousand miles of here."

"Yes, but . . ." Abe paused, then nodded, his lips

pursed together, a man seeing the light. "Well, it would sure explain the digging, wouldn't it? Maybe even this foolishness with the curse."

Abe's theory about the curse was simple and cogent. Assuming that the codex was really still there, Howard would have been shaken by the Institute's decision to resume the stairwell excavation, and become increasingly desperate as the dig progressed. What better way to protect his unclaimed treasure than for the Institute to lock up the temple again? And what better way to get the Institute to do that than to engineer the phase-by-phase fulfillment of an ancient curse? An article in *Flak* might not raise their hackles much, but how long would it have been before the story was picked up by the more responsible press as well?

And if implementing one of those phases also happened to result in the violent death of his old enemy Gideon Oliver on the ramparts of the Chichen Itza ball court, so much the better. If not, well, the point was still made, and another opportunity might always arise.

"You know," Gideon said slowly, "this goes a long way toward explaining Ard's murder too."

"You think Ard found out he was here, maybe even that he was behind the curse?" Abe asked.

" 'Return to the scene of the crime'—that was in his notebook. Who else could it refer to but Howard?"

Julie made one of her inexact attempts at finger snapping. "And what about that little blurb about the next installment? 'The Strange Case of Howard Bennett and the Tlaloc Codex,' or something like that. Stan must have found out Howard was here—maybe even that the codex was here too—and Howard killed him to keep him from talking about it."

"You know, it could be so," Abe said. "So far, nobody's come up with anything better."

Another small piece dropped suddenly into place for Gideon, one that he should have fitted in hours before. He snapped his fingers.

"Show-off," Julie said.

"The gun!" Gideon said. "The one Ard was shot with—Marmolejo said it was a .32—"

"—which is what Howard had," Abe said. "He had it with him when he went up to the temple that night. Nobody ever saw it again. An old Smith & Wesson, according to the report."

"That's right. That's *right*!" For the first time Gideon began to let himself believe it deep down. "Damn, it *is* Howard. He's right here in Yucatan. Do you realize this is the first time since the theft of the codex—"

"The attempted theft," Julie said. "The alleged theft."

"—that we've known for sure where he is? And he doesn't know we know. It's our first decent chance of getting hold of the bastard. And of getting the codex back." He nodded respectfully to Julie. "Unless the codex has been down there waiting for us all along, of course."

"Wouldn't that be something?" Abe said softly.

Gideon waved over a waiter hovering unobtrusively at the side of a pillared arch. "*Tres copas de brandy, por favor. Tiene Cardenal Mendoza?*"

When the drinks came, the three of them clinked glasses and Abe burst into a happy laugh. "Now I know

I'm surrounded by crazies," he said, his pale blue eyes alight. "A man gets a death threat, and he finally figures out it's from a murderer who's going around shooting people. What would a normal person do? Hide in his room, put on a fake beard, get the next plane. What does this guy do? He orders a round of cognac. Cardenal Mendoza, yet."

"Which you very willingly join him in," Gideon pointed out.

"Did I say I wasn't crazy too? Listen, where's Marmolejo? We got a lot to tell him."

"That's a relief," Julie said. "I thought maybe you two were planning to catch him on your own."

"Us?" Abe's mobile eyebrows soared. "What an idea. What are we, detectives?"

19

Marmolejo looked at the copy of the threat for all of ten seconds, then laid the paper down next to the brandy he had accepted but not yet touched.

"Yes," he said around his unlit cigar, "it's the same typewriter." He sat back in his chair under a wooden relief based on a wall painting from Bonampak, absently fingering his glass. "The question is: Why?"

"The codex," Julie said, looking puzzled. She had just gone through it with him. "It must still be—"

He waved her silent. "No, I mean the letter under the door. Why threaten your distinguished husband in this childish manner? Why not simply kill him?"

"To get the satisfaction of frightening him," Julie suggested. "Considering that Gideon was the one who started that committee, Howard would probably get a lot of pleasure out of terrifying him. Not," she added loyally, "that Gideon was terrified."

"You think so?" Marmolejo said. "I wonder. For me to get satisfaction from terrifying you, it would be important that you know it was *I* and not someone else who hunted you. But did Dr. Bennett sign the note? No; he gave no clue. For all we knew, it might have been anyone."

"But he couldn't afford to let anybody know he was here," Julie said. "We've already established that."

"All right," Marmolejo said agreeably, "but if he killed the reporter to keep his presence a secret, as you suggest, why call attention to himself this way?" He turned to look at Gideon. "If he wanted revenge, why not simply bash you over the head with the wrench—forgive me, Mrs. Oliver—and be done with it? Why risk identification with this letter?"

They were good questions. Gideon hadn't yet had a chance to think about them. "Well, of course he'd never expect Abe to compare the documents."

Marmolejo received this with a noncommital shrug. "He might think that *we* would. Eventually."

"So what's your theory, Inspector?" Abe asked.

The inspector shook his head, rolling the cigar from one corner of his mouth to the other. "Dr. Oliver, have you ever received threats from him before?"

"No."

"But then he gets so many that it's hard for him to keep track," Julie said.

Marmolejo took this in the spirit it was intended. "Then why," he asked, "does he suddenly begin now? Why not years ago?"

More good questions. "Maybe he never risked coming back to the States?" Gideon ventured. "Maybe this is the first chance he's had at me."

Another shrug from Marmolejo, and a change of subject. "Dr. Goldstein, if the codex is still buried at Tlaloc, I think our common interest would be best served if we retrieved it as quickly as possible." He produced a small matchbox, removed a tiny waxed match, and applied it to the end of his cigar. Marmolejo with a lit cigar was a rare sight. He was feeling expansive, and no wonder. The retrieval of the Tlaloc codex for his country would be a stunning accomplishment.

"I couldn't agree more," Abe said cautiously. "But the faster you dig the more risks you take. You wouldn't want to take a chance on damaging the codex."

Of course not; that went without saying. But was it not possible to speed up the digging without such a risk? What if he provided some of his own reliable men to help?

Abe, perfectionist that he was, was reluctant, but Marmolejo was persuasive. However dedicated the police protection might be, there was no way to provide foolproof security for either people or objects. Wasn't the fate of Ard proof of that? As long as the codex was down there, there was some risk that Howard might find a way to get at it, or even destroy it, deranged as he obviously was. And what about the danger to the crew's safety? Who could tell who was next, and when? But remove the codex and you remove Howard's *raison d'être*, or at least his primary reason to do anyone harm.

Abe wavered, then gave in. Starting the next morning, two of Marmolejo's men would report for duty in the temple, under Abe's supervision of course. With Abe's permission, Marmolejo himself would be there as well.

Abe, who knew when he didn't really have a choice, gave his permission. "But you know," he said, "there's something that's bothering me here. Garrison translated the curse last week on Monday night. The press conference was Tuesday, so it wasn't in the papers till Wednesday. And yet on Wednesday night Howard's already here, slipping notes under the door. How did he find out so fast? How did he get here so fast?"

The cigar was dead again. Marmolejo plucked it from his mouth between two fingers. "The question is: Get here from where? If he was already in Yucatan, there would be no problem."

"Already in Yucatan?" Abe repeated. "Why would he already be in Yucatan?"

Marmolejo did not always choose to answer the questions that were put to him. With business taken care of to his satisfaction, he lifted his brandy glass and grinned his monkeyish grin.

"To the recovery of the Tlaloc Codex," he said.

* * *

Worthy Partridge lifted to his mouth one of the four dried prunes that the kitchen staff added to his lunch box every day. "I, personally," he said, "will be only too happy to see the last of this wretched place." He shuddered. Behind pursed lips the prune was fastidiously masticated. "Remind me never to accept a free vacation again."

"Not me," Harvey said through a mouthful of white bread and sliced turkey. "This is great. How can you leave before they find out if the codex is there or not?"

"Easily," Worthy said sourly. "I don't want to be the next person Howard bumps off."

The subject was Marmolejo's announcement that morning that members of the crew were now free to leave Yucatan at their pleasure. Worthy was the only one planning to take advantage of it. He had made his airline reservation for the following day.

Harvey lifted wistful eyes to the Temple of the Owls. "Gee, do you think they're really going to find it?"

"Marmolejo promised they'd let us know if they did," Gideon said.

"Marmolejo," grumbled Worthy. "I wouldn't trust that man if I were you."

"Why? What's the matter with Marmolejo?" Leo asked.

"He's too small," Worthy said.

Leo laughed. "Huh?"

"I don't like little people. They move too quickly. Always darting."

The conversation had been going on in this desultory

fashion for half an hour. The crew was taking its lunch break in the shade of the acacias near the West Group after a morning of continuing the slow excavation of the ball-court foundations. Abe had asked Gideon to supervise this operation while he himself was in the stairwell with Marmolejo. The work at the modest ball court had been routine and dull, not even enlivened by Emma's accounts of her latest chat with Huluc-Canab.

She had decided to remain at the hotel this morning, and Preston had stayed with her. Emma had not been her usual dynamic self lately. This was partly because the rest of the group had begun to tune her out as soon as she opened her mouth, and partly because she was grievously disappointed in Huluc-Canab, who had told her that no real harm would come to any member of the group during their stay. Then, when Ard had been killed, she had challenged Huluc-Canab during their morning *tête-á-tête*, and he had pointed out that Ard had not actually been a member of the group. A rather glib and mealymouthed reply, in Emma's opinion. Gideon's too.

As they were getting up to go back to the ball court, one of Marmolejo's officers approached.

Would they care to come to the temple? he murmured politely in Spanish. They had found something of interest.

"*El codex?*" Gideon asked, and then, when the officer looked at him blankly: "*Un libro?*"

Yes, the policeman said, they had found a book. Very old, very beautiful.

Gideon whooped and reached for Julie. "I will never

doubt you again," he shouted, laughing. "You're brilliant!"

When they got to the temple, his exhilaration was momentarily chilled. He hesitated just inside the entrance with the strange feeling that he had circled back in time, that it was all going to happen again, as the Mayan calendar said all things did. Everything was the same: the air thick and gritty with dust—already he could feel it congealing on his tongue, crusting in his nostrils; the sulfurous yellow light from the portable lamps below; the wavering shadows on the walls and ceiling; the stale smells of antiquity, mold, and sweat; the tension in the voices from the stairwell.

Julie touched his wrist. "Gideon, what's wrong?"

He squeezed her hand and smiled. "Just a few ghosts."

They were easily enough exorcised by the sound of Abe's thin, excited call from the stairwell.

"Gideon, is that you? Come look, quick! Julie, you're there too? Come! Everybody, look!"

Trotting down the stone steps Gideon was further reassured by a pungent whiff of celluloid-acetone solution, the most common and comforting aroma at any dig. (Stale coffee was a close second.) It was used for everything from varnishing pottery, to gluing bone, to sealing waterlogged wood, to strengthening rotting hide. At the moment it was being sprayed out of a glass atomizer by Abe, in a well-thinned solution, onto something he was leaning intently over. The debris had been cleared almost down to the level it had been at in 1982, and Abe was kneeling on the lowest visible step, his bony knees cushioned on a folded towel. One step higher was Marmolejo, no less intent, and on the landing above them two dusty, sweat-stained policemen sat leaning against a wall sipping cool tea. The Mayan workmen who had been hauling out the dirt had been sent away.

Abe's narrow back was toward the stairs, blocking the newcomers' view, but when he heard the footsteps behind him he twisted to the side so they could see.

"So," he said, his eyes glowing, "what do you think of this?" He was as excited as Gideon had ever seen him.

With good reason. It was the codex all right, wedged in the angle between wall and step. Battered by the cave-in, crumpled at one corner, cracked at another, but basically sound. It was still open to the same place.

Gideon's burst of laughter drew startled looks from the others. Marmolejo in particular looked at him peculiarly, but how could he explain how funny it was? All that grave, dedicated work by the Committee for Mayan Scholarship, all the paper they'd generated, all that brilliant strategy to prevent Howard from selling the codex—and here it had been all the time, bruised and buried, but eminently safe under tons of rubble.

He stared at it, drinking up the sight; the ancient codex, the shadowy stone passageway, the vibrant old man. "Congratulations, Abe. What a—"

He stopped, frowning. Something had caught his eye a few feet from the codex. A small, unnoteworthy knot of gnarled, sticklike objects the color of driftwood, barely visible, protruding half an inch from the rubble that still covered the bottom steps and the base of the stairwell.

"Just a minute," he said.

He put a hand on Abe's shoulder and worked his way around him, gingerly stepping over the codex. The height of the uncleared rubble made it impossible to stand up straight. He hunkered down and brushed some dirt away with his fingers.

"Leo," he said, "would you twist that lamp so it's focused here?"

He ran his fingertips over the sticklike objects and pulled away some more debris. The others watched him, curious and silent. No one seemed to want to ask what they were.

"It's a right elbow joint," he said without preamble, "still mostly buried." He pointed to the visible ends of each of the bones. "Humerus, ulna, radius."

"*Articulatio cubiti,*" Harvey said automatically.

"Do you mean a—a *human* elbow joint?" Worthy stammered.

Gideon nodded.

"There's a *skeleton* under there?" Worthy had paled. In the lurid illumination his face looked like wax.

"I'm afraid so," Gideon said.

"Maybe it's—well, it's probably just an old one. You know, another Mayan burial."

"No," Gideon said, "it's only a few years old. I can—" But Worthy was already disturbed enough, and Leo and Julie didn't look too happy either. There wasn't much reason to explain that he could still smell the candle-wax odor of the drying fat in the bone marrow. And that would surely have been gone after a few years.

Besides, most of the joint cartilage was still there, and even a few shreds of ligament.

"It's recent," he said simply.

But not that recent. There was no trace of rancidity left, nor any sign of the insects and vermin that had performed the cleanup. And the cartilage was brittle and brown. The conclusion was inescapable—and self-evident, given a moment's thought. When he looked up at the faces peering down at him with sharp, puzzled concentration, it was clear that no one had failed to grasp it. He said it anyway.

"Whoever this is was killed when the tunnel caved in. Not before, not after. There can't be any doubt about it."

20

No one said anything for several seconds. The whirring of mental gears in the thick air was almost audible, Gideon's among them. *Who* was killed? Why? How? Had someone stopped Howard from stealing the codex, only to die for his efforts? Had there been a struggle? Had the weakened walls collapsed as a result, burying the codex and its defender together, so that Howard had had to slink off empty-handed, to wait for his chance to return? It was no more bizarre than some of their other theories, and it would explain a lot.

Only whose skeleton was it? Everyone was accounted for. Of the 1982 crew members, three were here on the stairway right now, two were at the hotel, and the others, those who had chosen not to return, were safe in the United States. Abe had talked to all of them by telephone when the dig started up. Then who . . .

It was Marmolejo who supplied the answer.

"So," he said softly. "Avelino Canul, at last."

Avelino Canul, the doughty little Mayan foreman who had supervised the local laborers during the earlier dig. Avelino, who had disappeared the day after the cave-in. The police had tried to locate him, but only halfheartedly. Given the corrupt and incompetent Colonel Ornelas's reputation, there had been nothing extraordinary about a Mayan (or anyone else, for that matter) who chose to run off rather than stay for police interrogation, even if he was guilty of nothing. And Avelino, it turned out, had had a few scrapes with the law in the past as the result of a long-standing fondness for rum.

The general consensus had been that he had gone to ground in his village just over the Guatemalan border, and when Howard's letter had arrived to explain things— so they'd thought—they had abandoned the search for him. As the colonel had pointed out, it he wanted to stay hidden in his own village, among his own people, there was no way the police were going to find him—even a half-Mayan policeman like Marmolejo. And in Guatemala they had no authority anyway. They had left it at that, but Marmolejo had always been vaguely troubled; it had not satisfied his need for closure. More than once he had wondered aloud to Gideon about the fate of Avelino Canul.

"Mr. Partridge," he said.

Worthy jumped. "Pardon? What?"

"Avelino and the other laborers were dismissed when the day's work ended. How do you suppose he got back here?"

"How do *I* suppose? What would I know about it?"

"You were here at Tlaloc, on guard."

"I—well, yes, but—it was dark. There wasn't any fence. The man was an Indian, used to the jungle. He knew the trails better than anyone. He could easily have come back without being seen."

"Yes, I suppose that's true. Well, why do you suppose he would do that? You think he wished to steal the codex himself? Perhaps they fought over it?"

"I'm sure I have no idea. Why ask me?" He swallowed hard. Marmolejo had frightened him.

"No matter, *señor*," the inspector said pleasantly. "I'm sure matters will become clear as we progress."

The rubble burying the bones was easy to remove, but it took an hour and a half because Marmolejo very properly insisted on exposing the skeleton bit by bit, layer by layer, with frequent photographs. The work was done by the two policemen, using their fingers as their main tools, and there was little for Gideon to do beyond observing and providing an occasional suggestion.

Meanwhile, Abe meticulously finished preparing the codex for removal and placed it with exquisite care in a padded crate supplied by the police. Simply getting it into the crate took twenty minutes. Quite a difference from the Howard Bennett approach.

When it was safely packed away, two other uniformed policemen—the entire Yucatecan State Judicial Police force seemed to be at Tlaloc—were detailed to carry it to the hotel safe to await the arrival of officials from the Institute. Abe, caught between curiosity about the skeleton and concern for the codex, opted for the codex and left with it.

Gideon and the others remained sprawled on the steps above, watching dreamily. An exhaust fan had been set up because of the celluloid-acetone fumes, and the air was now relatively cool and dustless. It was an oddly peaceful time, free-floating and slow-paced. There were still questions, but a big corner had been turned; they were now closing in on the answers instead of getting farther away. And of course there was the recovery of the great codex to be chewed over and relished.

By three, the skeleton was three-quarters freed, lying on its left side facing the ascending staircase, still partially embedded in the debris. Under the left wrist, the snapped metal expansion band of a wristwatch could be seen sticking out of the rubble. One of the policemen had reached to pluck it out, only to be stopped by a tart reprimand from Marmolejo. Didn't they know better than to *pull* things from the dirt? Everything would remain until exposed by careful digging. It was of great importance to view and photograph all objects in their natural relation to one other.

Gideon smiled to himself. Marmolejo would have made a hell of an archaeologist.

At three-thirty Marmolejo told the two policemen who had been doing the digging to quit. They had started early and it had been a long day; the rest of the job could wait until morning. They stopped gratefully and went to the landing above, settling down against the wall with the tea jug.

"Dr. Oliver," Marmolejo said, "I wonder if enough is visible for you to look it over?"

"Sure, if you want." He had begun to wonder when— or if—Marmolejo was going to ask him. This time he'd known better than to offer his services unrequested. He rose and started up the steps. "I'll go and bring my tools from the work shed."

"Ah, how long do you suppose your examination might take?"

"It depends. Three or four hours."

Marmolejo looked pained. He had been in the stairwell since before 7:00 A.M. "In that case," he said reluctantly, "I think we might better wait until morning. We can have it fully ready for you then."

"I could take a preliminary look now," Gideon said. He didn't want to wait until morning any more than Marmolejo did. "At least see if I can confirm sex and race. Age, maybe. That kind of thing. Then tomorrow I can get my stuff and do a more thorough job."

Marmolejo brightened. "*Por favor*," he said, then expressed to the others, firmly but discreetly, his reservations about having the Tlaloc staff remain as an audience, inasmuch as sensitive police business was about to be discussed. Perhaps they might continue their work in other parts of the site, or return to the hotel if they pleased?

When Julie got up with them, he signaled to indicate that she could stay, but she seemed relieved to go. Julie had a healthy enough interest in skeletal analysis (what choice did she have, married to Gideon?) but this was the first time she'd been in on the grubby nuts and bolts of it, and she hadn't been looking altogether happy about sharing a confined space with a freshly unearthed skeleton.

Marmolejo waited until they left, then nodded briskly to Gideon.

Seen up close, the skeleton was battered but well preserved, still held tenuously together at many of the joints by onionskin-like shreds of ligament. There was a tangle of rust-colored hair under the skull, but that told little. With the leaching and staining that would have gone on in this limestone rubble, who could tell what color it had been originally? Cross-sectional analysis would probably have something to say about race, but that would have to be done in a laboratory, under a microscope.

There was little in the way of clothing; just leather sandals and a blood-stiffened pair of shorts that had nearly rotted away. Shorts and sandals—had that been what Avelino had been wearing? Probably; it was what most of the men there had been wearing. If there had been underwear on this body, it was now indistinguishably matted to the outer shorts. As always, clothes on a skeleton made it seem less real, like a Halloween prank, but there was nothing whimsical about this. The rib cage was crushed, with some of the costovertebral articulations torn apart; the right pelvis was cracked and twisted away from the left; the left clavicle was fractured; the mandible was broken and gaping crookedly, with some of the teeth shattered or knocked out; and the left side of the cranium was caved in.

At least it was dry.

There wasn't much else to say about it that was good. The poor bastard had been squashed flat in the cave-in, and Gideon said as much.

Marmolejo looked at him without expression. *"De veras?"* he inquired wryly, managing it without opening his mouth around his cigar stub.

Gideon smiled. Yes, really. But there were a few other things of interest he might be able to come up with too. Best to start with basics. He squatted next to the skeleton, elbows on his thighs, and looked at the ruined pelvis. Gingerly, with Marmolejo's permission, he used a trowel to lift some of the decayed remnants of the shorts. They stuck to the bone a moment, then popped off.

"Well, it's definitely a male," he announced. That was simple enough. Everything about the pelvis shouted it: obtuse pubic angle, rounded ramus, rectangular sacrum, narrow sciatic notch. They should all be so easy.

Marmolejo nodded. So far so good.

Delicately, Gideon used the tip of the trowel to pick some cartilage from the pubic symphysis, the place where the right and left pelves join between the legs. Of all the surfaces on all the two hundred and six bones in the human body it is there, in that hidden and private place, that the signs of age and degeneration are most clearly and ineradicably engraved, decade by slow decade.

With the trowel held loosely in his hand he studied the narrow, rippled surface of the bone.

"Fifty years old," he said after a few seconds. "Give or take five years."

"Ah," Marmolejo said, pleased. "Avelino, he was forty-seven." He darted a sidelong look at Gideon. "Did you happen to know that?"

No, Gideon hadn't known.

Then he got down to serious work. He examined the long bones, roughly measuring a femur and a humerus against the yardstick of his own hand and forearm. With Marmolejo's approval he used his fingers to pull out some of the dirt that had lodged in the jaws, the eye sockets, and the cranium itself. He scooped out most of the dirt beneath the skull, leaving it somewhat precariously supported on a rim of debris. Each small load of dirt was placed in a separate, precisely labeled envelope for sifting by the police forensic team.

He had one of the policemen move the lamps so that the light shone horizontally across the bones, highlighting the ridges and hollows and irregularities that could tell so much, if only you knew what to look for. And then, lying prone in the dirt, propped on his elbows, he studied them, fingering the surfaces, probing them, thinking, calculating, speaking only to ask for increasingly finicky readjustments of the lamps. Twenty minutes passed. Twenty-five.

"A *preliminary* look will be fine," Marmolejo said.

After half an hour the inspector became openly restive, walking back and forth on one of the stairs; two small steps one way, pivot, two steps the other. Like a wolf in a cage. Marmolejo did not enjoy being an observer.

Gideon, engrossed in a set of unusual protuberances on the mandible, hardly noticed him. There were two bumps on each side of the jaw, right on the mandibular condyles—the knobs that fit into hollows on the sides of the skull to form the hinges of the jaw. He'd found nothing similar on the rest of the skeleton, so he knew it wasn't some generalized bone condition. Just two sharp little tubercles on each condyle, one on the outside, one on the inside. Only one thing could conceivably cause them, and that was the forceful, habitual use of the external pterygoids, the inconspicuous little cheek muscles that had their insertion points right there.

Peculiar, but probably of no importance. Yet he knew those spiky little buttons would nag at him until he made sense of them. Hadn't he run across something similar before? The memory was there, but just out of reach. All right, then figure it out from scratch. What did the external pterygoids do? They were part of the chewing apparatus, of course; thick, triangular little fiber bundles that protruded the lower jaw and moved it from side to side in the complex and improbable process of human chewing. But a lifetime of ordinary chewing wouldn't produce these bumps. So what he needed to figure out was . . . no, wait a minute. It had been that Pittsburgh case . . .

Marmolejo's impatience finally got the better of him. "Well, are you able to tell me *nothing*? Can we say for certain that it's Avelino, or can we not?"

"What?" Gideon surfaced slowly, his mind still on the tubercles. "Uh . . . no," he said.

"No, you're unable to say, or no—"

"No, it's not Avelino."

Wrong answer. Marmolejo's half-closed eyes opened briefly, then slitted again. The cigar stub jerked irritably. "Just like that? One look and the answer is no?"

Gideon glared up at him, matching irritation for irritation. If Marmolejo thought it was such a quick look he should have tried it on his elbows and belly. The back of Gideon's neck ached from keeping his head up, his left hand had fallen asleep, and when he lifted his elbows from the pebbly debris, they felt as if a set of tacks were being pushed into them. He stood up, rubbing the numb hand.

These remains, he explained crisply, were assuredly not Avelino Canul's, whatever the inspector wanted to believe. This had been a man anywhere from six feet tall to six-feet-two, judging from the quick-and-dirty measurement of the humerus and femur, and Canul wouldn't have been anywhere near that.

"I will check," Marmolejo said. "I'm certain I have his height in my files."

Gideon merely looked at the five-foot-tall Marmolejo. What difference did the files make? Couldn't he *remember* how small Avelino was? Who had ever heard of a six-foot Maya?

Besides, he pointed out, in almost every way the skull

was everything that a Mayan skull was not. The cranium wasn't wide and round—the Mayan brachycephalic norm—but long and narrow, a typical northern European dolichocephal. The cheekbones were curving, not squared; the palatal arch was V-shaped, not U-shaped; the orbits squarish and smoothly bordered, not sharp; the face as a whole was rugged and large-featured, not smooth and compact. In all, a classic Caucasoid skull, suitable for an illustration in a textbook.

And there was more—

But Marmolejo withered under the assault and lifted a resigned hand. "I submit," he said, and even managed a small, not unfriendly smile. "I know when I am beaten." He stared thoughtfully down at the skeleton.

"Who, then?" he murmured.

Gideon waited until the inspector's wide-set eyes swung up to meet his.

"It's Howard Bennett," Gideon said.

21

"What did you say?" Marmolejo asked woodenly.

"It's Howard Bennett."

Marmolejo took the three-inch stub from his mouth and scowled at it as if hoping to draw strength from it.

"Do you think it would be all right," he asked mildly, "if I smoked now?"

"Go ahead." Earlier, Abe had asked him not to smoke around the codex, but it was gone now, and the flammable celluloid-acetone fumes had been cleared away as well.

The inspector lit up with unusual thoroughness, taking two long pulls while he held the match to the end of the cigar. The first honest-to-God cloud of smoke Gideon had ever known to emerge from his mouth emerged. He waved the match out, put it in a little box, and slipped the box into a pocket of his *guayabera*.

"That," he said quietly, "is not possible."

"No, it's true, all right."

"We have had two letters from Howard Bennett," Marmolejo said patiently, "as you and your colleagues explained to me last night. One in 1982, one last week. Someone has just been murdered with what is almost certainly his revolver, the revolver he took with him five years ago. He was—"

"The fact that some letters were typed on his typewriter hardly proves he typed them." As Julie had tried to tell them. "And just because a bullet came from his gun doesn't prove he pulled the trigger."

"Of course not, but—"

"And there hasn't been a reliable sighting of the man since this place caved in. Now we know why."

Marmolejo grunted, about a quarter convinced.

"Look, Inspector, there are a lot of indicators here. The size is right. So is the age; Howard was pushing fifty. The race, the big-boned build, those are right too.

And then Howard was right-handed, as I remember." He gestured at the skeleton. "So was this guy, apparently."

Marmolejo frowned at the hand bones and seized on a specific. "How do you know? The right hand is larger than the left?"

"As a matter of fact, no. There are ways to tell, but hand size isn't one of them. For now I'm just going by—"

"The watch," Marmolejo said. "Obviously, it was on his left wrist. So you conclude that a person who wears a watch on his left wrist must be right-handed?" The cigar end glowed. This was the kind of reasoning he could have confidence in. "I would conclude the same thing."

"Right."

"But I would not trust my conclusion absolutely. There is no law that prohibits a left-handed person from wearing his watch on his left hand."

"Right again. It's a question of probability. But there are some shoulder-girdle measurements that should tell us about handedness for sure, and I'll do them tomorrow."

Marmolejo drew on his cigar and made an annoyed sound at finding that it was out again. A quarter of an inch shorter than it was before, it was rolled out of the way once more into the left corner of his mouth. "Now, look, Dr. Oliver, this is all very well, but it's hardly proof. *You* also are Caucasian, *you* also are large-boned and a little over six feet tall, I think. *You* also are righthanded, *you* also are the right age—"

"The right age?" Gideon protested. "I'm only forty-one."

"Close enough," Marmolejo decided for himself. "And with it all, does it prove that this is *you* lying here?"

"The age is wrong," Gideon maintained, "and anyway, I haven't been missing since this place fell in. And . . . well, there is one other thing."

Marmolejo grinned toothily at him, as if he'd known all along that Gideon was eventually going to pull a three-foot rabbit out of the hat.

As indeed he was. But he wasn't showboating, as the inspector thought; he was following the lessons of past experience. When you're going to present something to a policeman that requires more disposition to believe than he's shown so far, it's best to lead gradually up to it, to ready him for it step by progressive step, before hitting him with the clincher. He hoped Marmolejo was prepared.

"Did you know that Howard was a woodwind player?" he asked.

If he was surprised by the question, the policeman's dark face didn't show it. "No, I didn't know."

"He did, expertly. He used to play jazz clarinet with a group in a Merida nightclub every Saturday."

"Ah. And the fact that Dr. Bennett played a woodwind, this is in some way relevant?"

"Very. This guy"—Gideon indicated the crushed skeleton—"did too. For years."

Marmolejo's mouth opened slightly with a faint popping noise. Fortunately the cigar stub remained pasted to his lower lip.

"And if you put it all together," Gideon continued, "I don't think it leaves a lot of room for coincidence. We've got a white male here, around fifty, righthanded, about six-one, who's played woodwind for ten years at least . . . all of which also happens to fit Howard Bennett perfectly. And since Howard was last seen right here, at just about the time this skeleton was deposited, I don't think there's much doubt—"

Marmolejo found his voice. "*How* do you know he played the clarinet?" It wasn't quite a squeak, but it was as close as he was likely to come.

Gideon made it simple. The tubercles, of course. The other time he'd come across them, as he'd finally remembered, it had been during an examination of the scant remains of a firebombing victim in Pittsburgh. The man, a clarinetist with the Pittsburgh Symphony, had been tentatively identified by the police before Gideon was shown the bones, and Gideon, knowing nothing about him, had wowed the homicide detective in charge by casually asking what woodwind instrument he'd played.

But, really, it hadn't been a wildly difficult deduction once it occurred to him that the frequent, strong thrusting forward of the lower jaw might be connected to something other than eating. Playing a woodwind, for example. Perhaps there were also other possible causes for the tubercles, but he had yet to find one.

Marmolejo took this with better grace and more credulity than Gideon had expected. "All right," he conceded, "who am I to argue with the Skeleton Detective?" He made a clicking sound, tongue against teeth. "But where are our fine theories now? Who killed Ard, if Dr. Bennett didn't? Who attacked you?" He paused and laid his hand on Gideon's arm. "I don't want anyone on the crew to know this. Let them think we still believe it's Avelino Canul."

"That makes sense."

"And I'm afraid it would be inadvisable for anyone to leave after all," Marmolejo added to himself. "Mr. Partridge's permission will have to be revoked. I hope he's not too disturbed about it."

Worthy would never trust another small person, Gideon thought.

Marmolejo stood for a while, peering down at the earth-stained skull. "Howard Bennett," he said quietly. "Here all this time with his precious codex, killed trying to remove it by a cave-in he himself caused. I think the gods of Tlaloc must be laughing."

"Oh, I'm sure they're laughing," Gideon said, then pulled his last rabbit out of the hat. "But it wasn't the cave-in that killed him. He was already dead when the roof came down."

Marmolejo turned slowly to Gideon. "Murdered?"

"Murdered."

"How could you tell?" Julie asked. "Was he shot? With that Smith & Wesson?"

"No," Gideon said, "clubbed. Probably with the sledge-hammer. The left side of his head was knocked in."

"But all that rubble caved in on him. How do you know that isn't what did it?"

"Because he was *on* his left side, and the damage to the rest of his body shows the debris landed on his right side. In other words, he was already lying there, in that position, when it hit."

"Oh." She pulled the toothpick from a quarter of the chicken-salad sandwich before her and thoughtfully sucked the pickled onion from it.

They were on their balcony. Neither of them had been particularly hungry when he had gotten back from the site, and they had had sandwiches and milk sent up. Abe and the rest of the crew were in the restaurant, celebrating the finding of the codex with a champagne dinner insisted on and paid for by Dr. Villanueva, who had arrived at the Chichen Itza airstrip with several other Institute officials about an hour earlier. In the morning there would be a group breakfast, with speeches and congratulations, and then the codex would be borne in pomp to Mexico City for years of study and an eventual place of honor in the Museum of Anthropology.

"Now wait a minute," Julie said, having thought the matter through. "Who's to say the cave-in happened all at once? Maybe he was knocked down by a few falling pieces, and fractured his skull when his head hit the ground—and *then* the rest of it all fell on him. What's wrong with that?"

"Nothing, but he didn't just fracture it. It wasn't cracked, it was caved in—a depressed fracture. There was a hole in his skull, and some of the bone fragments were actually inside." No doubt driven into the brain to provide the immediate cause of death, he might have added, but why spoil her appetite? Or his.

"And a fall couldn't do that?"

"Nope. It's an axiom of the trade: When a moving head hits a fixed object hard enough, you get a crack; when a moving object hits a fixed head you get a depressed fracture. No, first he was slugged, then he fell, and then the place came down on him."

He took a bite of his ham sandwich. "Marmolejo thinks the cave-in was an accident; that Howard came on somebody trying to take the codex and got himself killed for his trouble."

"No, how could that be? If Howard was the one with the gun and the crowbar, how come he's the one who wound up dead?"

Gideon shrugged. "I doubt if he would have shot a crew member or even pointed the gun at him. Not unless he found him right in the act of taking the codex. He would have assumed there was some other reason for him to be there. It was outsiders he was worried about."

Julie shook her head. "It's so hard to believe. How could a member of the crew bring himself—"

"For two million dollars? People can bring themselves to do a lot of things for that."

He took a long swallow of milk. "Anyway, Marmolejo figures that whoever was on the other end of the sledge hit one of the props without meaning to. Howard and the codex fell down the steps, and five tons of rubble landed on top of them. That's his theory."

"And what's yours?"

"I think he's right. An eight-pound sledge can get away from you when you're using it in a fight, and with the supports already weakened it wouldn't have taken much to bring the whole place down."

He tossed a sandwich end onto his plate. "You know what I keep wondering about? That 'return to the scene of the crime' in Stan Ard's notebook. What was he talking about? Whose return?"

"Howard's, obviously."

"You think whoever's behind this had Ard fooled too?"

"Sure." She put down her sandwich and leaned forward. "To tell the truth, I never did put much faith in Inspector Marmolejo's idea about the killer just passing by and casually shooting him. Did Stan strike you as the kind of person who'd be outside working at seven in the morning? My guess is the killer made an appointment with him to lure him out there—" She smiled crookedly. "Gideon, is this what your cases sound like when you're working on them? As if you're reading lines in a particularly dumb movie?"

"Yup. Go ahead. "To lure him out there . . . "

" . . . so that he could shoot Stan, but first get him to write something that would seem to incriminate Howard."

"Like what?"

"Like what he did write. It worked, didn't it? Maybe he out-and-out told Stan that Howard had been seen around, hoping he'd write *that*—which would really have confused us. But—"

"But Stan, who never passed up the opportunity for a cliché, came up with 'return to the scene of the crime.' And I suppose the killer thought he'd better settle for that, shot him, and got out of there." Gideon nodded slowly. "You just might be right, Julie."

He put his feet up on the low table, crossed his legs at the ankles, and stared out at the twilit foliage. "Ah, that poor bastard Howard; he dies saving the codex, and the whole world winds up blaming him for stealing it. Thanks to someone who went to a lot of trouble to make us think just that."

"But why? That's what bugs me. I mean, I understand why somebody would do that in 1982: if everyone thought the codex was gone, nobody would bother to dig for it, and the killer could come back later on and get it. Fine. But why *now*?"

"Why *what* now?"

"Why bother to make it look as if Howard were still alive almost six years later? Especially in the middle of a dig that was bound to turn up his body sooner or later? And the codex too."

Gideon held up his hand. "Julie, Marmolejo and I went round and round for over an hour on this stuff, and we didn't get anywhere."

Julie brushed this aside. "Well, of course not. You didn't have the benefit of my brilliant insights. After all, who was the one who said all along that the codex was down there?"

"The same person," Gideon pointed out, "who said all along that Howard Bennett was behind everything that was going on."

"That," Julie said, "was unworthy of you." She rubbed her hands together. "Come on, Skeleton Detective, let's order up some brandy and get this thing figured out. We're on a roll here."

Gideon smiled and got up to go to the telephone.

"Right, that's just what this case needs: a little cognac and a little cogitation."

From the outset Gideon knew that it wasn't going to be much of a day. There had been a little too much cognac the night before, and maybe a little too much cogitation too. Abe had joined them at about ten o'clock, and they had stayed up talking until one-thirty; then Gideon and Julie had overslept this morning. That was what had started him off in a grumpy frame of mind, eliminating as it did their usual slow, luxurious introduction to the day: fifteen or twenty dreamy, voluptuous minutes in each other's arms, drifting and dozing, nuzzling and stroking, slipping sweetly in and out of sleep until the warmth of the morning began to flow in their veins.

It was Julie who had to run off first, to the ceremonial staff breakfast with the people from the Institute. Gideon, with an hour before he was due to meet Marmolejo at the site, stayed in bed by himself for fifteen minutes (it wasn't the same) before snapping fully awake with the frustrating feeling of having dropped a stitch, of having been on the verge of figuring it all out if only he could have continued whatever train of thought had been going along almost independently in his mind. For a few moments more he lay still, trying to recapture it. Something about Howard, something Howard had said . . . but whatever it was, it melted into tantalizing wisps and evaporated before he could get hold of it.

He got up, yawning, ordered coffee and a couple of croissants from room service, and breakfasted while he shaved. His mind was still humming with the problems they had raised the night before. Once again it had been all questions, no answers.

Foremost, of course, was the question of who had killed Howard. The logical best guess, although it had been hard to take it seriously, was Worthy. He had been alone at the site with Howard that night. And it was only Worthy's word that Howard had taken the gun and crowbar and gone up to the temple. Maybe it had been Worthy who had taken the weapons and then tossed the crowbar on the ground near the path to make it look as if Howard had escaped that way. Worthy could easily enough have tried to steal the codex and wound up murdering Howard and accidentally triggering the cave-in when he was discovered.

But so could everyone else, and that was the problem. Tlaloc was less than a twenty-minute walk from the Mayaland. Any of them could have doubled back from the hotel after Howard had dismissed them. Certainly, Gideon was in no position to know; he had slept for an hour after dinner, getting ready for the night watch.

And what about the old question that had been nagging at them in one form or another since the first day, when they discovered the surreptitious digging in the stairwell: Why had the killer waited until now to come back for the codex, when it would have been so much easier and safer last year, or the year before, or the year before that? Why—

It was a relief to hear a tap on the door. That would be the officer who would walk with him to the site. Despite the removal of the codex, which was surely at the root of it all, Marmolejo had not relaxed security. Last night no one had camped out on the balcony, but two policemen had wandered the grounds and hallways. And this morning Gideon was under strict instructions to wait for his escort before going to the site.

"*Un momento,*" he called, toweling the last of the shaving cream from his throat and taking a final gulp of coffee. On the way to the door, one more question struck him; odd that it hadn't occurred to him until now. He stopped at the writing desk and pulled his copy of the curse out of the center drawer. He ran his finger down it until he found what he wanted.

Fifth, the beast that turns men to stone will come among them from the Underworld.

He smiled faintly. Making that one come true would take some doing. Even if there weren't cops crawling all over the place.

22

The hot weather had returned. That was one more thing wrong with the day. Gideon glanced at his watch as they arrived at the site; 7:55 and already the air was like glue. Sweat dripped from the end of his nose. Under a lead-gray sky Tlaloc had the festering, derelict look of an abandoned garbage dump. The combination lock on the gate had been changed, but a guard materialized from behind the West Group to let them in. Inspector Marmolejo was already in the temple, he told them.

"Will you tell the inspector I'll be along in a minute?" Gideon asked his escort in Spanish. "I need to get a few things from the shed."

Against one wall of the work shed's storage area was a framework of wooden storage bins, doored and latched, but without locks, in which crew members kept whatever personal effects they liked. Gideon's was in the middle row on the right, and in it he kept his tools, tables, field guides, and osteological atlases, his thick, tattered old copy of Morris's *Human Anatomy* that had been around since graduate school, a glossier, rarely used copy of *Gray's Anatomy*, a poncho, a jacket for cool weather which he had wishfully bought when he arrived but had yet to wear, and a few fruits and sweets for snacking.

It was always a hodgepodge, but when had he let it get into this condition? Julie was right; he was getting sloppy. The front of the bin was literally plugged with the rolled-up jacket, the poncho, and the Morris. When he finished today, he would take twenty minutes to clean the whole thing out and straighten it, then keep it that way, the way a professional should. This was ridiculous.

It was also a little familiar. Wasn't it something he told himself most mornings? Well, maybe, but this time he meant it.

As he tugged at the stuff blocking the front of the bin, the train of thought that had eluded him earlier came suddenly back to him. He remembered what he'd been thinking—or dreaming—about. It had been that scene at the bottom of the pyramid in 1982, after they'd come out of the temple, when Howard had assigned shifts for guarding the codex.

"I'll take the first shift," he'd told them, and Worthy would take it with him. "Be back at nine," he had said to Gideon, and then with a smile: "Does that meet with your approval?"

Now what was it that was bothering him about that? There was something there, something he was overlooking, something that kept tickling away at him. He paused with his hand on the wadded-up plastic poncho. "Be back at nine . . . "

He shrugged and pulled. The poncho and jacket came loose abruptly; the heavy old volume of Morris thunked on the limestone floor, fortunately landing flat on its side. He reached into the bin only to find the interior stuffed with boxes, notebooks, loose tools, more clothing. What was all this junk anyway? Was that his hat? Had someone else run out of room and started using his bin? It was possible, he thought grouchily, but you'd think they'd notice it was already in use. There were other empty ones. He tossed the stuff out onto a work table and bent to peer inside, but the bins were awkwardly long and narrow—about eighteen inches high and wide, and almost three feet deep—and little light reached the back. Was that his instrument case wedged diagonally into the left-rear corner? Damn, he'd never have left it there like that; those things were delicate. And expensive. Somebody had been in here, fooling around with his things.

Puzzled and annoyed, he reached in with his left hand. His fingers brushed the pebbled leather of the case but couldn't quite grasp it. Who had designed these bins? With an irritated sigh he set his body, jammed his shoulder against the bin's opening and inserted his arm as far as he could, stretching, wriggling his fingers, trying to get hold of the case. And then froze.

Gideon was by no means slow-moving. He was athletic, his reflexes were sharp, and his mind was quick to react. Yet there were times when his analytical, left-brain-oriented intelligence outwitted him, using up precious milliseconds for thought or inquiry when he would have been better off letting his animal reactions take over.

It was one of those times. When he felt the first twinge of pain, stinging but superficial, as if someone had pricked the side of his hand with a pin, his response was to stop and consider. A loose tool? The pruning shears? No, something smaller. A probe? Maybe, but—

The second jab was sharper, not a stab as much as a pinch, and with it, astonishingly, there was an unmistakable tug. He jerked his arm out of the bin and something came out with it, hanging from just below the base of his little finger, squirming and wriggling. He flicked his hand, but the thing hung on, snapping violently from side to side like a loose spring. Shuddering, he whipped it against the framework of the bins, but still the snake held on, straight out of a nightmare, sinuous and muscular, its small, toothy mouth clamped tightly to his hand, chewing away. He whipped it against the wood again and then again, and at last it came loose, dropping to the floor with a fleshy smack. He thought it was dead, but it only lay stunned for a moment, a coiled, gleaming cylinder of red, yellow, and black, then came awake with a start, slithered rapidly out the doorway, and was gone.

Gideon looked anxiously at his hand. All he could see were four or five inconsequential-looking pockmarks, as if a playful puppy had tried its sharp new teeth out on him. There were only a couple of welling droplets of blood and not much pain—no more than an insect sting, and already fading.

Gideon scowled down at the hand. He knew next to nothing about snakes—wild animals were Julie's province, not his—but he knew enough, or thought he did, to know that a poisonous snake didn't chew on you; it struck with its sharp, hollow fangs and left two deep, distinct puncture marks, not a collection of frazzled little nicks like this one. The bite marks were one of the ways you told the difference between a snake that was venomous and one that wasn't. That much he remembered from his *Boy Scout Handbook*. And years before he'd had to incise and suck out the wounds of someone bitten by a rattlesnake, and the marks had been nothing like this.

Still, it wasn't something to be ignored. Infections developed easily in this climate. He would have Plumm take a look at it when he'd finished here, but for the moment a little antibiotic cream and a Band-Aid were called for. The first-aid supplies were in a freestanding metal cabinet in the other room. He went there, surprised to find himself a little trembly and short of breath. Odd that the incident had shaken him up like this. Jarring, yes, but not as painful as all that, and it had only been a little thing, maybe fifteen inches long. Pretty too. It had probably been more frightened than he had.

As he reached for the first-aid box on the highest shelf he stopped with a stifled intake of breath, convulsively hugging his arm to his chest. There was something terribly wrong. Without warning, his left arm, from elbow to shoulder, had burst into searing pain, as if someone had turned a blowtorch on it. He gasped from the astonishing, lacerating intensity of it and stared bewildered at his fingers. There was something the matter with them too; they were stuck together in a spastic muddle, crooked and misaligned, the thumb folding grotesquely down and in as he looked at it. All of it had happened with stunning suddenness.

He realized abruptly that his lips had been tingling unnoticed for some seconds, and that his eyelids felt peculiarly weighted. Good God . . . ! He might not know much about snakes, but he knew the classic symptoms of neurotoxic paralysis, and he had them all and then some.

Fifth, the beast that turns men to stone will come among them from the Underworld.

Fangs or teeth or whatever the hell it had in its mouth, the damn thing was poisonous—and he was turning to stone.

A new, colder layer of sweat oozed out on his forehead. He ought to stay quiet; movement would circulate the venom faster. But he had to get help fast. The toxin was working with incredible speed. Already the pain was less, which was a bad sign, not a good one. No, not less, but somehow distant, as if his arm were a separate entity enduring its own agony of fire, which was unfortunate but no concern of his. Poor old arm.

He jerked his head, frightened. He was getting dopey. Drowsy too. He had to act quickly. Find Marmolejo? Call the guard? Where the hell was Julie? She knew all about snakebites. But she was with Abe, damn it, at that . . . at . . . wherever she was.

With his right hand he brushed at the annoying sweat running into his eyes. Wasn't there something he was supposed to be thinking about?

"I'll take the first shift. . . . Be back at nine. . . . Does that meet with your approval . . . ?"

No, there was more to it than that. The question was . . . the question was . . .

He yawned. The question was what? He leaned his forehead against the cool metal of the cabinet. This was stupid. All right, let's see now, the question was . . . the question . . .

He straightened with an alarmed, about-to-fall jerk. Had he nearly gone to sleep standing there? Small wonder. It was stuffy in the shed, and hot. Cramped. Idly he glanced at his watch. Eight-forty. A little early for a break, but he could use—

Eight-forty? But hadn't he looked at his watch only a few minutes ago? Hadn't it said seven-fifty-five? Puzzled, he looked again. Eight-forty. Where had three-quarters of an hour gone? Had he actually fallen asleep leaning against the cabinet? He felt stiff enough, that was certain; his legs, his back, his arms, his hands, even his jaw. Stiff and achy too. Interesting. The question was . . . and off he floated again.

When he came out of it this time he was lying on the stone floor on his side, with his knees drawn up. The back of his throat was numb and clogged, and his chest felt as if it had a steel band around it. Breathing took effort, planning. Other than that, he felt comfortable enough. Quite relaxed, in fact; just a little chilly. That was certainly a welcome change. There was no pain. There wasn't much feeling of any sort to speak of.

He yawned and felt a gob of saliva run out of his mouth and dribble down his cheek. Embarrassing. Why all this saliva? He tried to swallow it down, but his pharynx didn't seem to be working any better than the rest of him. And now he couldn't close his mouth again, or at least he thought it was still open, and he could feel the spittle sliding over his cheek. This was getting downright disgusting. What if Julie walked in and saw him slobbering like a hungry St. Bernard, for Christ's sake?

But his mind was on another plane now, slipping free of his petrifying body and floating above him like a soap bubble, shimmering, clear, and wonderfully focused. He knew, in a vague way, that he almost had what he was looking for, that it was merely a matter of perspective, of filling in a piece or two.

"*Be back at nine . . .* " Or was that quite what Howard had said? Hadn't he—

A hand touched his shoulder. Marmolejo's face, shocked and rigid, was before him. How had he appeared so suddenly? Why did he look so awful?

"What's the matter?" Gideon said anxiously. "Are you all right?"

"What's wrong?" was Marmolejo's odd response. "What happened to you?"

This was nonsense, meaningless, some silly game. Gideon didn't have the patience for it. He closed his eyes, trying not to lose the thought he'd worked so hard to capture. It was important for Marmolejo to know. "Inspector," he said, "when Howard—when he told us to come back at nine—he–he—if you—"

But his lips were impossibly stiff, his throat like clay. And he couldn't hear his own voice. Was he really speaking? Was Marmolejo really there? He tried to see. His eyes seemed to be stuck shut.

"Inspector, listen—" He tried to speak, to shout, to explain. But he heard nothing except a dull, growing roar, felt no vibration of sound in his throat, sensed no listening presence.

After a while he stopped. Even with his eyes closed, he could feel the darkness blossoming and unfolding, like a flower in a slow-motion film. There was a terrific sinking sensation, not merely as if something inside him were falling, but as if the stone floor on which he lay, the entire work shed, had tipped, then plummeted over the edge of some immense pit. The crushing speed of the drop squeezed his chest until he knew his ribs were going to crack. Behind his closed and paralyzed lids the blackness expanded around him, as if he were a tiny, shrinking speck inside the starless, lightless universe of his own skull.

Is my central nervous system shutting down? he wondered with detached interest. Is this death?

Down he plunged, and down, and down, and down, and down.

Grimly, Marmolejo waited at the back of the hotel reading room for the speeches to end. The eyes of speechmakers and crew darted frequently at him. They had been uneasy since he had come to fetch Julie, and they had no doubt seen, as he had seen, how her face had whitened when he'd told her what had happened, and how she'd swayed momentarily before collecting herself and going off with the officer. And he supposed his own face was making them nervous, too, if it showed what he was feeling.

He was angry. Angry in a white-hot way that no policeman should be. Angry at himself for not understanding sooner; angry that he couldn't have headed it off before it came to this, to a good man's life hanging by a thread; angry at the cunning, clever, stupid killer behind it all; and angry, if the truth be told, that it took a semiconscious Gideon Oliver to figure it out and explain it to him.

The speaker from Mexico City sat down. Another one stood up. Who knew how long this was going to go on? The hell with it; he wasn't going to wait any longer.

He strode into the room, up to the table. The speaker's voice faded away. Everyone looked warily, expectantly up at him. Everyone except one person, with his back to Marmolejo, who kept his eyes blamelessly on the speaker. But a muscle in front of his ear worked rhythmically. Marmolejo put his hand on the thick shoulder. The man twitched.

"*Señor*," Marmolejo said formally, "will you come with me, please?"

Leo Rose tried to look surprised. He forced his mouth into what Marmolejo believed was referred to as a shit-faced grin.

"Sure," he said with empty brightness. "*Bueno-bueno*."

23

He wasn't falling anymore. He had bottomed out and was beginning to rise. No, he had been rising for a long time now, floating gently and serenely up out of the blackness. The awful pressure was gone from his chest. He could breathe again.

He was on his back, lying on something soft, his head and shoulders raised. A bed? He made an effort to open his eyes. Nothing happened. They felt as if they were stapled shut. Was he paralyzed? He tried flexing his hand and felt fingernails touch palm. That was nice. Something worked anyway.

Slowly—he was very tired—he raised his left hand to his face. It flopped against his nose as if it were asleep. He slid it over his cheek, managed with a few wrong turns to find his left eye, and with a finger pushed up the eyelid and held it there. The light made him wince, but how strangely, charmingly familiar everything looked: sturdy wooden chairs, pottery water jug on the table, solid walls, clean-cut planes, straightforward right angles. Everything was so wonderfully real and three-dimensional. He was in their hotel room and, yes, he was in bed. He could look down the length of his body. The pale-blue sheet covering him was pristine and unwrinkled, with crisp, straight creases where it had been folded. However long he'd been there, he'd been lying like a statue. He flexed his toes and was gratified to see the corresponding lumps under the sheet move accordingly.

He tried to look to the side but his eyeballs didn't work as well as his toes. He could turn his head, however, and when he did he saw Julie in one of the wooden armchairs, staring dully at the floor, her black hair unkempt. Behind her, the rose-colored light slipping in layered streaks through the louvered door was early-morning light, no later than six-thirty. A whole day gone by? Had she been up all night with him?

His arm felt like jelly. Keeping it up was too difficult. He lowered it. The eyelid plopped shut.

"Hi," he said. What came out was a croak.

He heard her start. "It speaks," she said cheerfully. "It moves." But he had seen the strain in her eyes, the pallor and fatigue in her face. He tried to tell her he was all right, but this time his tongue wouldn't work at all.

"Don't try to talk," she said. Her cool hand was on his wrist. "Dr. Plumm says you'll be fine."

Dr. Plumm? Was he sick, then? Was that why his eyes

didn't work? What was the matter with him, anyway? Like an automobile engine that had lain unused in a garage for a long time, his mind turned over, ticked, and coughed sluggishly to life.

He had gone to the site. He had stopped off at the work shed . . .

"Leo!" he cried. Another croak. "Julie, tell Marm—"

"Sh. Don't worry. They have him."

Have him? Who has him?

He must have said enough of it aloud to be understood. "Inspector Marmolejo arrested him," she said. "He's in jail in Merida. The inspector says you're brilliant."

"You mean I really told Marmolejo about it? I thought I was dreaming." That was what he tried to say, but it was too complicated to get out, and he gave it up halfway through.

"Sh," she said again. "Rest now. We can talk about it later."

He managed to pat the back of her hand—reassuringly, he hoped—and relaxed against the pillows. How about that? All the time he'd thought he was shouting soundlessly into that roiling black vacuum, Marmolejo had really been there, listening to him. And not only that, Gideon must have been right.

"Be back at nine," Howard had told them at the base of the pyramid. Only not quite. He'd begun to say it, all right, but he'd interrupted himself. "What time is it now?" he'd asked, and *that* was the missing piece Gideon had been searching for without knowing it; the piece that didn't fit.

Because if Howard had asked the time, it meant that he hadn't been wearing a watch, and if he hadn't been wearing a watch, then the broken one lying under the skeleton-wrist on the stairwell couldn't very well have been his. And if it wasn't Howard's, then whose was it?

Earlier Gideon had spent a lot of time wondering what it was that he and Stan Ard had had in common. There had, after all, been attempts on only two lives: Ard's (successful) and his (close enough). Why? Why Ard and Gideon in particular, and no one else?

Once he'd realized that the watch in the stairwell wasn't Howard's, the answer had been obvious. His mind had gone back to the interview with the reporter on the veranda. Ard had asked Gideon how he'd happened to know that the stairwell ceiling had begun to give way at exactly 4:12 P.M. Gideon hadn't been able to remember at first, but then he'd recalled. He knew, he'd told Ard, because he'd noticed later that Leo Rose's watch, broken in that first shower of rocks, had stopped at 4:12 P.M.

And then, having told him, he'd called Leo over and blithely repeated it in front of him. Leo had laughed pleasantly and gone into his waterfront-flexivilla spiel, but he'd been aware from that moment that Gideon and Ard knew something he couldn't permit anybody to know—not when Howard's body was going to be turned up any day. And when it was, there was going to be a broken watch near it. And that watch was going to say 4:12 P.M.

There hadn't been any way Gideon could be certain of all this, of course, but it had been a reasonable guess: if you find a watch with a snapped band next to the body of a murdered man, and it isn't his own watch, then—as any observant cop would point out in a flash—it could very well be the murderer's, broken and pulled off in a struggle. Ordinarily, murderers took pains not to leave such things lying around. But if the victim had been knocked to the foot of a stairwell by a sledgehammer, and if that flailing hammer had then accidentally slammed into a weakened prop and dumped five or ten tons of rubble down on the body, then retrieving a watch would be a bit of a problem. As would be anything else under the debris—such as a priceless Mayan codex.

The codex had already been recovered. The watch had still been there, and all it would take to find out if there was an incriminating 4:12 on it would be to go and turn it over. That was what he'd been trying to tell Marmolejo, and apparently he'd succeeded.

That still left plenty of questions, but his brain was aching with the effort of thinking. Julie was right. They could talk about it later.

He turned his face blindly toward her. "Been a long night?" he asked, enunciating carefully.

"Not too bad. Abe kept me company until a couple of hours ago, but I finally made him go get some sleep."

She squeezed his hand gently. "How do you feel?"

"Pretty good, actually. But my eyes don't seem—"

"Dr. Plumm said they might be paralyzed for a while, but not to worry about it. They'll be okay. Is everything else all right?"

"I think so. I'm just a little weak. And a little surprised to be alive." The words were coming more easily now.

"You can thank Dr. Plumm for that. He keeps a few vials of coral-snake antivenin on hand, just for times like this. Not that there are ever times like this, except when you're around. He really loaded you up with it. Had to get refills by air from Valladolid. You're also brimming with other intravenously administered goodies. You know, we very nearly had to helicopter you to the hospital in Merida for the iron lung. Dr. Plumm says you're a very lucky young man. I quote him."

"It was a coral snake that bit me? How did he know?"

"From the chew marks, I suppose."

"I thought poisonous snakes always left two fang marks."

"Nope, not Elapidae. They chew on you."

"Elapidae?"

"That's the family. Coral snakes are in the family Elapidae."

"Oh." He could feel a gauze bandage on his left hand. "Did he have to incise the fang marks, squeeze the blood out?"

"No, there's no point in doing that after the first thirty minutes. Anyway, it doesn't do any good with *Micrurus*."

"*Micrurus?*"

"That's the genus."

"*Micrurus*," he said again, more languidly. "You sure know the damnedest things."

It was very comfortable there, with his eyes closed and Julie holding his hand. He was relaxed and content, almost asleep. Those intravenous goodies, no doubt.

"Funny about the eyes," he mused. "Why would only

the oculomotor nerve be affected, and nothing else? No, wait a minute, the abducens must be screwed up too, because I'm not getting horizontal movement of the eyeball, which must mean involvement of the rectus lateralis. So . . ."

She laughed deep in her throat and lay her head on his chest. "I think I can stop worrying now," she said, still laughing. "You're back to normal."

The low chuckling turned to slow, shuddering sobs against his chest. Her hands tightened along his sides. "Oh, Gideon, Gideon, I was so—thank God you're—"

"There, there," he said drowsily, and lifted his hand to stroke her hair. "Everything's all right now."

And it was. He heard his own breathing become deep and regular, felt his hand slide flaccidly from her head, and seemed to observe himself descending back into the chasm, slowly this time, and peacefully, to a black and dreamless sleep.

24

The next two days passed in a gauzy haze, mostly quite pleasant. Abe was in and out, cheerful and comforting. A jolly and sanguine Plumm seemed to pop in every five minutes to paint Gideon's hand with gaudy green or purple tinctures, or to administer one of his arcane tests: prothrombin time, partial thromboplastin time, fibrinogen titer. Marmolejo, almost equally jolly, came twice—three times?—to talk about police matters. And always there was Julie, quiet when he wanted quiet, talkative and reassuring when that was what he needed.

On the third day, Plumm told him he was fit to travel, and a week's rest at home was probably his best way to ensure his being able to start the next quarter's courses on time. In any case, Plumm told him firmly, there was to be no thought of continuing work on the dig. Gideon's feeble protests, strictly pro forma, were brushed aside by Abe; Gideon was going home. Doctor's orders. No ifs, ands, or buts. The skeleton in the Priest's House could wait. When Gideon returned later to testify at Leo's trial, he could finish working on it if he felt up to it.

And so, five days after being bitten by a testy *Micrurus fulvius* in a Mayan ruin in the Yucatecan jungle, Gideon was on the green-and-white ferry *Yakima* as it made its silent, stately way across a misty, blessedly cool Puget Sound. The flight from Merida to Seattle, even with its airplane changes in Houston and Denver, had been mostly dozed away while Julie read, but the sight of the pearly green islands of the Sound had brought him to life, and they had begun to talk about Tlaloc again as the ferry edged out from the Edmonds dock.

"Isn't it funny?" Julie said, watching the creosote-stained pilings slip by, "We all thought the codex was at the bottom of things, but it was the watch. Just that stupid watch."

"Right," Gideon said. "Leo knew the codex was a lost cause, what with that all-out campaign by the committee. But the watch—that was important; that could tie him to Howard's murder."

"Well, I still don't understand why he took the chance of waiting so long to do something about it. Why didn't he try to get it years ago when there wasn't any digging going on?"

"But he wasn't taking much of a chance. When the Institute shut Tlaloc down, they really shut it down. 'For all time,' they said, which suited Leo just fine. And even if it reopened in fifty years, what could anyone make of the watch by then? The trouble was, they changed their minds in just five years."

"So he came back to try to find it before Abe got to it. That's why he was digging under the temple at night?"

"Uh-huh, but I think that was pretty halfhearted. He knew his watch had come off while he was fighting with Howard, and he'd have liked to have it back to be on the safe side. But it wasn't anything to panic over. He figured there wasn't any way to connect it with him."

"Until you showed up yammering about his watch stopping at 4:12."

Gideon glanced back at her from the window he'd been looking through. His eye muscles were still stiff, and he had to swivel his head to do it. He thought it gave him a certain dignity. "There is," he said, "no need to be unkind."

She laughed. "How would a bowl of Washington State clam chowder strike you?"

"As if I've died and gone to heaven," he said earnestly and began to get up.

Julie stood first and leveled a finger at him. "Stay. I'll go get some. I'll bring some hot chocolate to have afterwards, too. Dr. Plumm said hot liquids are good for you."

"Great." Gideon settled back at the window, feeling luxuriously convalescent and pampered. All he needed was a lap robe. Outside, a string of cormorants scudded along three inches above the water on some urgent avian mission, their black, snaky necks stretched out ahead of them and their wings flapping frantically to keep pace with the ferry. Above and to the north, a lone bald eagle wheeled slowly over the Sound, wings outspread, against swollen clouds.

Julie was right, of course. If not for that conversation about the watch, Leo might have continued to poke along, trying to get in a little more digging of his own, but not overly concerned. There was time, after all; the codex, the body, and the watch were all still well below the surface of the rubble. As Leo very well knew, having so selflessly volunteered to supervise the stairwell excavation.

But once he learned that Ard and Gideon were aware of the watch, he had to act more decisively. And so the threatening note had come within a few hours of that conversation, and the Chichen Itza attack had followed the next night. And when Ard announced that he was leaving Yucatan, Leo had to get rid of him immediately. He couldn't chance Ard's finding out—perhaps when he was back in the United States, out of reach—that a watch stopped at 4:12 had been found near a body lying in the stairwell. Even Stan Ard had been capable of putting two and two together from data like that. Poor Ard.

As for Gideon, his clock had run out the moment the watch had been uncovered by Marmolejo's men. God, how Leo must have panicked at that point—but of course Marmolejo had given him another night's grace when he'd put off digging it out until the next morning. And Gideon himself had told Leo just how to put that night to good use; he had forthrightly proclaimed his intention of doing a thorough skeletal analysis the next day . . . after getting his tools from the work shed.

Sealing his own doom, Ard would probably have called it, and the flea in Leo's ear had been enough. All he'd had to do was go to the back gate at Chichen Itza, buy a cute little poisonous snake in a cute little basket from one of the cute little kids (even with a vocabulary of *bueno-bueno*, how hard could it have been?), return to the site the same afternoon, stuff it in the storage bin with the basket lid loose, and leave it there all night to grow more and more agitated and enraged. Then when the blissfully unknowing Dr. Oliver returned in the morning . . .

"Question," Julie said, putting a tray down on the table. She set out cardboard bowls of clam chowder for both of them, along with crackers, plastic spoons, and two cups of cocoa, then slid into her seat across from him.

"I've been giving this a lot of thought," she said, "and

what I don't understand is why Leo was working so hard to make it look as if Howard was behind everything. I mean, he knew it was just a matter of days before we got to the skeleton. The minute Howard's body was identified, all that fancy footwork wouldn't count for anything."

"Ah, but he didn't expect Howard to be identified. You know, that clarinet-playing business was just a freak bit of luck. And Howard didn't have any identification on him."

"No, but Leo couldn't be sure of that."

"Yes, he could," Gideon said. "I was thinking about what went on after we found the codex in '82, and I remembered that the foreman asked for the workmen's pay. Howard said he couldn't give it to them because he didn't have his wallet on him. Well, if he didn't have his wallet, it was pretty unlikely that he had any ID. There wasn't any reason for him to have a passport tucked in a pocket. I'm sure that didn't get by Leo."

He paused for his first taste of the smooth white chowder. Plastic spoon, cardboard bowl, and all, it was wonderful, redolent of the sea and the Northwest. It was very good to be home.

"Besides that," he went on after a second spoonful, "Leo knew Howard had been wandering around Central America for over a decade, so no one was too likely to identify him through his dental records. No one was too likely to identify him, period."

"Except you."

Gideon demurred. "Luck," he said again. "And the fact that I knew the guy. But once I was out of the way,

Leo would have been free and clear. No one to recognize the watch, no one to identify the body. How could a Mexican pathologist who didn't know Howard ever figure out those bones were his? The corpse would be listed as unidentified, and poor Howard would be blamed for *that* murder too—his own—on top of everything else."

"But you'd already identified him. Killing you wouldn't—"

"But Leo didn't know that, remember? Marmolejo didn't want the crew to be told."

"Mm, that's right," Julie said.

For a while they attended quietly to their meal. Outside the window a misty drizzle spattered the metal deck. It looked cold. It looked good.

"Gideon, what do you suppose it was all about? What did Leo have in mind in the first place? Why did he attempt to steal the codex? What kind of plans did he have for it?"

"I don't think it was that kind of thing at all, Julie. No carefully worked-out plan, no complex motives. Nobody even knew a codex existed until almost five o'clock, and by nine Leo had already made his stab at getting it."

He shrugged. "I suppose Leo just heard Howard say he could get two million dollars for it— 'easy,' I think he said—and that was enough to set him off. Sneak back to the site, remove it without anyone seeing him, have it blamed on the *bandidos*, and then look into peddling it at his leisure. Or at least that's what he must have had in mind."

He pushed his empty bowl away. "There is one thing I still haven't figured out. The gun. How did Leo get it out of the country in 1982 and then get it back in through airport security? And what for? It was a hell of a chance to take."

Julie concentrated on chewing and swallowing a particularly tough piece of clam. "Oh, I know the answer to that one. He didn't."

"You mean he hid it somewhere around the site for five and a half years? I don't know, that seems—"

She shook her head. "No, I mean the gun got caught in the cave-in too, and then turned up in the rubble some time during the last few weeks. Leo must have been keeping a pretty sharp eye out for such things, and he probably grabbed it before the workmen even realized what it was. Using it on Stan was probably just an afterthought; one more way to incriminate Howard."

Gideon considered this. "Good thinking."

"It's Inspector Marmolejo's thinking. The gun turned up a few days ago, conveniently tossed under a bush just fifteen or twenty feet away from where Stan was killed. Inspector Marmolejo says there was limestone dust in all the crevices. It'd been buried, all right."

"Ah, good old Marmolejo. You're frowning. Something's still bothering you."

She nodded, spooning up the last of her chowder. "Well, what do you suppose that curse business was all about? Was it some sort of smoke screen? Was it a plan to upset Dr. Villanueva enough to close down the dig again? Leo couldn't really think anyone—besides

Emma—would take the curse seriously, could he? Or could he?"

"I don't think so," Gideon said. "And I don't think he was trying to make it look as if the curse were coming true; I think he was trying to make it look as if a desperate, demented Howard Bennett was trying to make it look as if the curse were coming true."

She nodded sagely. "That's just clever enough and crazy enough to be right. Hence the message from the gods on Howard's typewriter." She pulled the lid from her cocoa, sipped, and grimaced. Chowder was the Washington State ferry system's long suit; the cocoa came out of a packet that you stirred into a Styrofoam cup of tepid water.

Above them the ferry's horn hooted, loud and deep and throaty, and the big ship began its majestic turn into the Kingston ferry dock. Behind the little port town the rich green flanks of the Olympics rose and disappeared into the mist. It was snowing up there.

"Home," Julie said with satisfaction. "Had enough hands-on anthropology to last you for a while?"

"You better believe it," Gideon said. "You know the first thing I'm going to do when we get back?"

"Yes," she said with her no-nonsense look, "you're going to stay in bed for a few days, the way Dr. Plumm told you to."

"After that."

"Let's see. Build those bookcases?"

"Nope."

"Finish that monograph?"

"Nope. I'm going to straighten up my office. Everything in its proper place."

"Good."

"I'm cleaning up my act. I'm a new man."

"I'm glad to hear it."

He drained the last of his cocoa. "Besides," he said, and smiled, "did you ever stop to think what might be lurking in there under all that junk?"

aided, but why spoil her appetite? Or his

Join "Skeleton Detective" Gideon Oliver as he unearths a host of intriguing mysteries!

"Great stuff." —*New York Times Book Review*

"Elkins writes with a nice touch of humor...Oliver is a likeable, down-to-earth, cerebral sleuth." —*Chicago Tribune*

- ☐ **CURSES!**
  (B40-864, $4.95 USA) ($5.95 Can.)

- ☐ **THE DARK PLACE**
  (B20-955, $4.50 USA) ($5.99 Can.)

- ☐ **FELLOWSHIP OF FEAR**
  (B20-953, $4.99 USA) ($5.99 Can.)

- ☐ **MURDER IN THE QUEEN'S ARMES**
  (B40-913, $4.95 USA) ($5.95 Can.)

- ☐ **OLD BONES**
  (B40-687, $4.95 USA) ($5.95 Can.)

- ☐ **ICY CLUTCHES**
  (B40-040, $4.99 USA) ($5.99 Can.)

**Warner Books P.O. Box 690
New York, NY 10019**

Please send me the books I have checked. I enclose a check or money order (not cash), plus 95¢ per order and 95¢ per copy to cover postage and handling,* or bill my ☐ American Express ☐ VISA ☐ MasterCard. (Allow 4-6 weeks for delivery.)

___Please send me your free mail order catalog. (If ordering only the catalog, include a large self-addressed, stamped envelope.)

Card # _____

Signature _____ Exp. Date _____

Name _____

Address _____

City _____ State _____ Zip _____

*New York and California residents add applicable sales tax.

545

MARVELOUS MYSTERIES FROM EDGAR AWARD-WINNING AUTHOR MARGARET MARON

"So rich in detail…you can almost hear the North Carolina twang and taste the barbecue."
— *Houston Chronicle*

☐ **BOOTLEGGER'S DAUGHTER**
(B40-323, $4.99 U.S., $5.99 Canada)

☐ **SOUTHERN DISCOMFORT**
(B40-080, $5.50 U.S., $6.99 Canada)

**Warner Books P.O. Box 690
New York, NY 10019**

Please send me the books I have checked. I enclose a check or money order (not cash), plus 95¢ per order and 95¢ per copy to cover postage and handling,* or bill my ☐ American Express ☐ VISA ☐ MasterCard. (Allow 4-6 weeks for delivery.)

___Please send me your free mail order catalog. (If ordering only the catalog, include a large self-addressed, stamped envelope.)

Card # _____

Signature _____ Exp. Date _____

Name_____

Address _____

City_____ State _____ Zip _____

*New York and California residents add applicable sales tax.   632

MYSTERY AMIDST THE PYRAMIDS WITH ARCHAEOLOGIST/SLEUTH AMELIA PEABODY!

BY ELIZABETH PETERS

"If the reader is tempted to draw another obvious comparison betweeen Amelia Peabody and Indiana Jones, it's Amelia—in wit and daring— by a landslide."
—Peter Theroux, *New York Times Book Review*

☐ **THE SNAKE, THE CROCODILE AND THE DOG**
(B36-478, $5.99, USA) ($6.99, CAN)

☐ **THE LAST CAMEL DIED AT NOON**
(B36-338, $4.99, USA) ($5.99, CAN)

☐ **THE DEEDS OF THE DISTURBER**
(B35-333, $4.99, USA) ($5.99, CAN)

☐ **CROCODILE ON THE SANDBANK**
(B40-651, $4.99, USA) ($5.99, CAN)

☐ **THE CURSE OF THE PHARAOHS**
(B40-648, $4.99, USA) ($5.99, CAN)

**Warner Books P.O. Box 690
New York, NY 10019**

Please send me the books I have checked. I enclose a check or money order (not cash), plus 95¢ per order and 95¢ per copy to cover postage and handling,* or bill my ☐ American Express ☐ VISA ☐ MasterCard. (Allow 4-6 weeks for delivery.)

___Please send me your free mail order catalog. (If ordering only the catalog, include a large self-addressed, stamped envelope.)

Card # _____

Signature _____ Exp. Date _____

Name _____

Address _____

City _____ State _____ Zip _____

*New York and California residents add applicable sales tax.

594